Andrew Martin grew up in Yorkshire. He has written for the *Guardian*, the *Daily Telegraph*, the *Independent on Sunday* and *Granta*, among many other publications. His highly acclaimed first novel, *Bilton*, described by Jon Ronson as 'enormously funny, genuinely moving and even a little scary', was followed by *The Bobby Dazzlers*, which Tim Lott hailed as 'truly unusual – a comic novel that actually makes you laugh'.

In praise of *The Necropolis Railway*, the first Jim Stringer adventure, the *Evening Standard* said 'the age of steam has rarely been better evoked', while the *Mirror* described the book as 'a brilliant murder mystery'. This was followed by the *Blackpool Highflyer* and *The Lost Luggage Porte*r. The next books in the series *Murder at Deviation Junction* and *Death on a Branch Line* were shortlisted for the Ellis Peters Historical Novel Award and in 2008, Andrew Martin was shortlisted for the CWA Dagger in the Library Award. The sixth book in the series, *The Last Train to Scarborough*, was acclaimed as 'thoroughly engaging and entertaining' by the *Sunday Express*.

Praise for *The Necropolis Railway*:

'Beautifully constructed . . . Sometimes, the train really does get you there.' Alex Clark, *Guardian* (Book of the Week)

'Reader and hero are swept off their feet into a noisy, steamy, antiquated world of great danger.' Andrew Barrow, *Spectator*

'Martin skilfully evokes turn-of-the-century London as a mixture of enmity and camaraderie, despondency and boundless opportunity. In the background is a subtly drawn sense of changing times, of the rise of socialism, and the move towards women's rights.' *Times Literary Supplement*

'The author's research, that included participating in footplate experience courses, has paid off, for the book is very readable and the railway descriptions run smoothly.' *Ffestiniog Railway Magazine*

'A wonderful read ... Martin has a superb control of voice and atmosphere, and can turn the minutiae of the railwayman's labour to both comic and dramatic effect. If you enjoy Peter Ackroyd's (or indeed Wilkie Collins's) Victorian melodramas, this is just the ticket.' *Condé Nast Traveller*

'Martin weaves the dark menace of London expertly into this tale: the narrow streets and constant noise provide a perfect backdrop for murderous and sinister happenings.' *New Statesman*

'An unsentimental yet touching chiaroscuro evocation of London in the age of steam.' David Kynaston

'Hurrah for an Ealing comedy. Martin's back-bitten romance reads in black and white and is very endearing.' Philippa Stockley, *Evening Standard* (Books of the Year)

'A classy potboiler ... in the best formal traditions of Dickens and Collins (let alone Christie and Chandler).' *The Times*

'This ingenious and atmospheric thriller ... crackles with the idiom and slang of the period. An eccentric delight.' *Daily Express*

The Necropolis Railway

A Novel of Murder, Mystery and Steam

ANDREW MARTIN

faber and faber

First published in 2002
by Faber and Faber Limited
Bloomsbury House
74–77 Great Russell Street
London WC1B 3DA
This paperback edition published in 2005

Typeset by Faber and Faber Ltd
Printed in the UK by CPI Bookmarque, Croydon

The right of Andrew Martin to be identified as author of this work
has been asserted in accordance with Section 77 of the
Copyright, Designs and Patents Act 1988

A CIP record for this book
is available from the British Library

ISBN 978-0-571-22878-2

8 10 9 7

Acknowledgements

I would like to thank, in no special order, Dominic Le Foe of the Player's Theatre; George Behrend and Frank McKenna, railway authors; John M. Clarke (anyone wanting the hard facts on the Necropolis line should consult his excellent short book, *The Brookwood Necropolis Railway*); Professor Chris Lawrence of The Wellcome Trust Centre for the History of Medicine at the UCL; Jonathon Green – a font of slang from all eras; Keith Gays and the staff of the North Yorkshire Moors Railway; Clive Groom of the 'Footplate Days and Ways' steam engine driving courses; ex-train drivers Les Willis and Ron Johnson; the archive staff of the National Rail Museum in York; Tim Baker-Jones of the W. H. Smith archive; the staff of the Highgate Literary and Scientific Institution; the staff of the Silver Moon Women's Bookshop, which is now within Foyles; Matthew Sturgis for some tips on Edwardian mores; Elizabeth Cook, Barbara Blackford and Anna Rawlinson of the Highgate Bookshop; Bill Simpson (ex of Nine Elms Engine Shed); David McWilliam of the Institute of Directors; the staff of the London Ian Allan bookshop; Dave Notarius and the staff of Motor Books; the Reverend Paul Walker; and Messrs French of Lamb's Conduit Street, WC1, undertakers.

All departures from historical accuracy are mine.

Author's Note

The London Necropolis and National Mausoleum Company became the London Necropolis Company in 1927 and still exists under that name. It ran funeral trains from just outside Waterloo to Brookwood Cemetery from 1854 to 1941, using locomotives and footplate crews supplied first by the London and South Western Railway, then the Southern Railway.

The service, roughly as it was in 1903, provides part of the backdrop to this story, but it should be stressed that no events such as those described here ever took place, nor did any people such as those presented here ever exist.

I am deeply indebted to the LNC for letting me employ the earlier name of their company in amongst my swirling imaginings.

by the same author

Bilton
The Bobby Dazzlers

THE NECROPOLIS RAILWAY

Chapter One

Saturday 14 November 1903

With the letters from Rowland Smith in my pocket, I had a lively ride from York to London: just four and a half hours in all. The engine was one of the new Atlantics of Mr Ivatt, and when she came down Stoke Bank I put aside *The Railway Magazine* I was reading, and leant out the window at the carriage end to experience the amazing velocity.

After Peterborough I took down my box and opened the parcel my dad had packed for me, which turned out to contain three tubs of Melton cream for my boots, and two tins of Nugget's polish, also for my boots. My dad was red-hot for smartness, smart boots especially. There was an alarm clock too – which was the next best thing to Dad coming with me because he'd always woken me up himself at home – and a green Lett's pocket diary, which might seem an out of the way sort of thing to give somebody, November sort of time, but I knew it was the kind of thing Dad would have thought gentlemanly.

I opened the first page, which was headed 'The King and the Royal Family, showing ages and annuities', and stared at it for a while, thinking: well, it's all right, but I would rather have a map of the railways. Then I took out from my pocket the letters from Rowland Smith, which had been sent to me, not from the place he worked, but from his home address: Granville Mansions, Dartmouth Park. Whenever I saw that I thought with wonder, 'In the house of the Lord there are many mansions.' It was in the Northern Division of London. I put the letters away after a few more minutes of marvelling but took them out over and again throughout the journey.

We came into Platform One at King's Cross, which was as I had expected, but what I had not expected was that half of

London would be there, and most of them attempting to force me into the Ladies' Waiting Room, where I had no right nor any desire to be.

When I finally struggled free, the first thing I saw was the road packed with darting waggons, then, over the road from King's Cross, and three times the size, St Pancras. I could not believe there had ever been so many bricks in the world – it must have had more than the Eskdale viaduct and I knew for a fact there were more than five million in that. The clock said five to three; I turned back and looked at the clock on King's Cross, and that said five *after*, and I thought: now, that is strange, because it was impossible to imagine either the Midland or the Great Northern making a bloomer over the time, of all things, but one of them must have, and it seemed that I was only getting in everybody's way by standing there and fretting over it.

Then I spied a stream of hansoms pouring out of a little arch at the bottom of St Pancras like beetles from under a stone, and decided I would take one for the first time in my life. But as soon as I stepped into the road between King's Cross and St Pancras, I was put into another cab – one of a completely separate lot – by a lad who had lately been holding a horse's head and eating a fish. Now he was tipping his head back, and, blowing spinning bits of fish into the air from his mouth, saying, 'If this keeps up, we might be in with a fighting chance, eh, guv?'

He was talking about the sun. It had been raining in Yorkshire but the day was set fair in London, and I might just as well have stepped off a boat train, such was the newness and strangeness of it all.

'Where you off to?' shouted the fish-eating kid.

I said, 'Waterloo,' sounding not like myself, but even the horse seemed to have heard of the place for he set off without coaxing.

There were just too many people in London, and that was all about it. Sooner or later, I thought as we rolled away from

King's Cross, they will have to bring this madness to a halt and get everything put straight. All the buses were marked 'Vanguard' and there was no end of motor cars. There was no end of everything else either, so that after a sprint of a start we soon settled down to a crawl, and I added a second half crown to the one I already had in my hand for the fare, fearing the price might be to do with time spent as well as distance covered.

After twenty minutes or so we came up to the river, which was something more like ten rivers side by side, all brown and glittering and packed with rolling, smoking boats, with big factories on the Waterloo side. Through a gap between two of them, I could see the engine shed of Waterloo rising above the factories and houses like a lot of giant greenhouses at an angle to the river, but the greenhouses gave out after a while, and then there were metal girders, and the automatic hammer was somewhere in there: you'd hear the bang, and then the black cloud would come up after every one.

On the other side of that rusty bridge – and I believe that in my excitement I forgot to breathe all the way across – I realised I had gone from what they called the Northern Division to the Southern Division, and when I remembered that Rowland Smith lived in the Northern Division yet *worked* in the Southern Division, I began to think of that gentleman as being even grander than I had already imagined, and resembling the Colossus of Ancient Greece who stands over whatever river it may be.

We came onto what I now know as Westminster Bridge Road, where trams were surging up to the people like steeplechasers. We had also struck the smell of Waterloo, which came from the station and the chimneys on the river. It was the smell of bad beer, or good pickles, or something that kept you thinking, mingled with engine smoke and another smell that was like the sea captured by factories.

We carried on under a long, low viaduct with a slow-goods hammering overhead, and when we emerged I saw a great vibrating building with steam and smoke rushing out of a line of chimneys. I had thought this would be another factory, but a sign on the roof told me it was the 'Lambeth Skating Rink'. We did not reach that building, however, but turned sharp right, going immediately under another black viaduct with another goods pounding overhead. This viaduct was enormous, and, when we came out from under, the day was not as bright as it had been before.

This dark street, which was called Lower Marsh, was all in the shadow of that great viaduct, and so the people there lived in a world of under and over: under went the houses and shops, the pubs, the people and the lines of stables, and over went the trains with a constant clanging. The shops spilled out into the street and had more goods outside than in: everybody was selling everything to everybody else, and everybody was shouting to make themselves heard over the trains. The most important thing in the street apart from the viaduct seemed to be a round pub called the Citadel: a big, orange-glowing beer-barrel sort of a place with a sign saying Red Lion Ales and Reid's Stout over and over again – I would soon learn that in London they are never happy to just do something once.

Above the pub, above the street, and really above all, was the great station itself, the spider in the middle of the viaduct web. I knew it to serve the grandest railway in the world, the London and South Western, and yet I was surprised, for there was nothing glorious to it. Waterloo seemed to have no front and no back. It did have a roof – in parts – but there were many huge tarpaulins rising and falling in the dirty breeze over the rambling mass of bricks and glass. Under these great tents, I was sure, they were making the station bigger still, and I did not doubt that it would finish up the mightiest in the Empire. Already, as I knew from *The Railway Magazine*, Waterloo received 700 trains every day, compared to 250 at King's Cross. St Pancras received . . . a good many, I did not know the exact number, and I realised, alone in the dark little

6

cab, that it would be a very long time before I would be able to look it up, for I had only brought the latest two numbers of *The Railway Magazine* in my box.

But there was no time to fret over that because the cab man called down to me through his hole. He might as well have been talking in a foreign language, but did not sound happy, so I gave him the two half crowns, thinking: well, he'll give me some of it back, at any rate. Having taken the money, though, he just opened the door. I thought: he'll hand over the change when I've stood down; it's probably that way about with hansoms. I climbed down in front of a pharmacy that seemed entirely given over to selling Vianola Soap, and watched the cab man turn in a circle, thinking: as the horse turns he'll count out the change, but the fact of the matter was that he was lighting his pipe as the horse walked, and then he was gone altogether, and the whole of my five shillings with him. I did not have much time to worry about this, though, because I now saw a sign that hit me like a bullet: Hercules Court.

I cannot now say how, on the journey down from Yorkshire, I had thought my lodge and my landlady might actually be because any memory of it has been blotted out by the thought of how they actually were. The lodge was on a corner, half in Lower Marsh and half in Hercules Court. The wall facing Lower Marsh was covered in posters, all saying, 'Smoke Duke of Wellington Cigars', except for one going out on a limb with 'Stower's Lime Juice, No Musty Flavour'. I knocked on the door of this giant cigar box and a lady opened it, releasing a smell of wash day. She was certainly not from the common run of landlady, and while she did not look well-to-do, she looked clever – her faded skirts did not matter. Her eyes were very large and yet she herself was very small, and that to me was the right way about. It would have been very easy to lift her up, I thought, but I perceived instantly that nobody would ever dare to try.

She stood aside and looked away as I dragged my box through the doorway. On the floor was brown linoleum, and the wallpaper was black, with big, glowing orange flowers. This continued up the stairs, which were so narrow that my landlady's skirts touched both walls at once. She opened a door and showed me into a room.

'It's quite commodious,' I remarked after a while, for this was the best that could be said. The wallpaper was a design of roses on a trellis; there were two windows opposite each other, not at all clean. I walked towards one of them and my landlady said, 'As you see, they give on to the garden.'

There being no grass or plants of any description, but just bricks and a coal shed, this was more of a yard, I thought. I knew about yards because we had one at home. Immediately beyond this one was a brick wall that must have been sixty foot in height, if not greater, with an oil lamp burning towards the top of it. I was just trying to think of a way of asking about it when the landlady said, with a faraway look, 'Soap works. You'll have no trouble from it.'

There was a truckle bed and a broken bamboo table with a candle end in a saucer. No gas. There was one picture over the bed which showed a glum sort of castle in a brown field with two sad-looking men standing alongside it. I walked a little way towards the bed, and saw that underneath this scene were the words 'Harrow School, 1723'.

My landlady said, 'It's a pound down,' and then, as I gazed at a small pool of water on the floor, 'I believe that you have a start on the railways?'

'I'm to begin as a cleaner,' I said.

But people don't understand how it lies with engine cleaners – they didn't then and they don't now – and I could never leave it at that. 'Cleaning', I went on, as my landlady looked down at her boots, 'is the first stage on the road that leads to firing an engine. After some months, I anticipate becoming a passed cleaner, which will mean I can do some firing duties, and then, if all goes satisfactorily, I will perhaps move on to driving on a low link: shunting work, I mean, little goods and the like. At the top of the mountain that I am endeavouring to climb –'

At that, she flashed a look at me: a kind of warning I suppose it was, looking back. But I pressed on.

'At the top of that mountain are the express drivers, the ninety-mile-an-hour chaps, that is, and I have the confident expectation of becoming one of those myself, but I will have to spend many years proving that I'm the right sort, and if I have faults my watchword will have to be that I will seek to mend one every day.'

'Yes,' she said at length, 'well, it's a pound down.' She would have no fussing about; she wanted the money in her hand. I paid up, and she wrote me a receipt there and then, very fast and determined. As she wrote, leaning on the mantelpiece, she explained the rules of the house while I looked at the water on the floor, then up at the crack in the ceiling from where it came. There had been one other gentleman staying in the lodge – a schoolmaster who rode a bicycle – but he was leaving that day. Like this gentleman, I could have my laundry done if I left it out on a Friday evening. Wash day was Saturday. Today was Saturday but there would be no more done since the boiler had just been drained.

In the kitchen, my landlady said, there was hot water that could be brought up in bowls, and some margarine, bread and preserves to which I could help myself. I asked whether there was cocoa, and she said, 'No.' I said I was partial to it in the mornings, especially Rowntree's, at which she gave me such a look that I immediately added that I could do quite well without after all.

This lodge, she then told me, was owned by her father and he also owned another lodging house in which he lived and where she spent most of the week. He was not well, and presently kept no servants: there had been a skivvy for both houses but she was sick, therefore my landlady spent a good deal of time at her father's place. But she would be in this lodge every Saturday to do the washing – for the other did not have such a good kitchen – and to collect the rent.

When she had left, I quickly unpacked my box. Then, to put

me in the right frame of mind for my new life, I sat on the truckle bed and began reading, in one of my two *Railway Magazines*, a long article about one David Hughes, 'A Great Western Railway Engine Driver Who Received the Royal Victorian Medal'. Seldom has any driver put up harder running than Mr Hughes over any territory, but it was difficult to give him my full attention, what with all the shouts and screams and railway clamour around me. After a while I took up my two numbers of *The Railway Magazine* and tried to stand them on the mantelshelf with a lump of coal as a prop, but they would not stay upright, not being bound, as all my others were in the regulation red leather, all standing proudly in rows on the shelves of my cosy little bedroom in Baytown.

But I tried hard not to think of that.

Every now and again, as I brushed the dust off the mantel and thought, despite myself, of the balmy life I had left behind, there would come a great smashing wave of laughter and shouting rolling out of the pub just along the road. This presently mingled with another train thumping over the viaduct, and the clanging of a church bell.

It was only four o'clock. But it was four o'clock in Waterloo.

Chapter Two

Monday 16 November

On my first morning I climbed out of bed at five, an hour before my alarm rang, and put on the old black suit of Dad's that I would be wearing for work. He'd said I ought to wear a collar and tie, and I'd said that sort of thing was for the porters, the little men of the railways, and that I would not keep a collar on my shirt but would wear a kerchief, and we had agreed on that. I had two caps with me down in Waterloo: my best cap and my other one. As it was my first day and I was nineteen and felt myself on a heavenly mission, I stood up, put on my best one, and prepared to look in a glass to see how much I resembled a fellow of the right sort. But there was no looking glass, and it would have been too dark to see into one even if there had been, which was all just as well.

Then I sat back on my bed and watched my new alarm go around to six o'clock. It *did* go off at six, which made me feel a juggins for not trusting it, but I had a dread of having to be woken by a call boy on my first day.

I stepped out of the front door, and there was my welcome to Waterloo: a man in an Ulster, stiff with mud, was banging a metal bar against the iron ladder that went up the side of the viaduct. The fellow was saturated, and the queer thing was that he quite looked the part, for his coat was bell-shaped and swung in time with his blows. Above him, the cold wind raced under and over the dirty tarpaulins that bandaged Waterloo.

I turned away from this scene and, thinking things would pick up with the sun, I began to walk. It took me one day to realise that the quickest way from Waterloo to Nine Elms Locomotive Shed was along the river. On that first morning, however, I attempted to walk there through ordinary streets, following the viaducts whenever I thought I might not be going right, but this proved no simple matter since they were tangled up with the buildings. The dismal streets were full of dark warehouses instead of ordinary houses, and full of men and their horses and waggons bringing things into Waterloo or taking them away and making a great din about it, and what with the noise, the strangeness of the streets and my fearfulness of being late, I was in a very fretful condition when I finally came upon the main gates of Nine Elms.

It was Monday 16 November 1903, bang on seven o'clock, and I could've done with some cocoa inside me. I walked past a pub called the Turnstile, ever closer to those golden gates, although they were far from golden, of course.

'Who are you, mate?' he said, a funny little bloke who was suddenly in my way.

'I'm new, I'm to come on as a cleaner.'

'I might be able to help in that.'

'Oh, yes?'

'It depends who you are, though.'

This funny little fellow, who had, I believed, the accent of the true cockney, was very keen to have my name, so I thought I would give him it, and then I would be able to get on: 'Jim Stringer,' I said, and held out my hand.

His name was Vincent, and he had a little nose, little eyes, a round white head with dints in it, and a big grin on him that came and went like electric light. His cap was right on the back of his head, and even though he was only a young fellow like myself he had precious little hair.

'I'm looking for the foreman,' I said to him.

'Now what foreman is that, mate?'

'The foreman of the shed, I think.'

He gave me a long, funny look as if I'd said something a bit fishy. 'You want to book on?'

'That's it.'

'I'll show you to the timekeeper,' he said. 'His name's Bob Crook, but he's Mr Crook to you.'

There were a lot of people coming and going around the

gate, but it seemed that I was stuck with this eager little chap. He took my arm and steered me into a long, hot building at the side of the gate. There was one room inside and, starting from the back of it, there was a clock, then a man on a stool under an electric light, then a small desk with a ledger on it, then a metal table scored with a chequerboard pattern on which sat hundreds of numbered metal disks, each about the size of a sovereign. The walls were glazed bricks, there was a good fire going, and everything looked hot and shiny, including the man at the table, who was dipping his long face into a steaming cup of tea.

'Good morning,' I said.

Instead of replying, the timekeeper carried on very carefully drinking his boiling tea. Meanwhile, his clock ticked. It was as if he liked the sound of it and wanted everybody else to pay close attention.

'Stringer?' said the timekeeper, after about half a minute had ticked by.

'Yes, sir,' I said.

'You're number one hundred and seventy-three,' said the timekeeper, and he stood up, gave me a disk, and sat back down.

Well, he wasn't friendly, but he'd been expecting me at any rate; he wrote the time next to my name in the ledger while Vincent started booting the fender.

'Will you be going off-shed?' said Mr Crook, without looking up.

'I don't think so,' I said.

He wrote something else down in his book.

'I'm very sorry, Mr Crook,' I said, 'but what do I do with this?' Feeling like an ass, I held up the token.

'You return it to Mr Crook,' said Vincent.

Thinking this a queer bit of business I started to give the token back to Crook, but as I did so, he cried, 'Not *now*, for Christ's sake.'

'You hand in the token at the *end* of your turn,' said

Vincent. 'Come on, let's be off.'

We turned towards the door – the fellow Vincent wanted me out of that spot for some reason.

'Number one hundred and seventy-three,' said Crook, just as Vincent was pushing open the door.

I looked back at him.

'That makes you the new Henry Taylor,' he said, and both his eyebrows jumped.

'Who's he?' I asked.

'Another bloke we had on,' mumbled Vincent, who was holding the door open.

'And where is he now, Mr Crook?' I asked the timekeeper.

'Interesting question, that is,' he said, getting a bag of shag out from under his little desk.

'Nobody knows what happened,' said Vincent, 'and that's all about it.'

The wind flying through the open door was playing havoc with the timekeeper's fire but the gentleman himself didn't seem to mind. I looked above the fireplace and there was a noticeboard with details as to special trains, signalling alterations, and an article about the weather torn from a newspaper: 'GOOD PROSPECTS FOR MACINTOSH TRADE,' I read.

'That Taylor kid,' said the timekeeper, digging his pipe into the shag, 'well, at first – around the back end of August, it would have been – they thought he'd gone home, fearing himself not up to the mark for an engine man, but it's more likely if you ask me that he's gone to the bottom of the river.'

'What river, Mr Crook?' I said.

The timekeeper looked up at me with a frown while his fire blew back and forth, and I remembered about London, which had a great many of most things but only one river.

I did know that the timekeeper knew of Rowland Smith, and the peculiar circumstances of my coming to the London and South Western Railway, but I decided to say my piece: 'I'm from Yorkshire, Mr Crook,' I said, 'and this is my second

14

railway start. I was on the North Eastern to begin with – not on the traffic side but portering.'

But Crook was still thinking about the earlier matter, for he nodded in a vague sort of way, saying, 'The Taylor kid . . . nineteen. Good-looking boy. I've heard the mother's half dead herself over what happened. She'll be crying over him at this present moment, if you want my guess.' And he turned to look at his clock, as if to make quite sure; then he picked up his tea and put it down again. 'It's one for Sherlock Holmes, if you ask me,' he said, and both his eyebrows went up again.

As the timekeeper began lighting his pipe, Vincent had me out through the door, shouting, 'I'm taking him to the Governor, Mr Crook!'

We started walking across a patch of sooty nothing between the timekeeper's room and the beginning of the tracks. 'There's a job waiting for that bloke making up shocks on the penny horribles,' said Vincent. 'He's bloody wasted here.' He stopped and looked at me, and said, 'What made you chuck portering up north? Or did you get stood down?'

'I wasn't stood down. I wanted to get on to the traffic side.'

'I've heard of chaps leaving the railways,' said Vincent, 'and I've heard of a lot more that got the boot, but I never heard of anyone going from one territory to another like that.'

Feeling suddenly glum at this, I thought: no, nor have I.

I remembered how Dad, in high excitement, had gone to Whitby Library to look up Rowland Smith starting with the Peerage, but had not found him there or anywhere else. I had seen Dad that night drinking beer on his own, which was unusual and meant he was anxious.

We started wandering across the windy greyness, and what met my view was familiar from the pages of *The Railway Magazine* but at the same time different. Two hundred yards to our right was a broken-down loco shed with about twenty roads going into it: I knew from my reading that engines went into there but they did not come out, for the Old Shed was a locomotive's graveyard. The tracks went into it on either side of something I hadn't read of: a house that must have been a remnant of earlier streets. It made a strange sight because, even though the windows were bricked up, smoke was racing from the chimney.

Beyond the Old Shed was the New Shed, which was semiround and a real gobstopper, with twenty roads fanning into it from two turntables. As I watched, two engines were chuffing into the grey haze that was around the shed, and two were chuffing out, heading away towards a horizon filled with black engines, more than anybody knew what to do with, just waiting, like some great army, for the work of the day.

The New Shed was dark, except for holes in the roof where the daylight came shooting in, and the smell of coal and oil had me worrying about the burning feeling that came with each intake of breath. All around was the sound of coal smashing into locos from above, coal crashing out of them into the pits below. We walked along next to a row of fancy lampposts, all lit, that ran between two lines of engines, and it was like walking along a street except with locomotives instead of houses, and all sprinkled with glittering black. I could hear twice as many men pounding away as I could see, and then I solved the mystery: half of the fellows were working under the engines with candle ends to see by.

Vincent led me to the top end of the shed, by which I mean the back of it, where there was a kind of black cricket pavillion with a name painted on the door: 'P. T. Nightingale, Yard Master'.

'Governor,' said Vincent in an under-breath as we went in, 'and Governor's Clerk.'

It was very bright and warm inside, with two fires going. There was a man in the corner with his back to me. He had an amazing quantity of white hair that looked like fleece, and was sitting at a high desk on a high stool and coughing. I could not help but think that if his desk wasn't so tall he wouldn't need such a high stool. Before me was another man sitting on a normal-sized chair at a normal-sized desk. He was also a more normal-sized fellow. He was wearing a brown bowler with no hair coming out from underneath, and he had a little face but very fiery; his head looked like the top of a match.

He looked up at me, and Vincent pointed at him, saying, 'Give Mr Nolan the token.'

Mr Nolan looked at it and called out, 'Number hundred and seventy-three,' at which the gentleman in the tall chair, still coughing, turned around. Mr Nightingale was a boozy-looking sort, and I thought: I'm standing in the red-faced room. But he was handsome all the same, and more of a hawk than a nightingale.

Now Nolan was holding the token out towards me again.

'Take it back,' said Vincent.

I was pretty tired of this token by now, but did as required. Then Vincent said to the Governor, 'I expect he'll be on general cleaning so I'll take him off to Mr Flannagan.'

Vincent turned on his heel, but the Governor leant forward on his high chair, and it was like a signal moving to stop. His face was all twisted up. 'And who the hell do you think you are?' he said, 'the bloody District Locomotive Superintendent?'

'No,' said Vincent, with no question of a 'sir' to follow.

I had not expected this kind of thing from Nine Elms men; I had expected them to be all one, like the Brigade of Guards.

'You take him to stores, and find him a rule book,' said the Governor to Vincent, 'then take him to Flannagan, who can show him about, but his duties are to be set directly by me.'

'He's not coming onto the half, is he?' asked Vincent, and I didn't know what he meant, but he said it in a peevish sort of voice that would have got him stood down immediately on the North Eastern.

There was another long look between them. 'I will come down from here in a second,' said the Governor, 'and I will put you on your fucking ear.'

This was not the way it should have been; it was not the way at all.

Nolan the clerk came in quickly: 'Why do you want his

duties to be set from this office, Mr Nightingale? Is there any particular reason for it?'

'Bampton Twenty-Nine and Bampton Thirty-One,' said the Governor – at which Vincent cursed in an under-breath – 'have not been coming off-shed to a standard of cleanliness befitting their special duties.'

'I've been going at those of late,' said Vincent. 'I've had no complaints.'

Ignoring this latest incredible remark coming from low to high, the Governor, looking at me, said, 'I'd like to see these two shining like thoroughbreds when they go to work, and I will arrange with the drivers of these locomotives for you to have a number of rides out on them. Is that clear?'

It was not clear at all, but I nodded a 'Yes, sir' as the Governor began coughing once again. As soon as we were out of there I asked Vincent who Flannagan was: 'Charge cleaner,' he muttered, and I thought again of this Henry Taylor, and wanted to ask how a Nine Elms man could just go missing, but I could see that Vincent was sulking like a camel and not keen to say anything more. As I looked at him, he turned his back on me and began walking away between two lines of locomotives.

I fished in my jacket pocket for the first of the letters from Rowland Smith, and viewed again the miracle that had brought me to this cold, crashing shed: 'I think I have the power to bring you on without resorting to the usual formalities . . . Testimonials will be required, however . . .' The letters fluttered in the icy breeze, looking suddenly very flimsy indeed. Noise was coming from all parts of the shed, like the banging of hundreds of broken pianos, yet for the time being there was not a soul in sight. Any idea that I had made a mistake – and a dangerous one at that – in coming to Nine Elms must on no account be allowed.

Chapter Three

Baytown

It seems a horror to think of it now, so many years on, but the whole of my life is divided into the times before Rowland Smith came strolling along that platform at Grosmont, and the times after. 'Before' started in 1884, the year in which I was born, my mother died, and the railway came to Baytown.

Baytown, which the gentry called Robin Hood's Bay, was just a few tall thin houses – a quiver of arrows on the edge of the sea – and if one dog barked, everybody heard it. Dad thought he was the cream of Baytown because he was a butcher and not a fisherman. He told me that the trouble with Baytown wasn't that it stank of fish but that it stank of fisher-*men*, and perhaps that's why I started to like the trains, which called at this funny, fishy little town but didn't have to stay.

If you stood on the front with your back to the sea you could see the train come across the top of the cliffs from Hawsker in the north, stop at Baytown, then head south to Ravenscar. Only two people watched them with me and the first was Crazy May, who *was* crazy, maybe because she had one eye lower than the other, and who all day long crushed crabs on the beach for the seagulls and couldn't remember whether it was the trains that were scared of the horses or the horses that were scared of the trains.

The other was Mr Hammond, who had been a swell in his day but had made a mistake in London which was never to be spoken of, but had put him in Queer Street, so that he could no longer be in business. When I was tiny he took me on the train to the West Cliff marshalling yard at Whitby and we would watch a little J72-class cutting fruit and fish specials. That was the engine for me because it had a name: Robin. As we watched, Mr Hammond smoked cigarettes and told me the differences between a handbrake, an engine brake and a vacuum brake, and so on. He was very amiable considering I was just a kid. 'The smoke box is at the *front* of the engine,' he would say, 'and the firebox is at the *back*.' He must have told me that hundreds of times before it sank in.

Later on, Dad and I would ride the train to Darlington to watch the Atlantics flying down the main line. After every one that went past, I would look up at him and say, 'What about that, Dad?' and the poor fellow always had to think of something to say, for I had no mother after all.

I had no aspirations to a life at sea; I did not want to be a butcher either. I would look at the letters on Dad's shop – 'Stringer: Family Butcher' – and wonder what there was 'family' about it. I remember the barrels of ice in the cold room at the back and the fire in the shop at the front – those two always fighting each other, it wore me out to think of it somehow. My ambition instead was to be on the railways. I read everything I could lay my hands on that had for a subject trains, and had *The Railway Magazine* every month for 6d, which my Dad paid for because he thought it was improving. Not that he wanted me on the railways. Dad wanted me in his shop, but he changed his tune when myself and three other lads from Baytown were offered five bob each to build a bonfire for Captain Fairclough's firework-night carnival.

Fairclough lived at Ravenhall, and the whole headland was his garden. The fire took a while to get up, but I was told it was still smoking on the seventh, and I expect that's why the Captain sent me a letter, having heard from one of the other lads that I wanted a start on the North Eastern. Fairclough had more connections than York station, and he said that he would be willing to write to the general manager of the North Eastern Railway telling him I was an eminently suitable person to go on.

Now, if Captain Fairclough, who had done something at Khartoum and got the QMG for it, had suggested informing the Governor of Armley Gaol that I was a very good person for a fifteen-year stretch, then that would have been it as far as Dad was concerned: I would have been *off*. But he did still want me clerking in some way. 'I would prefer you in a post offering some prospect of advancement to stationmaster,' he would tell me, 'and I do not mean stationmaster at Robin Hood's Bay.'

'But the fellow up there, Langan, has thirty shillings a week,' I would say, 'and with his coal auctions he does a lot better than that. They're not lawful, of course, but that's all right.'

I would say things like that so as to tease Dad, and in hopes of making our pretty part-time slavey, Emma, start laughing, because then she was even prettier.

Dad took to spending evenings in the back parlour with *The Railway Magazine*, and in the morning he might say, in a thoughtful sort of way, 'There are twenty thousand bikes taken into Newcastle station every year.'

'I know that, Dad,' I would say.

'Who do you suppose is in charge of them?'

'The bicycle booking clerk, Dad. Who else is it going to be?'

'He would have to be quite a respectable party, looking after that amount of bikes.'

I did not want to be a bicycle booking clerk, so I would give no opinion on that. I wanted to be a driver, and I knew I could do it. I'd practised on my safety bike by coming down Askrigg Hill without touching the brakes or without hands on the handles, and without a lamp if it was after dark. I secretly felt that I was built for high speed: my eyesight, I felt certain, was six-six, and I knew I had the lean looks of an engine man. But Dad got his way, and I applied to the North Eastern for something that would lead me into the clerical line all the same. I had my certificates, and my testimonial from that famous gentleman, Captain Fairclough, and my letter was very well greased: 'I feel that I am able to hold my own in a gentlemanly way . . . I am seventeen years old, and need scarcely say that I am a total abstainer . . .' (Which was

21

true give or take the odd sip of dad's Sunday night jugs of ale).

I was called to York by some johnnies in top coats who said there was a chance I could go on immediately as a lad porter at Grosmont, but first I had to answer such out-of-the-way questions as 'What is the difference between up and down?'

I got my start the following week.

Chapter Four

Monday 16 November
continued

I asked a fellow where I might find Flannagan, the charge cleaner, and he just pointed to a whole row of huts at the top of the shed and walked on. Then Vincent reappeared, coming around the corner of a long-boilered locomotive. 'All right, mate?' he said. 'You're still looking a bit lost.'

He seemed in high spirits once again; he was a very changeable sort.

'Come here, mate,' he said, and he showed me into one of the huts in the line. There was a thin stove, and a seat like a shelf going all around halfway up – and that was it, except for a lad who was pretty much all teeth.

'This is where the firemen who do the half-link turns mess,' said Vincent. These words came out all of a tangle, and I hadn't untangled them before he went on: 'It's quite a decent spot,' he said, chucking his cap on the bench, 'except for this one thing. Have a good look about, and tell me what's missing.'

'Well,' I said, 'any number of things are missing,' which made Vincent look put out, and the toothy kid go red and walk out of the door.

'The main thing lacking in here,' said Vincent, who hadn't said a word to the toothy kid, 'is a kettle, and there is no kettle because there is no place to *boil* a kettle, are you with me?' Vincent knelt at the stove and flipped open the door, which fell down on its hinge and came to rest sticking out. 'So we put our billies on here,' he said. 'They take at least ten minutes to boil, and we do one at a time.'

I couldn't see why he was telling me this, but tried to keep up an interested face.

'Now, if it ever happened that all the lads came in here at

once,' said Vincent, 'this is the order in which we would brew up: first billy on would be Clive Castle, who's a passed fireman who sometimes does firing turns on the half, depending on how busy they are with the Brookwood runs. He's sort of half on the half and half not. Next it would be Joe somebody – just can't quite remember his name – who also fires up at odd times. Then it would be the last fireman, the bloke who's just gone.'

'He's full-time on the half though?' I said.

Vincent nodded.

'What's that fellow's name?'

Vincent gave me another of those long looks that he went in for. 'Mike,' he said after a while, and it caused him a lot of pain to say that word.

'Next billy on,' he continued, 'is mine because I was passed for firing on the half-link six weeks back, but I've been kept back on cleaning – though really I'm just kicking my heels – until everything's put straight in the office. Now if *you* should ever come up from cleaning to firing on the half you'd put your billy on the stove next, making you fifth in line and last.'

I told him that if I ever came up from cleaning to firing on the half-link I would probably bring my tea in a bottle, and he didn't like this one bit. Then I said, 'Look, what *is* this half-link business? Engine men work in links, and a link is a sort of bundle of duties. You can't have a *half*-link, and no one's told me I'm to be on it in any case.'

'You sure of that?'

'Honour bright.' But I could tell that he still didn't believe me.

'But you are on it,' he said slowly. 'I know that from the special cleaning duties you've been given. And why shouldn't there be a half-link: it just means a little link, that's all, and I'll tell you what: I'd rather be on half-link than bottom-link.'

'Bottom-link?'

'The bottom-link's the one above the half-link. Slow-goods: cutting coal waggons in the dark, hour after hour.'

'Why in the dark?'

'You get in amongst moving coal waggons and it's bloody dark, I'll tell you.'

'But what does the half-link *do*, then?' I asked, for he still hadn't got to that.

'The half-link isn't like any other link. It does a dog's dinner of local turns, but most of its work is on that one particular special sort of run.' He stopped here and gave me a queer look. 'But you don't need telling about that, mate.'

I asked him how he made that out, and he said, 'You're being put to cleaning the engines for that run, and doing nothing else, by the sound of it, except getting more than your fair share of rides on them, which is probably so you can get up to firing before you're properly ready for the job. Where did you say you were from, mate?'

'Baytown.'

'Now I've never heard of that spot.'

'Gentry would call it Robin Hood's Bay.'

'Still never heard of it,' said Vincent. 'Does it have electric light?'

'*Whitby* has electric light,' I said, but he hadn't heard of Whitby either.

'What brings you down here?' Vincent asked, and I found that I was taking against the fellow in double-quick time. I thought: Rowland Smith brought me down here, with his letters that all of a sudden seemed so mysterious. It would have to come out in time, but I mumbled something about there being more chances for a lad south than north, adding: 'This special run you spoke of – it's all goods, is it?'

Vincent thought about this for a while. 'It's mixed.'

'Mixed *goods*?'

'No, mixed goods and passengers. It's not what you might call . . .' He seemed to drift away for a minute here, but he came back galvanised: 'Of course, with the sort of running I'll be putting up, I'll be off the half-link and on to suburban runs in under six months, you bloody watch. After that the sky's the limit.'

25

'The Bournemouth Belle!' I said.

'You've got it, brother. Eighty miles to the fucking hour, and the big penny in the pocket. Do you want to see where the half-link drivers have their twenty minutes?'

'That would be fine,' I said.

The half-link mess turned out to be hanging in the blackness off the side wall of the engine shed. It had a wooden staircase leading up to it, and a metal pipe connecting the back of the shed with the floor, and I wondered: now, what is holding this thing up, the pipe or the staircase? because neither looked up to the job.

'We can't go in, of course,' said Vincent when we'd got to the top of the stairs, 'but we can look through the window.'

There were proper tables and chairs, though of a rough sort. Two men were sitting in the mess, both smoking pipes and reading newspapers, the nearest one's being all about sport – 'GOLFING NOTES', I read, and 'ROWING FROM THE UNIVERSITIES' – while the chap at the far end was behind a newspaper of a smarter sort: 'EAST LONDON WATER, PRESENCE OF DANGEROUS BICCILLI'.

The sportsman was side-on to me so I could see that he was a wide, pinkish bloke with curly yellow hair, and a face that seemed to have burst a long while ago. All I could see of the other was his paper, with pipe smoke rising above it, and two thin legs shooting out from underneath with shiny boots on the end of them.

'That's Barney Rose,' said Vincent, pointing to the sporting paper, 'and that there's Arthur Hunt,' he added, pointing to the second man, and I could tell from the way he spoke that this fellow Hunt was really the man for him.

'Are they the only two drivers on the link?'

'The only two full time on it, yes.'

'And they've only got one fireman between them?'

'Apart from the relief blokes who come and go.'

In all my years of reading *The Railway Magazine* I had never heard anything to match it.

'And that one fireman is the fellow called Mike that we've just seen in the firemen's mess?'

On the subject of this toothy lad Vincent just nodded, and I could tell that it wasn't a matter of dislike but something more.

'Henry Taylor,' I said, 'the one who went missing . . . Was *he* firing on the half-link before he vanished?' Here I came in for another of his stares. Henry Taylor was the great unmentionable, but Vincent did bring himself to a shake of the head eventually.

'Cleaning,' he said.

'So I've been taken on in his place?'

Another pause. 'That's it,' said Vincent.

'Don't these fellows ever do any work?' I said, turning back to look at the two engine men.

'They're on their twenty minutes,' Vincent whispered. 'I told you that.'

We carried on watching them. They had both turned over pages. 'WRESTLING NOTES', I read on the sporting paper; on the other, 'TODAY'S SPEECHES'. Then TODAY'S SPEECHES collapsed and I saw the thin, wolfish face of the man behind the paper, like a dagger. He didn't glance at me but nodded quickly at Vincent before disappearing again behind the journal.

This nod was electrifying in the effect it had on Vincent, who blushed as if that man had been his best girl. Then the other one, the comfortable one, put down his paper and nodded, but this nod was for the two of us, and quite genial. He stood up and opened the door, while the other just carried on with his paper and his pipe.

'Well, lads,' said Barney Rose, 'Ranjitsinjih has hit thirty-four off one over for the second time in three weeks.'

I tried to think of something to say.

'I just had to pass on the news to someone,' said Barney Rose.

'He's new,' said Vincent, pointing at me, and making no

27

attempt to continue with the cricket talk. 'He's cleaning for the link.'

There was a short silence; Rose moved his hand to his face, then away again. 'What's your sport, young man?' he asked, finally looking at me.

'I'm not so hot at any game, sir. I concentrate on my work.'

'But even so,' said Rose, in a dreamy sort of way.

'I have most energetic aspirations,' I said, still hoping to bring the talk back to what it ought to have been, 'and my supreme goal is the footplate.'

'Oh, my eye!' said Rose, before adding more quietly, 'Another Henry Taylor! He was always pretty keen to come up.' He was sweating and smiling in a strained way. 'Taylor was quite an ardent lad like yourself . . . but that's all right.'

'I believe that any young railman aspires to the footplate,' I suddenly heard myself saying, 'and I see no mystery in that, because I hold the life to be a grand one of freedom, healthy effort, endless variety, and delightful good friendship.'

'Where on earth did you get all that?' asked Rose, and he really did seem astonished at my remarks. But I was watching the hard-looking fellow at the far end of the room who'd put the paper down once again and started staring at me. His shirt had no collar but it was clean and pressed. He looked like a grey wolf, and was obviously the right sort, but I did not like him, whereas I had always assumed that I *would* like men of the right sort.

'It has been indicated to me,' I carried on, giving this fellow back as straight a look as I could, 'that I might be climbing onto the footplate of a slow-goods in six months from now, and that I could be wielding the shovel pretty freely from then onwards.'

Hunt took his pipe out of his mouth, and pretty well demanded, 'Who has given you all these promises?' For a working man, he talked like a swell, but with too much of London in his voice.

'Mr Rowland Smith,' I said.

From the look the man gave me – a look of nothingness – I at first assumed he did not know the name, but that I could hardly credit.

'Mr Rowland Smith,' I said, 'is a director of the company that employs you, sir: the London and South Western Railway.'

'And you', he said, settling back on his bench in a way that made me realise that this wooden room was the kingdom over which he ruled, 'are his little friend?'

'It is not –'

'What wage has he started you at?' the wolf cut in.

'Fifteen shillings,' I said, at which he caught up his paper sharply, spitting at the same time, then muttering something I could not catch, save for a single word which I could not help but think was 'devil', however much I wanted it to be something else. The man was at his paper for only a second, then he was moving fast towards me, saying, 'There need be no further –'

There was more, but again I couldn't catch it for he had booted the door shut in my face.

Chapter Five

Grosmont

Rowland Smith came to Grosmont on 30 August 1903. Even after all these years, and all that went on at Nine Elms and the Necropolis, it's the day I remember, and it runs through my mind like one of the old bioscopes – going too fast, I mean, which is how it was at the time.

Thirtieth of August was a Sunday, and I had been in the ladies' lavatories at Grosmont, as usual on the quiet days, getting the sand out of the sinks, trickling the Jeyes into the khazis, shuffling about with my bucket and dreaming of the main line. I had to give most of my attention to the ladies' conveniences because the Board would from time to time send out a Mr Curtis to inspect them. As far as I could tell this fellow did nothing all day but pounce on North Eastern stationmasters and peer into their ladies' conveniences – a very out-of-the-way line for any respectable gentleman to be in.

I was thinking what a rotten sort of day it had been. The bike ride in had been worse than usual because it had been so hot. The sign in Baytown pointing to Grosmont said seven miles but when you got to Grosmont the sign pointing back the other way said nine miles, and I reckoned that was the one telling the truth.

So I'd been moping about all morning with a bad head from the heat, being vexed by the booming rams on the hills and the chiming of the station clock on the 'down'. At 2 p.m., I came out of the ladies', and old Eddie Murgatroyd from Beck Hole Farm came up to look at the time, which it seemed he wasted a lot of time by finding out. Later, a limestone train came through, leaving behind it even more silence than there'd been before. At two-thirty I was sitting on the bench on the 'up' making a show of cleaning some lamps with a

31

linseed rag, when the stationmaster, Mr T. T. Crystal, turned up and placed himself in front of me. Because my heart was not really in my work I'd been getting endless scoldings from Crystal over the past few weeks, and I could tell I was in for another.

'I want them all filled and the wicks trimmed,' he said, pointing to the lamps.

'I know, Mr Crystal,' I said, looking down at his boots.

'Well, you didn't bloody know yesterday. I had to do the futting job myself.' Mr Crystal was chapel; he never gave a proper curse.

Behind his boots, a cornfield moved in the wind, like a bright yellow sea, restless and dazzling, and I knew this meant danger. I turned my head slightly to the right and counted all the buildings in Grosmont, which I had done many times. There were fourteen in all: eight houses, two shops, two churches, one public house and a tunnel.

'Where's your knife for trimming the wicks?' said Crystal.

I took the penknife out of the pocket of my waistcoat, and that checked him, but not for too long.

'Are you liking it here?' he said.

'I am, Mr Crystal,' I said to the boots. 'I am very much.'

'I hear you're interested in speed records.'

'Very much, Mr Crystal.'

'I have to say, that is not evident from your work on these lamps. What's your plan?'

'What do you mean, Mr Crystal?'

'I mean in life.'

I wanted to get on to the traffic side, as I have already said, but there was no point mentioning that to Crystal, because as far as he was concerned I was dreaming of a life in the ink-spilling line.

'I wouldn't mind being SM at Newcastle Central, Mr Crystal.' I'd sort of gone dead as I came out with this, because I instantly knew it was the wrong thing to say, that position being a long way beyond the expectations of even Crystal himself, but even though I am the type that usually buttons up during a scolding, I carried on in the same flat voice, really as though I was trying to bring about the explosion I knew to be close at hand. 'It is one of the most notable stations in the country. I think I have it in me to reach that position in twenty years' time or so, with application and a following wind.'

'A following wind?' shouted Crystal. 'You'd need a bloody hurricane!' Then he pointed to his blooms. 'When you've done with the lamps, water those pansies in front of the bike store because I'm futting telling you this: I'm not dropping the certificate for the first time in ten years on account of you.'

He walked off to the ticket office, and, as I filled the watering can from the stand pipe on the 'up', I heard him muttering to somebody in there about something, which was queer because there was no ticket clerk on a Sunday – Crystal did the job himself. I started watering, thinking: there are no flipping flowers at Newcastle, the atmosphere does not permit it, not with above 1,000 trains a day being worked through there, Newcastle Central being one of the foremost stations on NER metals instead of some half-forgotten halt with not above a dozen trains through each day. I stood up, and replaced some of the lamps that had been on the platform, and as I did so I could hear hooves and wheels going away from the cab yard. Ten minutes later, a johnny in a grey suit emerged from the ticket office and came drifting along the platform. Watching him walk was like listening to funny music playing. He went straightaway into the gentlemen's and something made me put down the lamp I was supposed to be cleaning, pick up my bucket and walk in after him. Somehow I knew that my moment had come – but also that it only *was* a moment.

The smell of the Jeyes and the darkness after the dazzle of the platform had me in a daze, and I could see him in the corner, making water as if he was performing a circus trick, with his fine grey coat all ruffled up behind him like a bustle, hands on his hips. I was watching the back of him but then he turned around, allowing me my first view of his face. It was smooth, and nearly too handsome to be real. His suit was fancy and expensive, but in a quiet way. I couldn't put my finger on the matter, but I believed there was something magnified about his jacket. His necker was large and yellow and worn loose, and I thought: he will not be a pipe or cigar man but will smoke cigarettes. Here was £500 per annum, in any event.

'You're for York, sir?' I said.

He smiled at me and lowered his head; he seemed impressed that I had worked this out, but then we *were* on the 'up'. 'I'm waiting for the two forty-eight,' he said. 'Is it on time?'

'Yes, sir,' I said, although only Mr Plumber in the signal box, who would have had the bell when the train left Whitby, could have said that for certain.

There was a long pause, and I could hear the clattering of the Esk, almost like a machine.

'You were up here on some matter of business, sir?' I said.

'I came here to bury my mother,' he said, and, seeing the confusion this shocking revelation had thrown me into, half smiled and more or less bowed.

'Connecting at York for London, are you, sir?' I asked hastily.

He bowed again, as if I was quite marvellous to have worked this out, but it was no great feat: only London would have been grand enough for him.

'You'll have a good journey,' I said, putting down my bucket, 'although the four-coupled engines of the Great Northern are not at present matching the speed of our own.'

'The North Eastern's?' he said.

'Our four-two-twos have been achieving seventy miles an hour with regularity.'

'It's admirable to have such a knowledge of one's own company.'

'I got that from *The Railway Magazine*. I have it on a monthly subscription.'

'Very creditable in a young man.'

'It is sixpence a month,' I told him, and then wondered whether I ought to tell him this came out of my dad's pocket. 'I have them in the regulation bindings,' I added.

I then asked whether I might show him to the waiting room, because I did not cut the right sort of figure standing next to that bucket.

'What a glorious sight,' he said, looking at the flowers as we stepped back onto the platform.

'For the past ten years,' I said, 'Mr Crystal, the stationmaster here, has had a certificate from the Board for them. Last year he was commended in three categories.'

'Mr Crystal sounds like an excellent fellow,' he said.

'Yes,' I said, because he probably did *sound* like one.

As I spoke I was thinking very clearly: Crystal has his knife into me and I shall not progress under him. There will be a new lad by the end of the year, and I will be stood down and lose my railway chance for ever unless I do something.

My boots rattled on the wood, but those of the toff, which were buttoned at the side, made no noise as we entered the waiting room. All the windows were open, but the fire was orange and seething, and the coal and paraffin smell made the place so stifling that we would have been much better off outside. But it was too late for that.

'Do you want some more coals on the fire?' I said – a strange remark, all things considered, but anxiety had brought on a brainstorm.

The man wiped his brow with a blue handkerchief. 'Why not?' he said, and I thought: now, that is gentlemanliness for you. He removed his hat, causing his hair to spring up, and that is how I remember Rowland Smith. You took one look at his surprising curls, and you thought: Brilliantine – he needs Brilliantine on his hair.

I picked up the poker and prodded some coals.

'I could see you on a footplate,' he said.

'Oh, I feel I could put up some wonderful running, sir,' I said, 'giving a thin, even fire at all times, with the coal put exactly on the spot where it is needed.' Fancying myself quite a bit, I picked up the tongs and moved one lump from the back of the grate to the front, as if that really meant something.

'My name is Rowland Smith,' he said, and at the same moment, almost laughing, took two steps forward and shook my hand.

I was so startled by this that at first I forgot to give my own name in return.

'If you like high speed,' said Smith, unbuttoning his coat, 'then why are you portering?'

Now this, I thought, is the very question.

Smith took out a silver cigarette case – I had been right over this – and began to hit one of the cigarettes on the back of it; it was engraved on the front. The black floorboards were going one way, the sunbeams another. He struck a match.

'I know it will be a difficult transition to make, sir,' and I carried on without a particle of fear, 'but I am committed to a life on the footplate.'

It was the most important remark I had ever made, and the following words, mixed with smoke, came out of Smith's mouth: 'The path that leads to success must be pursued through all its asperities and obliquities.'

'I shall remember that, sir,' I said.

A silence fell between us and I perceived that the time had come to make one further leap. 'Do you have any involvement with the London networks, sir?'

He gave me a half nod, and said, 'Have you heard of the South Western Railway?'

'The *London* and South Western? Only this week I was reading of the excellent timings for ocean passengers between Plymouth and London.'

'Indeed. Have you ever been over South Western metals?'

'No, but I've read so much concerning that excellent company that I do feel acquainted with its territories.'

'In *The Railway Magazine*?'

I nodded.

'I thought so,' he said. 'They're always looking out for engine cleaners to come on, you know, and these fellows are on the footplate as passed firemen, working, for example, slow-goods in not above six months.'

'You have a *very* close acquaintance with the network?' I said.

'I am a railway man through and through,' said Smith.

Well, you do not look it, I thought, and I looked this thought of mine straight *at* him, and he could see it for what it was: a sporting challenge.

'I'm getting on pretty well here,' I said. 'Of course, footplate work would be much more like it, but my father was anxious . . .'

At this I faltered, but Rowland Smith nodded and said: 'Go on.'

'He wanted me at a desk, sir.'

'He is no doubt a respectable gentleman.'

'He is a butcher.'

Smith made a face that I fancied meant: well, it's better than nothing.

'The South Western needs firemen,' he said, 'which is to say that it needs drivers.'

'But I am *here*,' I said in desperation. And at that moment the rooks circling over the trees, half a mile above the signal box, started making their lonely noise, and the whole place seemed like a graveyard that I had to get out of.

'I will have a letter sent up to you care of this station from the headquarters of the South Western,' said Smith. 'What is your name?'

I gave him my name along with many assurances that, if given a chance, I would not be found wanting; then his train came. In a flurry I helped him up into a first-class compartment, passed his box to him, and he gave me no money, as befitting a platform hand who was really an engine man in disguise. When the train left, I returned to the empty waiting room and sat there alone until the heat from the fire and the heat from the sun had faded away, at which moment, try as hard as I might, I could not remember what either one had felt like.

Chapter Six

Tuesday 17 November – Friday 20 November

On my second morning as a Nine Elms man, I woke to find that the pool on the floor of my lodge and the black mark on the ceiling had been added to considerably. I looked out of the window: it was raining hard, and London in the rain, with all the colour and light gone, frightened me. So too, and for the first time, did thoughts of a life on the railways.

It was as though I had brought down a curse on myself for coming out with the name of Rowland Smith, I decided as I pulled on my boots. Arthur Hunt, who may have looked like a wolf but was the only man I had so far met who was the right sort, had dismissed me from the rough steps of the half-link drivers' mess and gone back to his paper. Vincent had stared after me, while the somewhat friendlier fellow, Barney Rose, had given a half smile through the window as if to say, 'I'm sorry for you, mate, but what can I do?' I had spent the rest of the day wandering around Nine Elms in a daze, with only the token in my pocket to say I had a job at all.

I went out into the dark street. The saturated man was there, banging his stick, and the queer thing was that from the look of his face you could tell he was aiming at solemnity. There was a great roaring coming from within the station. It was somewhere between the wind trapped in a chimney and the elephant house at a zoo. I bought a cup of coffee and a cheese sandwich from the barrow under the railway viaduct in Westminster Bridge Road, from which a whole gang of people seemed to get their living. On the other side of the street were three women, not going anywhere. They were next to a brazier with half the cinders tipped out of it. They were all beautiful, but too thin and too dirty, part of the very street.

As I looked, one of them said something to another, and

this second one turned and gave me a look I could not understand. Later, I thought there might have been a question in it – a notion that set my head spinning.

I drained my cup and set off on my new route from the lodge to Nine Elms: into Westminster Bridge Road with the trams already racing in the rain, then down the steps to the Embankment, with the black river to my right, and the wet, dark gardens to my left. Continuing west, I struck a district of factories: a distillery with high windows that made yellow patterns on the dark water, two gasworks and a brewery. I felt very compressed as I walked along that narrow path between the silent factories and the river, but it did save ten minutes on my journey.

In the gatehouse I tried to give a cheery 'Hello' to Mr Crook. I had decided to put from my mind the first day; I would start all over again in the hopes of this time seeking out some men a bit more like driver Hughes in *The Railway Magazine*, as well as getting a leg in with the ones of a more ordinary sort. But Crook just kept his head bent over his metal chequerboard. He had pinned up over the fireplace a new article concerning the weather: 'MORE FOG', it said, but I hadn't noticed any so far, only rain. When he gave me the token, it was with no friendly word, or any word at all.

Things got worse too, for I was stopped on the ash patch before the sheds by a red-headed fellow who said he was Flannagan, the charge cleaner. He was at an angle because he had one leg longer than the other; he also should have been Irish with a name like that but he was not. None of these things was his fault but they made me take against him, and he had certainly taken against me.

I said I was on my way to see the Governor, having been instructed to report to him each day, and Flannagan staggered for a second in front of me before saying, 'He's not in, he's taken sick. I'm putting you to tidying up coal.'

'But am I not to clean the Bampton tanks Twenty-Nine and Thirty-One?' I said.

'They're perfectly clean as it is,' replied Flannagan, and there was no answer to that. 'Get yourself a shovel from stores.'

The stores were in a long building slotted in the gap between the two middle roads in the shed, which were slightly further apart than all the others. There was a desk with a sort of black brick tunnel behind it that was full of everything that could be carried and had a fire going at the back of it. There was a man in there asking for a set of fire irons: dart, pricker and paddle. The dart was the subject of a jolly chat between him and the storekeeper, and the pricker and paddle caused a near riot of laughter when the storekeeper finally turned them up. But when this fellow had gone the storekeeper stood before me like a pillar of stone.

'I'd like a shovel, please,' I said, and he gave me the evil eye for a while. Then he moved off to get it and when he returned, I said: 'Don't you want my number?'

'I know your fucking number,' he said.

I couldn't ask him why he spoke in that way, for I didn't trust my voice not to shake.

There was a row of coal pens near the coaling stage where all day long the biggest blokes in Nine Elms stood on coal waggons on an embankment and flung the stuff down into the engines that drew up on the lines below. On the first day of this duty – which was really just a way of making a fellow eat dog – I put myself wholeheartedly into the job, but it soon came to me that there was no difference between the bits of coal I'd tidied up and the bits of coal that I hadn't, and I began to spend half my time crowning rats with my shovel.

I would also kill time by trying to name the engines I saw coming off-shed. There were several 0-4-4 tanks of the M7 Class, many O2s of the same wheel arrangements, and all kinds of 4-4-0 tender engines, including K10s and the T9s, or Greyhounds, which seemed to be the maids of all work about the place. Being so close to these wonderful motors and having prospects of riding out on them should have put me in great snuff, but all I could think was that each had two men on the footplate, and here was I without a mate.

As to the blokes who came by my coal heaps on foot, I soon gave up nodding at them. They were passing me all the time: riding bikes, pushing barrows or just mooching along close enough for me to smell the smoke from their pipes, but the only one who stopped, apart from Flannagan – who'd stagger up to scold me on the untidiness of the coal from time to time – was a tiny man with a suitcase who said that if I was to have any hope of becoming a passed cleaner, I'd better have some books. It was heartening that he had in mind my ultimate goal, but the books in his suitcase were expensive. I bought *Continuous Engine Brakes*, though, which he said was very galvanising and was willing to let go at one and six.

This I would glance at while taking my suppers of fried tatters and bacon alone at a dining room near my lodge.

I kept myself to my lodge or the dining rooms, for I'd had a bit of a fright on only my second day in Lower Marsh. In the evening, thinking to have a bit of a look about, I had come across three men of the world under the viaduct. Their clothes were rags, but their boots were big and shiny, and the one nearest to me, who had the face of a doll and very glittering eyes, looked down at his boots and up to my face with a grin, as if he meant to bring the two together. I had them down as a kicking gang, and was sure they would have set about me had not a constable come by at that moment – he never said a word, but the three walked backwards away from me as he passed, letting me keep their bootcaps in view for as long as possible.

I hadn't funked it; it had never come to that, and maybe it had been a put-on from the start. But I was shaken up, for I had never seen the like before. In Bay, the men who built the Eskdale viaduct would have their battles on the beach, but the people in the town were never touched, and though there'd be blood spilt it was more like sport. If it had all happened before my Nine Elms nightmares had begun I would not have believed that any such thing could happen in the shadow of a great railway station.

Afterwards, I started to get the district of Waterloo right. Yes, there was cleanliness and newness all about: the public baths and the laundry that looked like a great ship were two streets away, and there was high-class this, royal that, advertisements for Beecham's Pills and all those soaps. But these were frauds. The real Waterloo was in the semi-drunks colliding with donkey carts, the shop sign speaking of 'knives, steel saws and choppers', the roaring from the pubs, the shouts I heard from my windows at night, all coming from smashed-up, wrong-speaking mouths – 'I'll put the fixments on you, you bloody rotter!' And the station itself. Too many builders had been at it, and all with a different idea. It didn't look like a railway station at all; it didn't look like anything. But still the trains rumbled in over the viaducts – one a minute or more, it seemed to me.

I sat wondering whether I should write to Rowland Smith – I had his address after all – to ask whether shovelling coal and braining rats surrounded by unfriendly faces was what he'd had in mind for me when we'd met in Grosmont. I would ask him straight out. Later in the evenings I would think of going to the pub at the end of the road, the Citadel, but the amazing wildness of it and thoughts of Dad, who enjoyed his jugs of Old Six at home but did not hold with public houses, kept me in my lodge.

This itself was a very queer spot. None of the rooms in the house was locked, but there again there was nothing *in* any of them apart from the one next door to my own. This, like mine, had a view of the soap works, which at least were always quite silent and sent out no smoke. The floorboards were very bad, and there was quite a big looking glass, so you got a double dose of the empty black fireplace. Looking into it I saw that my face was yellower than it had been before – yellower, and blacker too, in parts. This was what it meant to become a man, but I was not getting the coal in the way I would like, namely, swirling up from a rattling, open firehole door on a happy run down to the sea, with my mate watching the road beside me and a bottle of tea waiting on the drip plate.

Towards the middle of that first week, I had the notion of taking my twenty minutes in the Old Shed, where I would be free of that pill Flannagan for a while, and I might carry on with *Continuous Engine Brakes*. It was dinner time on Wednesday when I first stepped into that shed full of crippled engines and walked past the old house, which was like a guard, or a kind of warning.

The Old Shed was kept in darkness at all times, so I had a bull's eye with me, and with this I picked out the broken engines. They all stood in queues that led nowhere, and the closer you got to the top of the shed the more they looked like kettles. I couldn't put a name to most of them, for they all had parts missing, some even their wheels. The parts that remained had all been scrawled with chalk numbers that I could make no sense of.

One that caught my eye was a strange 2-4-0 with mighty rim-splashers. It reminded me of a bike. I leapt up onto its footplate and gave a yank on the dead regulator. Then I turned and pointed my lantern tank through the open firehole door. There was a nice bed of dry rags in there, so I climbed inside, pulled the door to, and set about making myself a cosy nest on the grate.

The firehole was of the usual sort of size, by which I mean it would have made a bedroom for one of those half-size people they have in circuses, being perhaps eight feet in length, four and a half foot high, and three and a half wide. All about the metal walls of the firehole hung ghostly grey ash – the place seemed to keep a memory of every fire that had burned in there. For ten minutes I munched on my snap and tried to make sense of a drawing of the Westinghouse Automatic Brake. Once, I heard a clatter from within the shed that fairly made my hair stand on end, but after a second's thought I knew it to be rats.

The Westinghouse Brake comes with many complications, and presently I fell into a doze. How long it lasted I don't know, but I woke up in the greyness feeling: this is too complete. There ought to have been a circle of light around the firehole door but it was firmly closed, and a firehole door cannot be opened from the inside, for all that is meant to *be* inside is the fire. I tried to kick the door but my quarters were too cramped to allow it. I tried standing and stretching but could not unbend my body in any direction.

Then I saw a little twist of smoke coming up throught the grate, and I knew that after the Taylor kid it was my turn. I was about to suffocate, then to disappear altogether. I cried out once, 'No!' and as I did so the smoke leapt into my lungs, and afterwards it was all coughing, with the smoke now coming up from all parts of the grill. I could not see the sides of the metal box in which I was locked, but as I kicked and pounded against them they seemed to close in on me. I could not breathe, and nor could I stop myself from trying to breathe. Shaking and dying, and trying to pray, I lay down on the floor of the box, and all at once the smoke changed colour around me. It was streaming freely over my head and away from me, turning like twine, and I found that with my coughs came breaths. I sat up and saw the fire door open once again and the smoke drifting slowly through. I rolled through the doorway and found a pair of shaky legs on the footplate of the engine. The backs of my hands were bloody but I could only feel and not see the blood, since my bull's eye was broken. From the top of the shed I could hear the scuffling of boots in ash, and laughter.

Railway blokes, I knew, were likely to go in for all kinds of japes with a new man on the job, but this little exploit had nearly finished me off.

Chapter Seven

Saturday 21 November

On the Saturday, Vincent rolled up again, once more in the mood for a chat. He settled down with his snap on the top of the coal pen I happened to be at, which was downwind of the coaling stage so my face was black and my eyes were red.

'I can see you're up against it today,' said Vincent.

'Clear off, will you, mate,' I said, but in an under-breath. It came to me that I just didn't trust this little fellow; I couldn't say for certain whether he was behind the exploit in the Old Shed but he was top of my list.

'I'm cleaning a big Birmingham class,' he said. 'Been at it for two days, and the job's nearly done. I'm going at her with rape oil just now.'

'Coming up nicely, is she?' I said in a weary kind of way.

'Top hole,' said Vincent.

That was all tommy-rot, for the engine he was speaking of would be black and you can't clean a black engine in a black shed, but I said nothing, and carried on shovelling while he watched me in a superior way.

He began eating, and I spotted that his dinner was a clanger, which is a pastry with jam or apple at one end and bits of meat and potato at the other. They'd had them on the North Eastern too – and up there a clanger was an engine man's dinner. There was no law against eating one if you weren't on the footplate, but it was all wrong in my eyes.

'I could do with some goggles, I tell you,' I shouted at Vincent, as the yard pilot banged another wagon up to the coaling stage.

'That's a funny bit of kit for a railwayman,' he roared back, as the blokes began chucking down the coal.

'In France,' I said, 'engine men wear them on the footplates.'

'Go on!' said Vincent.

'Honour bright,' I said, and Vincent repeated these words with a sneer, adding: 'You read that in the *Boy's Own Paper*, I suppose.'

'*Railway Magazine*,' I shouted back, but he didn't hear, or pretended not to. 'In France,' I said again, 'they call the drivers *ingenieurs*.'

'Give it a bloody rest, will you?' said Vincent, who'd gone moody again. He bit into his clanger, then quickly put it down, and I thought: I know what's happened – the jam's shot through the meat end. Serve him right, too.

'I suppose you think cab roofs should be all over,' said Vincent.

'Well,' I said, stopping shovelling because I was desperate for a proper chat, really, 'that would be up-to-date, at least.'

'Only trouble is, you'd have drivers falling asleep all the time if they didn't get a soaking or a bit of a blow to keep them going.'

'How could that happen? In America the drivers sit on *seats* in the footplate, and they don't fall asleep.'

'Seats? Can you imagine a first-class man like my uncle Arthur sitting down at the regulator?'

'Uncle!' and I fairly gasped the word out, for Vincent did not look like the sort of happy-go-lucky young fellow that has an uncle, and Arthur Hunt did not seem like the amiable sort of bloke you imagine as having a nephew.

'I'm wondering how those two ended up on the half-link,' I said. 'Your uncle especially. He looks all right to me, and you don't get taken off the main line just on account of a hard nature.'

Vincent gave me one of his looks. 'Arthur won't lick the Governor's boots, and Barney's no toady either, but he's easier meat for the bastards on account of being a more obliging sort of bloke.'

'They were both top-link men at one time, though?'

Vincent nodded: 'Lodging turns,' he muttered. He was a

very suspicious fellow, slow as Christmas at giving out facts.

'So they're both in hot water, are they?'

'Drowning in it.'

'Why don't they get stood down?'

'Too popular about the shed. There'd be a bloody riot if Arthur went, especially. Barney's got to look out for himself a bit more.'

'Why?'

'Five years back he crashed the express just before Salisbury.'

'A bad smash, was it?'

Vincent nodded: 'Made the hills rattle; he was never the same after that.'

'How do you mean?'

But Vincent said nothing to that. I looked at him, trying to fathom his face, which was like a white billiard ball, right down to the little blue chalky marks. 'This summer,' Vincent went on after a while, 'they said he ran over in the yard here, and they tried to get him for that.'

'He went past a stop signal?'

'That's what somebody said – some little splitter.'

I asked who, but he wouldn't say. He may have been slow with information but it was coming now, and it was, in a sly way, against Barney Rose. The half-link, it seemed to me, were pretty thick with each other, but Vincent preferred Hunt to Rose. I found I had a great appetite for all that he could tell me, and I wasn't sure whether it was a strength or weakness in me, but it was something altogether new.

'Barney's all right though,' he went on. 'He doesn't mind the Brookwood runs.'

Now, he'd mentioned that spot before.

'Where's Brookwood?' I asked.

'I don't know why you don't look it up in *The Railway Magazine*,' said Vincent; 'it's sure to be in there.'

We both turned away at that moment, for an 0-8-2 monster tank was coming up like nightfall. As the coal blokes began to fill its bunker, Vincent stuffed what was left of his clanger under his jacket, but it was no good, because the dust gets you from all sides.

I put in a few minutes more with the shovel before I spoke to him again. 'The Governor said nothing about me shovelling coal on these heaps.'

'But he's on sick leave just at the moment,' said Vincent, and a little smile sneaked quickly across his face. 'Maybe you should have watched your step a bit with Arthur.'

'But I've only ever said half a dozen words to him since I've been here.'

'Maybe they were the wrong half dozen,' said Vincent, bringing his clanger out of his pocket again. 'Or maybe there's a bit of a mystery about why you're here in the first place.'

'What are you getting at?' I asked, but of course I knew very well because the thing was a mystery to me as much as anybody.

'I mean, look here,' said Vincent, 'you meet some johnny up in the bloody middle of nowhere.'

He meant Smith, who was the cause of all my troubles in some way, but I tried to pretend that my thoughts concerning that gentleman came without complications. 'He wasn't some johnny, he's a director of this company.'

Vincent put his pipe on the coal, and gave me one of the hypnotising looks he went in for. 'No, mate,' he said, 'he's not.'

With this, all the ground went from beneath my feet; but I tried not to let on. 'Who is he then?'

'I can't believe you don't know all,' said Vincent. 'You must have had a few chats with the gent.'

'I've had one chat with him,' I said, 'and some letters were sent.'

'Smith used to be part of this show,' said Vincent, 'the London and South Western Company, I mean, and he still comes back to cause trouble from time to time, but now he's with another lot.'

'What other lot?' I was desperate for the answer, which

might make everything plain, but Vincent first caught up his bottle and had another long go at his tea.

'Ever heard of the London Necropolis and National Mausoleum Company?' he said after a while.

'No.'

'They run the bodies out to Brookwood Cemetery. Well, they do the ceremonials; we lay on the trains, and the half-link runs 'em.'

'And I'm to work on this funeral train?'

'If you ever get off these coal heaps,' said Vincent with a horrible little grin.

Vincent stood up and put the cork in his bottle. 'You've been sent to work on that show for a reason.'

I was still too busy trying to imagine 'that show' to be thinking of reasons, but I said in a daze: 'What?'

He didn't answer, but instead asked, 'This fellow Smith . . . he's not been in touch since?'

'No.'

'And he was helpful towards you?'

A funeral train. I had heard of a funeral train, but not a funeral *train*.

'I say,' said Vincent, 'was he helpful towards you?'

'A proper gent in all regards.'

'Think he might be a Tommy Dodd?'

'A what?'

'Don't know? Then count yourself lucky. Let's say that you're here because he's got friends who've pulled strings, and now, you see, Arthur doesn't like that because he can think of other people who should have had this start before you.'

'Like who?'

'Like friends of *his*.' Vincent was watching me like a coal rat. 'Friends of his from London. You see, we don't go up there and take *your* work, poking our nose into your ways . . .'

I thought of Grosmont, and how the sun had shone every single day as I worked my notice and the rooks had risen off the trees at dusk like cinders off a fire, and then I thought of

Smith, and how he had gulled me from start to finish. He had heard of my liking for high speed, yet had brought me down to work on a funeral train. But *why* had he done so?

'Hunt thinks I earn too much money for a new lad, doesn't he?' I said. 'That's one of the reasons he's got his knife into me.'

'No,' said Vincent, 'he thinks you earn too *little*, and that nobody should agree to come on at that rate. But you did, and so did those other out-of-town blokes – bloody Taylor and bloody Mike.'

Then I saw a big man stumbling towards us wearing a bowler that was more on his hair than on his head: the Governor. As he began to climb the coal hill, Vincent turned to face him; the two closed, and I thought the Governor looked fit to explode as he reeled back and crowned the side of Vincent's head, roaring, 'Get back to your fucking duty!' For a moment I thought Vincent was going to be up and at him, but he did saunter off eventually, cool as a cucumber, and the Governor led me into the shed to finally start me on the long road to engine driving, by which I mean that he started me cleaning Bampton Number Twenty-Nine.

The Bampton tank was green. It looked somewhat like an M7, being thirty-five tons of muscular-looking side tank, but there was something not right about it. The dome was too big, like a big, ever-growing bubble rising out of the boiler, threatening to burst.

I spent the rest of that Saturday going at it with paraffin rags on the motion and frame, and tallow on the boiler, and thinking about the private war I'd struck. The missing man, Henry Taylor, was to do with it, I was sure, and so was Mr Rowland Smith. When I was not thinking of that I was revolving in my mind funerals and trains, and how the two might go hand in hand.

For all my troubles, I was glad to be cleaning at last, and I would like to have set to with Brasso on the controls as well, but a fire-raiser came onto the engine at four o'clock and ordered me off the footplate. He didn't seem to mind, though, that I watched him about his work as best I could from down on the tracks. The lights were all lit and the shed was almost pretty – quieter than usual, too, for there didn't seem to be many blokes about.

After a while the fire-raiser looked up from the firehole door, where he'd been spreading out the coal, and shouted, 'I hear you're from the North Eastern.'

'That's it,' I said, and I was glad he was willing to chat, but anxious as to what he'd heard about me.

'Some good running up there,' he said, and his voice came out with an echo to it, as though his head was half in the firehole.

'Our first Rs', I shouted back up at him, 'did almost a hundred and fifty thousand miles between Newcastle and Edinburgh with no valve-wear to speak of.'

But by that remark I had somehow killed the conversation, for there was no answer.

Having no other duties, I hung around that funny little hunchback, Twenty-Nine, sitting on the buffer bar drinking tea until late in the evening, and watching the fire blokes come out of their mess at the top of the shed, which must have been a pretty uncomfortable spot, as it had a great fire burning at all times inside it. They were off to raise steam in the engines going out on 'dark days', which is what nights were called at Nine Elms, and they carried torches or sometimes buckets of burning paraffin held on wooden spars. They never used the engines' proper names but called out nicknames instead, and the talk was all of Jumbos, Piano Fronts, Town Halls and the like. As the evening progressed they were shouting about the Turnstile too, the pub near to the Nine Elms gates. I had seen it, of course, but that was all.

I was just thinking this was a bit of all right, that maybe things were looking up, when Arthur Hunt came out of the darkness with a black-bearded fellow. One nightmare glance went shooting between us, then he and his mate leapt up onto Thirty-One, and he took her off somewhere – I did not care where.

That night the streets were full of girls, and I suddenly knew how they got their living. From my lodge I saw washing flying on the line in the yard. There were three pairs of my landlady's knickers and three of her blouses, and they were all lit up by the light on the soap works wall. But there was no sign of the lady herself.

Chapter Eight

Tuesday 24 November

The following Tuesday I walked in on Crook, bent over his board. He seemed to be playing a game of chequers against himself, but then there came a fearful shriek; he glanced out of his window, and what he saw galvanised him into speaking.

'The Bug!' said Crook, and his eyebrows jumped, giving me high hopes of a conversation.

'What's the Bug, Mr Crook?' I said, for I had stopped siring him.

'A four-two-four tank,' he said after a while, looking over my head as he spoke.

'Anything special about it?'

'It contains at all times Sir Roger White-Chester.' He was back at his chequers game now.

'An important gentleman, is he, Mr Crook?'

'Board member,' said Crook, who was now back to mumbling, 'and more important than the locomotive superintendent, Mr Drummond, who was meant to have that thing to himself.'

'What does Mr White-Chester do?'

'Comes in weekly to inspect the shed.'

'To inspect it for what?'

'Slackness,' said Crook.

'Slackness of what kind?'

'Your kind would do,' he said, looking up at me. 'Standing about talking when you should be on the job.' And he went back to his tokens.

Walking out of Crook's place, I saw the Bug directly: a little squashed-up tank revolving on one of the turntables with a lot of smoke twisting out of its chimney in a spiral. I walked into the shed and found the Governor coughing outside his office with papers in his hand. He was walking me over for another cleaning turn when there came a second shriek from the Bug. It was pounding up towards the shed now, with us directly in its sights.

The Bug lurched to a stop and a johnny in a top hat and frock coat leapt out of the side and started striding along the very road on which we were standing. At first I thought there was something the matter with his face but this turned out to be his moustache.

'Sir Roger,' said the Governor in an under-breath.

The arrival of Sir Roger White-Chester had an electrifying effect on the shed. He came in shouting, 'Very good, very good!' and yet all the blokes in the shed had disappeared from view. He caught one poor bloke who was pushing a barrow-load of rags, though, and quizzed him about something before setting off again with his 'Very goods!' which echoed all about in what you'd have thought was an empty shed.

'What does any man who's up to the mark have to fear from talking to him?' I asked the Governor.

'Do you want me to introduce you?' he said.

It was fortunate – for I certainly did not want to be introduced – that White-Chester turned around at that moment and walked back towards daylight and his Bug. The aim, I supposed, was not that he would see others but that others would see him, and stop their slackness as a result.

At three o'clock or so I was sweeping the footplate of Bampton Thirty-One – which was like Twenty-Nine, only red – when Barney Rose came for it. I first spotted him coming through the shed towards me with the Governor and Mike, but when I looked again there was only Mike with him, and that toothy fellow leapt into the cab while Rose called out, 'Fancy a trip?'

'I'm sure I do,' I said, and straight away went bright red. This was very unexpected after all the surliness of earlier days. Alone of all the cleaners in the shed I didn't work in a gang, and I was desperate for company.

After we'd coupled up to two blank, black carriages and two passenger carriages, neither of which I got a proper look at, and finally got ourselves untangled from the Nine Elms sidings, I felt as if I'd been living in that shed around the clock for years. I had forgotten how blue the sky could be. As we rolled along the top of the black viaducts, we were level with the roofs of the houses, among which great factories squatted, like giants sitting down among pygmies.

Rose took it pretty easy on the footplate, never looking at the fire, not seeming too bothered about steam pressure, saying hardly anything to Mike. Seeing a fellow like Barney Rose at the regulator was like marvelling at a ship in a bottle: you couldn't understand how it had come about.

I realised that very likely I was only on this trip because the Governor had ordered it, but Rose was pretty friendly towards me, just as he had been on my first day – friendlier than he was towards Mike. He said that he couldn't believe anybody who came from Yorkshire was not a great hand with bat and ball. He wouldn't look me in the eye, though, I did notice that.

Mike was amiable too, but all wrong about the footplate. As he shovelled, he spilt coal everywhere – kept stumbling on the lumps like a drunk – and he just kept piling the stuff on, sending the steam pressure through the roof. He wasn't right in his looks, either, which is probably why I couldn't stop staring at him. With most people, you never see the teeth; with others you see nothing but. Mike was one of the others.

I left off staring with Rose's next remark: 'We're off up to the Necropolis station at Waterloo,' he said. 'What we've got on here are two hearse waggons and two passenger carriages, which will make up a funeral set for tomorrow.'

At last I was seeing the work of the half. 'Are there bodies inside the funeral carriages?' I said.

Rose grinned at that.

'We don't run the stiffs *into* the Necropolis station. We run them out. The trip is from the Necropolis station to the

Necropolis itself, which is at Brookwood in Surrey.' He knocked his pipe out on the regulator, sprinkling the baccy over his boots in his unparticular way as he asked: 'Now, Necropolis is a Greek word, and it means what, Mike?' He looked at his mate for the first time, who gave a sort of shrug.

'Boneyard, I expect,' said Mike.

'It's a terrible thing, this Board School education,' said Rose, as I tried to place Mike's accent. It was certainly not London. 'Necropolis means city of the dead,' he continued, 'and that's what we have at Brookwood: the biggest cemetery in the world.'

'What locos are commonly used on the run?' I asked.

Rose shrugged. 'The Bampton tanks: Twenty-Nine and this one – also known as the Green Bastard and the Red Bastard.'

I said, 'They *are* a pair of beasts, really, aren't they?' but I knew I could never call an engine a bastard, and didn't think a chap of the right sort ever would. (I was wrong about that, however, along with many other things.)

'They're not fast,' said Rose, 'but that doesn't matter because the funeral trains never go above thirty, unless Arthur's at the regulator.'

'He's still on the expresses to Devon – inside his head, I mean,' put in Mike. 'You've not lived 'til you've been put off a footplate by him.'

He smiled after saying this – it was an odd smile, because of the need to cover up his teeth – and then went red. Rose looked at Mike again but said nothing, and I thought Mike had gone a bit far in poking fun at Hunt, even though he was a pill.

'Would Henry Taylor ever have been on this Necropolis run?' I asked Rose, for I seemed to have more in common with the missing man than I would have liked.

He said nothing for a while, then: 'All cleaners get rides out.'

Now Mike spoke up, and Rose gave a strange little sort of gasp as he did so. 'Henry liked the cemetery,' he said.

He had the eyes of Rose and myself on him now.

'Why?' I asked.

'It's beautiful there. You've got, you know, grass . . . trees. It's something a bit different.'

'What was this fellow like?' I asked.

'You shouldn't say that,' said Mike, and it was the first bit of sharpness I'd had from him.

'Shouldn't say what?'

'Was.'

He'd stopped putting on coal now; he was leaning on his shovel. 'We got to be good mates, me and him, and I've had the coppers on at me no end of times, twice in the last month, trying to get to the bottom of it, and they haven't finished with me yet. If you'll take a pint with me sometime,' he went on, 'I'll tell you all about him, because he really was a first-class fellow.'

At which Rose cut in: 'We got the road for the Necrop?'

Mike leant out of his side and nodded back to him.

The Necropolis terminus was two private lines and two private platforms of no great length. It was just outside Waterloo, and the branch that led into it veered off at the last moment from the thirty or so roads going into the great station. We came in with Mike reading all the signals, the steam hammers from Waterloo beating away and echoing for miles in the hot, dirty air around the factories and houses.

The little station had a simple metal and glass canopy on each platform. It looked like a place that everyone had recently left, and when Rose shut off steam late, giving the carriages a bit of a whack against the buffers, I thought: he's trying to wake somebody up. Even though it sounded like it might be a breakdown job, though, nobody came out from any of the black doors on either platform. After a couple of minutes, however, a little tidy man in blue did come out. He looked about him a bit, then hopped down behind the tender to start uncoupling our set, and Rose told me I could go off for a quarter hour and take a look about.

I walked down the platform we'd come in on, past a row of doors in a low, blank building. The first two doors were closed, but the third was open, so I looked in. There was a fat young fellow standing in a shadow holding a broom. He was being given a scolding by an older, taller, dismal-looking fellow. They were both in black suits – neither of the best cloth – and there were posters on the walls showing folks at funerals. 'Mourning Suits Made by the Gross', I read, and 'Dickins and Jones, Mourning in All Its Branches'.

'The address is to begin in ten minutes,' the older man was saying, 'and the room is not swept.' He sounded devilish surly.

'Well, I did sweep it,' said the fat fellow.

'When?'

'Earlier,' said the fat fellow.

'Today?'

'Bit earlier than that.'

'During the summer the room was very frequently found to be in a terrible condition. At that time it was not found necessary to give the address every week . . .'

'Well, then,' said the fat kid, 'it was not found necessary to sweep the room every week, either.'

'But now the address is once more weekly; it is also of a considerable duration –'

'So I've heard,' said the fat fellow.

'– and being so, it is quite intolerable to give it in a dusty room or a room that is too cold, as is very frequently its condition.'

'Well, the fires are not down to me,' said the fat fellow, 'and two weeks ago you said it was too hot.'

'If the room is overheated, the address attracts a class of person it is desirable should not attend.'

'What class is that?'

'A cold class,' said the other, slowing down, and sounding glummer by the second. 'A class with a limited interest in extramural interment, and a much greater interest in getting warm on a sharp evening.'

'Bloody hell,' said the fat fellow, but he had a jolly sort of face, I thought, for somebody working in a spot like this.

I moved on to the next door, which was also ajar. In the darkness I made out a table, on top of which was a tangle of candelabras and a stack of thick yellow candles laid on their sides. Underneath the table was a pile of long dried rushes and two clocks of black marble that reminded me of tombs. In the corner of the room was another table, and at this one a small, worried-looking man of about seventy was reading a book while eating what must have been an early supper. It looked like chops, but where they came from I could not guess. From the door next to him, another man entered, and I at once had a feeling of great danger when I saw that it was Rowland Smith. He had on more business-like togs to the ones I'd seen him in at Grosmont, but they were still exquisite. Half-hiding at the edge of the doorway I listened.

'That's a very good mixture you have there, Erskine,' he said to the worried-looking man.

'Mmm,' said the man, because he was eating – and very fast. 'Now, on the Underground Railway, Rowland –' he continued, before stopping to pour salt onto the side of his plate. 'On the Underground Railway,' he began again after a while, 'which is the nearest station to the Temple?'

'Temple,' said Rowland Smith.

'Yes,' said the worried man. 'Which is the nearest station to it?'

'The nearest station to Temple is Temple itself.'

'This is where my spy glass comes in,' said the worried man, and he put down his knife and fork and picked up a lens on a stick. He looked through the glass at the book of maps that was before him. 'There is no station close to the Temple at all except . . . Oh, yes, I do see now. When did they build that one?'

'I don't know exactly, Erskine. It's been there for some time, I believe. On the matter of the fifty poles that are to be conveyed tomorrow to Palmer –'

But the worried man was not having this. 'Is Stanley preaching the gospel?' he asked instead, pushing his book away. 'I saw you speaking with him earlier.'

'The address is shortly to begin.'

'Good attendance?'

'There will be the usual number, I expect. If that. He says the room is too cold, and not swept.'

'Yes, he seemed very agitated.'

'He is always in that condition.'

'Indeed, and I fear the matter goes deeper than an unswept room,' said the worried man, going back to his chops. 'The difficulty is the manner of the address.'

'And the subject,' said Smith. 'But it would look amiss, I think, after all, to drop it or even reduce the frequency.'

'That is your settled view?' said the worried man.

'Yes.'

'You have no thoughts of bringing him into your scheme of economy?'

'No.'

These two are not the greatest of pals, I thought.

'Have you moved yet?' said the worried-looking man, chewing ten to the dozen.

'Yes,' said Smith. 'Last week.'

'I have not had notification of the change of address.'

'It is not much changed,' said Smith. 'I'm still in the same mansion block.'

'Then why the deuce did you move?' said the worried-looking man.

'It is a better flat. It is on the lower floor, giving on to the garden, and it is to the rear, so it is quieter.'

'A southerly aspect, I trust?'

'Easterly,' said Smith, at which he looked up and saw me in the doorway.

'You know, as to the poles to be conveyed to Palmer,' the worried man said, 'I must, as Chairman, take heed of the points raised by Mr Argent –'

'Excuse me, Erskine,' said Rowland Smith, and he came hurrying across the room towards me.

He was very friendly, as before; and when he lifted his hat his hair sprang up, also as before. 'How are you settling in?'

'Tolerably well, sir, thank you,' I said, for I was at least man enough not to say I was having an awful time of it.

'And the lodge is a pretty good one?'

'Quite all right, really,' I said.

'You've come in on the footplate?' He pointed to Thirty-One, and I nodded.

'Just for a jaunt, or have they got you firing all ready?'

'Just for the jaunt,' I said. He really seemed to know nothing at all of railways. 'Mr Smith,' I said, 'when you were good enough to take an interest in me before, I was given to . . . I was . . . I formed the impression that you were connected to the London and South Western Railway.'

Rowland Smith was always able to bring out the best from me, in a roundabout way. It had taken a lot for me to say that, just as it had taken a lot for me to ask him to take me on in the first place.

He smiled and nodded. 'As you might know, this and that company are closely interconnected, the South Western running the trains to Brookwood by contractual arrangement with the Mausoleum Company. Some five months ago I found myself in the position of being able to do some work, advisory in nature in the main, for the board here, and I put myself forward. On finding I had been succesful, I of course resigned my seat on the board of the South Western so as to avoid any collision of interests.'

I thought: it is not normal for a man like this to speak to a man like me in this way.

Smith suddenly laughed, and in a most amiable manner. 'You yourself would have stayed at the South Western?'

I could not help but nod, crimson-faced I should imagine.

'But then you speak as a lifelong subscriber to *The Railway Magazine*,' said Smith, seeming to bow at me as he did so.

The worried-looking man appeared at the doorway. 'If you must talk to me about those poles, Rowland –'

'Yes, Erskine. I'm just saying hello to this young fellow here: Mr Jim Stringer. He is a very hard worker, entitled to every possible encouragement. He works with the chaps that drive for us, and he's always after footplate runs, so we'll be seeing a fair bit of him.'

This obviously did not excite the elderly gentleman all that much; in fact it made him look very sad. As he looked on, Smith asked, 'Will you meet me, in order to let me ask you some questions?'

'Questions as to what, sir?'

'Oh, concerning the life at Nine Elms.'

'Where?' I said, and I must have fairly gasped out the word.

'My flat. The address is on the letters.' He reached into his jacket and a pocket book flopped open in his hand. 'You must come to my place,' he said again, 'and you must come by cab.' He held out his long, fine right hand, and I saw a ten shilling note there.

I shook my head and took a step back; a cab (with an honest driver) could be had for sixpence a mile. I was young but I was not stupid, and it seemed to me plain that he wanted me to sneak on my fellows and would pay me to do so.

'I'll write to you,' he said, putting the note back into his pocket as though quite used to having his offers refused. 'Do carry on with your tour,' he said. 'It's quite an interesting set-up we've got here.'

Chapter Nine

Tuesday 24 November
continued

I could not stop thinking about what Rowland Smith had in mind for me in his flat in the Northern Division of London, but if anything could have taken my mind off it, the little Necropolis Station was the thing. It certainly was a very interesting show.

I walked around the buffer stops to the second platform, where there was another row of low, dull buildings. I had been given permission to look about, so I opened one of the doors and there was a coffin. Above it, an electric light swayed on a chain that had a black cable entwined in its links. The coffin lid was off and, stepping forward, I saw a white face – I could not say whether a man's or a woman's – with a mass of blackness below. There were chairs like thrones on either side, and I marvelled to think that this place was a waiting room of sorts. I looked again at the mighty electric light, thinking: all this modernity for the dead. But I longed for the roaring of gas, and I stepped out of there in double-quick time.

I walked around the block of buildings on that platform and saw what from my side looked like a low wall but was in fact the top of a twenty-foot drop. At the bottom was a dazzling white courtyard with, on the far side, a fancy pink-brick building with a big arch cut through it. As I looked down, a black coach-and-four shot through the arch into the courtyard. The driver got down, and when he removed his black top hat I expected more blackness, but there was no hair there at all. It was as if he was letting me know: just between you and I, my unknown friend above, I am completely bald. He put the hat back on, left the carriage in the middle of the courtyard, and everything went still again save for the hot horses, stomping now and again in the shafts.

65

Two minutes later a door on the right-hand side of the court opened, and two men in black came through it. Three more men in black came out from the tunnel, and one of these was talking all the time, but I couldn't see which one. The men stood still for a second; but their shadows, which were like the hands of clocks, kept growing. Then the bald fellow led the horses into stables at one side, and a coffin was taken out of the back of the carriage by the other four, who put it onto their shoulders and carried it quickly through a doorway in the bottom of the wall of which I was on top. I seemed to be watching a funeral taken at a running pace, but with all proper dignity preserved.

The door below me closed, and then I heard a muffled, buried groaning getting louder and louder. This groaning changed to more of an open-air scream for a second, before the four men and the coffin burst out of a door right behind me that was in some part of the platform buildings. They'd come out of a rising room – in America they call them elevators. The coffin men turned and aimed towards me. For a second it was as if they were bringing their casket to me, asking me if I'd like to try it for size, and I was glad when they continued down the path towards the buffer bars. I now spotted an iron ladder coming up from the floor of the courtyard to where I was standing, and I thought: I'll go down.

This place spoke of mystery, and it needed to be got to the bottom of, and so did that ladder.

The courtyard was white and empty, except for horse droppings. I thought: for neatness and cleanness you must have up-to-date transport, but then I remembered Nine Elms. I went across the courtyard, through the arch, and out into the street. I couldn't quite get my bearings. I knew by the noise and the pickle-and-beer smell and the train thumping across the viaduct to one side that I must be in the same territory as my lodge. The front of the Necropolis building was straight out of the *Arabian Nights* – all domes and swirls and bricks of pink, as though it was embarrassed, for the street it stood in was plain enough. I tried to get the place straight in my head. It was like a castle with a courtyard, and this pink part with the arch running through it was where the portcullis would be. Yes, a castle with a portcullis, a courtyard – and a small railway station running along the top of its back wall.

'Excuse me,' said a pleasant sort of voice at that moment. 'Is today Tuesday?'

I turned around and saw another man in black – no under-taker this time, but a parson.

'I am looking for the Tuesday Address on Interment,' he said. 'Do you know where it is held?'

'Upstairs in there, I suppose,' I said, pointing at some of the lighted top windows of the pink part.

'It *is* Tuesday, isn't it?' said the parson.

'Do you mean *today*?' I said, because I was learning to be cautious with all remarks.

'The last time I came it wasn't on,' he said, 'or at least it wasn't on here, but perhaps it sometimes happens elsewhere.'

This parson, who was a very vague gentleman indeed, now walked under the arch and through a doorway in its side. I followed, and saw that he had entered a kind of vestibule with electric lights burning. It was all good wood; there was a triangle pattern everywhere in the panels, which meant something – the sign of a secret society – and on the wall just to the left of the door was a glass case with funeral notices inside. There was a smell of carbolic and old flowers.

I walked in, and up the wide wooden staircase. There was nothing on the first floor save closed double doors and a great fan of flowers trapped in a glass globe. If they could have had black flowers, I am sure they would. The sprays were perfect but I didn't like the way they didn't move, and I began to think more favourably of old Crystal and his fluttering blooms on the 'up' and 'down'.

There were two lots of double doors on the next two land-ings, and two more on the fourth floor, which was the top one. On one of this pair was a card fitted into a slot, reading:

'Extramural Interment: An Address by Mr S. Stanley'. From within, I could hear what I felt certain was the voice of the sad busybody I had glimpsed earlier scolding the fat boy, but this time he sounded slower, and lower and grander. He was saying, 'As it is appointed unto all men once to die, the subject of interment is one of universal interest. It comes home to every human breast, not only with a solemn but an emphatic closeness. Whatever, or whosoever, the head of a family in this vast city may be – whether high or low, rich or poor, young or old or in the prime of his days, he must . . .'

I knew what was going on: this was the company crying its wares. I put my eye to the chink in the door, and although I could not see the speaker, I could count the number in his audience. There were four, including the parson I had spoken to in the street.

I turned to the second door and, opening it, came upon a room in which were one loud clock and a lot of large books. Screwing my boldness up to the highest pitch, I entered this little library, which seemed more out of bounds, than any other part of the premises so far. The volumes were marked with every year from 1852 to the present. I picked out 1888, and opened it.

'On Tuesday 19th of March,' I read, 'at a meeting of the directors –'

Just then I heard a voice.

I looked up from the book, but what I had heard was only the voice of Stanley coming through from the next room. He was in high force now. 'Within these numerous and loathsome decomposing troughs, for centuries past in the heart of the capital of a great Christian nation, the most depraved system of sepulture has existed that has ever disgraced the annals of civilisation . . .' (His speech being very old fashioned, I couldn't properly follow the meaning.) 'During which time the amount of poisonous gases evolved from putrefaction into the civic atmosphere, beyond that absorbed by the soil, exceeded . . .' Here there was a short pause, before Stanley continued with a dismal booming, *some seventy-five million cubic feet.*

I read the book as long as I dared, and could not make sense of it. It was all lawyer's talk. But it wasn't all books, this room. The clock was on the mantel, which was very grand, and there was one black pot to the left of it and another to the right. Over the mantel were pictures of swells, five in all, with dates underneath. The first picture was titled 'Colonel Tidey', and he was dated 1799–1862. Well, that was his life, but there was another line, stating that he had been 'Chairman of the London Necropolis Company from 1854 to 1861'. Colonel Tidey was a bearded gentleman, as were the next three. The fifth only had moustaches, and had been photographed, not painted. His name was Sir John Rickerby, and he had gone from life, and of being chairman, in the same year, 1903, the only one to have done the two in one. Well, I thought, it's 1903 now, so he could have died this very morning, although that would have needed quick work by the picture framers.

I thought of the worrit I had seen eating a chop and talking of poles to Mr Smith, the fellow called Erskine; he was the present chairman – he'd felt the need to remind Smith of it – so he would take the next spot on this chimney breast. I stood and looked at the pictures, deciding at length that each of the five seemed more down-hearted than the last.

'Nothing more or less than to remove the sepulture of the dead from the homeseats of the living!' the voice from the next room was booming, in a desperate sort of way. I stepped out of the room with the pictures and the books, returning to the top of the stairs. 'Be assured, madam,' Stanley was saying – and he was back to his fast, busybody voice now – 'that a hopeful spirit is *somehow* maintained. By liberal expenditure of printer's ink has it been made known . . .'

When, five minutes later, I walked back along the first platform at the Necropolis station, I was amazed to see, beyond Thirty-One, the Bug sailing away from the station, with White-Chester leaning out from one side, holding onto his topper and looking back towards the Necropolis station, and

Rowland Smith doing the same from the other side. Smith wore no hat, and his curly hair was flying.

On Thirty-One, Barney Rose and Mike were waiting with steam up. They were not talking and Rose, I fancied, looked pinker and more crumpled than usual, perhaps because he was sitting on the sandbox and staring silently into the fire. 'Saw you talking to your Mr Smith, there,' he said, looking up at me. 'Most amiable, he seemed to be.' He was smiling, but more from habit than happiness, I thought. 'He works here, now,' he continued, 'but he's still great mates with White-Chester.'

'The two of them have just gone off in the Bug,' I said.

Rose nodded, then he looked up and grinned. 'Dapper gentleman, ain't he?' he said, as some of his former cheeriness seemed to return. 'Yes, I'll say that for him, quite the masher, is that young chap.'

Rose was suddenly speaking to me as a man and I made an effort to answer in kind: 'Quite the ladies' man, too, I should guess,' I said.

'Oh, well,' he said, looking back up at me, 'I don't know about that, but I'll tell you this: he's tough as a bulldog under all those fine coats of his, a very good fellow to have batting on your side.' He nodded at me as if to say 'congratulations on that, at any rate', before slowly standing up and walking back over to the regulator.

As we pulled away, I leant out of the cab and watched the Bug disappearing into the complications of the down-main with a great sense of desolation in me; of being a very small person in a very great city, where everything hurtled at too great a rate, and people moved from station to station, life to death, all in the blinking of an eye, with nobody to notice or care, or say that the world had been lost to madness, because the madness had by degrees become the normal thing. And nor could you step aside from it. You kept up with the game or you got flattened, as surely as if you'd stood on the tracks before one of Mr Ivatt's mighty Atlantics.

And so I would try to keep up with the game.

Chapter Ten

Saturday 28 November

On the Saturday following – by which time I had recorded all the strange events in my Lett's diary, with notes as to possible meanings in the many spare pages at the back – I walked through the door of my lodge after a long and lonely day of cleaning at Nine Elms to find my landlady in the kitchen. She was about her Saturday clothes-washing, stirring the boiler with a black wooden stick, and very prettily too, with her head turned away from the rising steam, which had somehow unloosed her curls.

'Mr Stringer,' she said, nodding slowly.

I nodded back, and she gave me a glance which I took to mean there was something a little too forward in the way I had looked at her, so there was nothing for it but to leave the kitchen.

A few minutes later, however, when I was lying on my bed listening to the rumbling of the trains and looking once again at the notes in my diary (which had quite replaced *The Railway Magazine* for me), there came a knock on my door. 'Come in,' I said, standing up, but she would not.

She had put her hair to rights; the style was complicated but most effective. 'You forgot to put out your washing again,' she said.

'I'm sorry,' I said. 'Would it be too late to do it now?'

'I'm just about to drain the boiler.'

'Oh.'

She was looking all around the room, as if she had never set eyes on it before, but I was interested to see that she did not once look at the water on the floor. Should I say that it was a little hard to be paying six shillings a week, with a pound down, for a place with a puddle next to the bed? I was struggling for the right words here when she thrust a piece of paper at me, saying, 'Mr Stringer, would you be so kind as to post this somewhere about the premises of your railway company? It is an advertisement.'

'Yes,' I said, 'I would be very pleased to. Do you mind if I read it?'

She shook her head.

'Unusually excellent furnished bed and sitting room with garden view offered to respectable person,' I read aloud. 'One minute from Waterloo Station. No servants kept, every comfort and convenience. Very moderate terms.'

'Well?' she said.

'What room is this concerning?' I said.

'The one alongside this one, of course,' she said.

'The one with the looking glass?' I said.

'It has a very *pretty* looking glass,' she said. 'Ought I to mention that?'

'You've put down "No servants kept",' I said, 'but –'

'I am not a servant,' she said, most indignantly.

'No,' I said, 'of course not. I only meant that your terms do include laundry.'

'I will wash clothes,' she said, '*if* they are put out.'

'I think it's an excellent notice,' I said, handing back the paper, 'unusually excellent, in fact, and I know just the spot for it at Nine Elms.' I had in mind the noticeboard in the timekeeper's office. I put the notice into my waistcoat pocket, and my eyes drifted once again to the water on the floor. I noticed that my landlady's had done the same. 'I wonder what causes the water on the floor?' I said.

'A broken roof,' she said.

She was certainly very direct. She walked into the room and put the toe of her boot into the puddle in a very hypnotising way. She looked up at me and her face was caught mysteriously between smiling and not. 'It's the trains have loosened the tiles on the roof,' she said. 'What I call the drayhorse engines do it – those fearful draggers that bring the heavy waggons over the arches and set every house in the district shaking.'

'You mean the slow-goods?' I said.

She did not seem very sure of that.

I somehow took her to mean that she fancied the expresses at any rate, and I asked if that was true.

'Well,' she said, 'I suppose I do. If I have to go to Bournemouth then I wish to go in a hurry.'

'You've been there?' I said, 'On excursions?'

She nodded.

'The Greyhounds can do it in two hours,' I said.

'Well, ours took four on the last occasion,' she said, walking rapidly towards the door as though I personally had been responsible for the slowness of her journey to the sea.

'High speed is my passion,' I said, to try and stop her going.

'But you are presently retained . . . not as a driver?'

'As a cleaner,' I said eagerly, 'but cleaning is the way to driving, did I not tell you that when I arrived at this lodge?'

She nodded quickly, and said, 'The subject of trains is of great interest to some people – or so I would imagine.'

And then she was gone, but the puddle was still there on the floor.

Chapter Eleven

Monday 30 November

For the following week I had the worst turn of the lot: the five o'clock in the morning go-on. On my first day of early turns, which was Monday 30 November, there was more coming and going in the shed than I had seen at any later hour, with 200 locomotives under the roof, and the fires were being started on all sides. The men were stoking up the whole of London, setting the world turning for another day, and by their looks they seemed to say they could manage the job quite well without me.

I went in to see the Governor first thing. As Nolan scribbled away, the Governor said he was giving me a rest from Twenty-Nine and Thirty-One for a while, for there weren't enough funerals. This was no great shock: those two only went out three or four times a week in any case. He put me on to general tidying and making straight, and as I was leaving he called out, 'Watch yourself off-shed today. It's thick as a bag out there.'

I walked back to the mouth of the shed, and saw that the dawn had come but it had been one of those frauds, where too much blackness makes way for too much whiteness. I couldn't even make out the turntables. A bell was being rung behind me, echoing in the shed. A couple of engines were coming off-shed, rolling out on the tracks to either side of me, big as black clanking houses on the move and giving me a sheer blank fright as they swept strangely past, proving the power of the fog, which swallowed them in an instant. A minute after, I heard an explosion.

A man to my left threw off his cap and began to run. On Filey Beach when I was twelve, my dad offered me a sporting challenge: first to touch the spars of Lighthouse Pier from a hundred yards off. For the first time my father did not let me win, and I saw what a man could do, even a little, sometimes-silly butcher in a brown billycock. This fellow was faster than my dad. He was leaping the rails, flying across the front of the fog, then disappearing diagonally into it. A crowd was coming up behind me to watch, and I turned around and saw Crook. It was a shock to see him away from his clock. 'Detonation,' he said to me, and his eyebrows did their little jump.

Detonators were put on the tracks as a back-up for signals on foggy days, and an explosion meant an engine had struck one. I didn't breathe as I awaited the sound of a smash, which was like waiting for death itself, because there was curiosity and horror too. I believed smashes came as the sound of a great bell being rung, and now I was about to find out for myself. But thirty seconds went by and we heard nothing, and I felt I ought to be doing more than standing there and waiting, so I stepped away from the shed.

I knew, once in the middle of the fog, that the bad business wasn't over. There were shouts, lamps swinging, the sound of people scrambling forward, then stopping. I was hard by the locomotive now, and I saw it was an engine commonly called a Jubilee, one of the two that had rolled out of the shed beside me. There were men all around it, with more crammed onto the footplate. A man was being moved around in there, propped up, turned about, and I could see the little ambu-lance box being passed across from one fellow to another. Then I saw the head of the man being moved: it was Mike's, and it was all wrong; blue, like a bad potato.

The body that was connected to the head flopped – the legs were for a second forgotten, and dangled from the cab – and it seemed too small, although in fact it was the head that was too big. But it scarcely mattered either way: the two could not remain connected for very much longer, since the one would henceforward want nothing to do with the other.

Now there was a fellow coming up from behind who said, 'Did you hear the barker?' Somebody else I didn't know said,

'That's what we all heard.' 'No,' said a voice that could have been the first one, 'we heard the shooter and the fog bomb blowing off together.' Another said, 'There was no shooter. He just came off the bloody engine.'

I looked up. Arthur Hunt was leaning against the Jubilee's tender and staring at me as if he'd never left off doing it from that time I'd first seen him in the half-link's mess. The dirty business done, the fog was clearing all the time, racing away. Barney Rose was at the other end, next to the cylinder casing. He had his pipe going, but looked rattled all the same, and I knew I should have left him alone, but I couldn't. I had come to a place that was full of hatred. One man had disappeared and another had died, and this last was a good deal more popular than myself. It wasn't bravery that made me walk towards Rose; it was something like what they call the life force itself.

The fog may have been lifting but the Jubilee was giving out whiffs of steam, and there was Rose's pipe smoke to add to the morning ghostliness. When he spoke he looked away from me. 'I was under orders from the Governor to let Mike take her off-shed,' he said, 'just while I walked along her and took a good look at the motion . . . something a bit queer about the noise it was making . . .' He left a long pause, then he started again, still looking away: 'He was like Taylor and like you: a very ardent lad.'

He gave a funny little sideways smile that made me feel ill, and I said, 'What do you *mean*?' I suppose I was shouting, but the fog seemed to require it.

'No holds barred,' said Rose, shaking his head and seeming nearly to laugh. Another bloke came up to us, and Rose carried on talking, still with that hateful half smile. 'Well, Mike being new to the regulator, and a little heavy-handed with it, I got left behind. I never saw him hit the fog bomb, only heard it, and when I got nearer he was flat out by the track, with the engine heading away for bloody Bournemouth at ten miles to the hour. He'd come off the footplate and hit the next rail.' He looked up at the two of us, then down again. 'Talk about beginner's luck,' he said.

Beyond and above us, on the footplate of the engine, I could make out that they were still holding Mike, still turning him this way and that as if he might somehow come back to life if they got him at the right angle.

'How did he come off?' said a voice.

'Tripped on coal, if you ask me,' said Rose.

I remembered that I had seen Mike's messy ways with the shovel for myself.

A lantern was coming towards us; behind it was a man coughing – the Governor. 'It's Florence fucking Nightingale,' said a sharp voice – the voice of Arthur Hunt. Mike was being brought down off the footplate, and somebody was shouting, roaring angrily. The Governor yelled something to Rose, then leapt onto the footplate of the Jubilee. Rose followed him up more slowly, looking completely all in. Two minutes later the engine began rolling backwards towards the shed. Rose was at the regulator, and the Governor was looking out at all the blokes. 'The impedimentia of illusion are being removed from the stage!' he roared, by which he meant get back to our duties.

A shout went up – many intemperate words, and all against the Governor. I wasn't one of the shouters but it made me feel good to be part of the crowd. For the first time I was a Nine Elms man. Well, I mean . . . it was for once not myself but another who was the object of hatred. 'Get that fucking slave driver off there,' said a voice from the crowd of men, which could have been Hunt again, but I could not be sure. Then I saw the swinging bulls' eyes of the constables coming up, and I thought: it is very like the end of the shows in the music halls with the chuckers-out coming in, and I remembered Mike's legs hanging off the side of the cab, and how they were like Mr Punch's little broken legs that would sometimes flop over the front of the small stages in the seaside booths, making you sorry for him in spite of all. But Mike was a good fellow to begin with, in my eyes at least; Taylor had been another by all accounts, and maybe that was part of the killer's programme, to get the nice ones, in which case I had better stop playing the milksop.

The coppers took the numbers of the blokes around the loco, and asked everybody what they'd seen. Two hours later a detective with a white beard who looked like a sea captain, accompanied by the Governor, came to see me while I was ripping rags on my own in the rag store, and I told them everything I knew and nothing of what I thought – because I could have given them quite a bit to chew on.

The Governor called me a good lad, and started coming on strong about the half-link blokes right in front of the detective. He said that Rose was not up to the mark, that there would be an inquiry, and it would be the finish of him. He also said that Rose had overrun in the yard at the start of August, which I'd already heard from Vincent, who'd said somebody had split over it, and now the Governor, working up to boiling point in the rag store, came out with the name. 'It was that poor sod Henry Taylor who spilled the beans to me – it was his job to do it, but look what happened to him. He was a good lad too – would have been up on the footplate in double-quick time.'

By now his colour had reached the danger level, and he started coughing, as the detective, who seemed to know of all this anyway, smiled, and told him to calm himself.

I had one question burning to be asked: 'Where's Vincent today?'

'On leave,' said the Governor.

'So he's not about?' I said, and the Governor said nothing, but looked across at the detective.

As I went back to tearing rags, I fell to thinking – because I had to think about everything – how Mike was careless with coal. On the footplate, he was one of those clumsy fellows whose boots always seemed too big. But it did look as if he'd been jacked in, and with him went the best hope of finding out what had really happened to Henry Taylor. Why would Barney Rose not look at me? And why had Arthur Hunt been off-shed with no engine underneath him? And then Vincent, who was certainly no friend of Mike's . . . that mysterious little fellow had five days holiday a year, and had taken one of them on this foggy November day . . . And then why had Arthur been off-shed with no engine underneath him?

One thing seemed certain: with Mike gone, the half-link was left with nothing but relief firemen. Vincent would have to go up. At the same time, though, there were 500 men at Nine Elms Loco Shed, and any one of them could have been the killer. Come to that, there were thousands of fellows in London who were off their boxes, and the wall around Nine Elms was low enough to let in any of *them*. Bob Crook, after all, was no sentry – you did not need to see him unless you were booking on.

When I'd finished thinking all these things – all destined for the back of the diary, to be mulled over for hours – my mind emptied for a while, except for the small part of it needed to keep me tearing rags. I did not quit the work but in due course a feeling of stark terror came over me, and with it thoughts of the shadows in the courtyard, moving and growing.

I had seen the devil of violence and yet I knew it was only the start.

Chapter Twelve

Thursday 3 December

I did not see Vincent until that Thursday. He was in the cleaners' mess eating his snap, and as I entered he walked out straight away, leaving some onion skins behind. That was probably because he'd heard I'd been on the footplate of Thirty-One, or because he was still not firing on the half despite the death of Mike; or just because he had his knife into me the same as everyone else. I didn't have the opportunity to tell him what I thought about Mike, which was just as well, because Vincent was the fifty-face man, and you couldn't tell him your innermost thoughts.

At the end of that day I kept a new promise I had made to myself (for I had nobody else to make it to): I went into the Turnstile, the pub just outside the engine-shed gates, and I dare say I was one of the few fellows ever to have stepped in there alone and with no prospects of a chat. It was a bare, blank place with two bars separated by a screen: there was no difference between the two, but one was for footplate men, the other for all the rest of the blokes. I don't know why, but I liked it; I thought it was the heart of something – and it was packed out.

I had only seen pubs from the jug-and-bottle doors, where Dad would send me from time to time, but as I said, he did not hold with taking a drink inside a pub. He wasn't church and he wasn't chapel or anything at all in the religious line; I suppose it came down to this: that a pub was a place where smart boots cut no ice.

I had stepped into the part that was for 'the rest'. Fighting my way to the bar, I got myself what the fellow in front had asked for: a glass of 'half and half'. I didn't know what either half was, but after one sip I knew I'd better go carefully with it. The engine men, on the other side, took their ale in pewters. I looked all about me, watching the blokes chat, and wondered how it had come about that I was watching these revels but not joining in the fun. Presently I spied Flannagan, the charge cleaner. With his funny legs, this fellow was made for leaning up against a bar and that's what he was doing. As he talked to two young fellows I'd seen about the place cleaning, fetching tea for Flannagan and so on, I thought that perhaps one of my troubles – when it came to understanding all the exploits going on about me *and* getting myself some pals, which probably went hand in hand – was that I had not yet stood a drink for any Nine Elms man. The fact was that I had not stood anybody a drink anywhere, but I knew it was a manly sort of thing, and this was the place to start.

'Two gallons of linseed oil,' Flannagan was drawling, 'one gallon of paraffin, about a pint of bloody Brasso . . .' As I moved towards him with a weird sort of smile fixed onto my face, his talk gradually got slower as though he was a clockwork toy winding down, and when I was right alongside him, he stopped completely, with nothing but a look of disgust left on his face.

I had forgotten that the fellow to be bought a drink had to want to have one bought for him. So I turned away, and it immediately seemed that Flannagan got wound up again. 'Half a ton of rags, about a mile of bloody emery paper –'

'You're exaggerating now,' said one of the lads near him.

'I'm fucking *telling* you,' said Flannagan, 'and it still comes off black as night. That fucking engine was *built* dirty.'

'Get away, Mr Flannagan,' said one of the young fellows – but in a scared voice.

Back at the bar I tried to steady myself after this latest calamity. Looking up, I spotted Arthur Hunt in the drivers' part. Vincent was on one side of him, Rose on the other. Vincent shouldn't really have been in there, since, although he was passed, he hadn't gone up. But he was Hunt's nephew, and what Hunt said went.

Hunt was smoking a cigar, his sharp nose going forwards

and his hair swept back. Vincent was quiet, just watching his uncle as though he was a god.

Barney Rose was looking semi-drunk, but Hunt was a different person altogether in the company of another engine man, even one as slack as Rose. I put my anxieties about the pair of them aside, and saw two engine men enjoying a drink after their turn, picturing them both on express rails, skimming down the lawn to Bournemouth.

'Dear old Teddy?' Rose suddenly said to Hunt, and it was evidently a great crack because they both laughed a good deal. It was strange to see Hunt do this because his face altered out of all recognition. Rose said, 'Chamberlain.'

'Joseph Chamberlain?' said Hunt in a thoughtful sort of way, rising as he did so and walking towards the bar. 'Now if that gentleman had not had all the advantages this world has to offer,' he called back to Rose, 'then I think –'

'I've got it,' called Rose. 'Plumber!'

Hunt purchased two more pewters of beer. 'I'm not so sure,' he said, going back with the ale. 'I mean to say, there's a fair amount of skill in that.'

Rose took a long pull on his beer. 'Plumber's mate, then,' he said after a while.

'What are the duties of a plumber's mate?' asked Hunt.

'Carrying spanners,' said Rose. 'Brewing up for the plumber.'

Hunt nodded. 'And do you need certificates for it?'

'I'm sure that a couple of testimonials would suffice to get you a start in that line.'

'But where would a clot like Chamberlain get a decent testimonial?'

'Mr Balfour might give him one?'

'Mmm,' said Hunt, and I hoped he was going to smile again, because I liked to see what happened to his face when this novelty occurred. But thinking better of this, I finished my drink and left before he could look up and see me and have his evening spoiled.

Chapter Thirteen

Saturday 5 December

On the Saturday, I booked off at four-thirty and turned my back on Nine Elms, which was full of rumours and coppers, and walked back to my lodge along the riverside. Along the Embankment, which was as busy as any road, I watched the black water sliding up and down the hulls of the rolling, smoking boats. Waterloo was a stranger place than Nine Elms, with a stranger smell, and the god of it all was the stone lion watching the black river from the top of the Red Lion brewery. The sun was going down, but that smoke was still going up, and the traffic and the people were all still going strong as the sky turned pink.

I turned away from the river into York Road: hundreds and hundreds of people were coming at me under hats. I stopped under my coffee viaduct and there was yet another new person – a young woman – standing behind the stall.

'Money in the tin?' I said.

'That's it, love,' she said.

Her eyes were very blue, and very white around the blueness. When I'd paid she tipped her head and stretched out her arms like a dancer, pushing her bosoms to the front of her semi-clean white dress. It's not often, I thought, that you see anyone so very beautiful do anything so strange. I moved along Lower Marsh with my coffee feeling ashamed of my thoughts. I bought some Vianola soap from the Vianola Soap Pharmacy over the road from my lodge, because I had planned an extra good wash for myself before taking a pint down at the Citadel. I had found myself quite galvanised by my drink at the Turnstile, despite the difficult circumstances; several things had become clearer in my mind, although I had found, when I came to put them in my Lett's diary, that they amounted to nothing much. The thoughts were along the following lines: that although Barney Rose was under the gun at Nine Elms, he had a better friend in Arthur Hunt than I had first thought.

At any rate, I resolved that there would be no harm in taking a drink more often after my turns. I was moving away from Dad by degrees, but that was only right. He would not stop *being* my dad by any of this.

I looked up at the wall of my lodge, and saw that an advertisement for 'Go West Cheese' had been put on top of some of the 'Smoke Duke of Wellington Cigars'. 'Stower's Lime Juice, No Musty Flavour' was still there.

My lodge was dark and hot. Instead of going straight up the narrow stairs to my room, I went into the kitchen for a bowl of washing water. My landlady was there, folding clothes. The boiler was bubbling away in the corner giving the place the drowsy air of a Monday morning. The place was more like a factory than a kitchen, with no decoration apart from a line of tins on the mantelshelf and a framed bit of embroidery above the tins reading 'Commit Thy Way Unto The Lord'.

I gave my 'good evening' and paid my rent; then, in keeping with my new idea of boldness, said, 'It's quite all right either way, but did you manage to get any cocoa in?'

My landlady looked up at the tins on the mantelshelf, and I did the same: Bird's Eye Custard, Marigold Flake, somebody's candied peel, Goddard's Plate Powder, raisins, currants.

'No,' she said.

'Oh, well,' I said. 'I would like to collect a bowl of hot water to have a wash, if that's all right.'

She put the kettle on, then leant up against the table, saying, 'And how is life on the railways?' She looked very grave; very beautiful, too, in a strange way. Every one of her expressions seemed to contain a lifetime of meaning. She said again, 'How is life on the railways?'

'Well, it's not all honey,' I said.

Two racks full of airing clothes were swinging slowly above our heads. She went over to the boiler, moving the clothes inside around with the stick, watching me. She laid the stick on the side of the boiler before walking over to the table. This was covered in blue cloth. There were two piles of folded towels on it, and a red book. My landlady touched one of the piles of towels and let it tumble on top of the book. Then she looked at me and nearly smiled, which was more thrilling than if she really had smiled. Suddenly she whirled around and started moving the tins on the mantelpiece. I could see the tops of her gypsy boots, and, being embarrassed, I embarked on one of my Gladstone speeches, for which I cursed myself even as the words were coming from my mouth.

'I am endeavouring to rise in the estimation of my mates, not by boasting of my accomplishments but by being at all times civil and obliging, ensuring that when my driver comes to collect the engine on which I have been working, not only are the motion and boiler thoroughly cleaned, but also that the footplate is swept up and the boiler front plate –'

'Mr Stringer,' said my landlady, 'you are very boring.'

'Oh,' I said.

'How would you feel if I told you all the details of my working day?'

'I would be very interested.'

'Right,' she said, with considerable force. 'Today I started at six, when I realised that you had left out your laundry for me to wash.'

'But you told me to do that!' I protested. 'And there were only two shirts and two undershirts.'

(My long johns I had been too embarrassed to put out, and I had been endeavouring to clean them myself when my landlady was absent.)

'I collected it from upstairs,' she went on, 'and put it together with the household load. Then I sorted the whites from the coloureds, and gave everything a good scrub with the brush on the washboards. I broke off to start the fire under the boiler, before boiling up the whites, giving them a good poke about all the time with the stick, and using plenty of soap, which I cut off the big block. After that I rinsed and blued to bring the whites up to white. Next the coloureds had to be done, and after that everything was rinsed and put through the mangle. Some went out on the line to dry, and some were put up here.' She pointed to the swinging airers. 'Next, I cleaned out the copper and scrubbed it for next time.'

'But it's still going –'

'When I had finished,' she said, cutting me off, 'I looked again at all your clothes, and realised they were still in a terrible state, so I did them all again.'

'It's because I'm cleaning engines,' I said.

'By transferring all the dirt to yourself,' she said. 'Why do they not give you something to wear other than ordinary clothes?'

'I don't know,' I said. 'In America, footplate men do have uniforms.'

She looked at me very curiously.

'They're blue,' I added, wanting to keep my explanation to a minimum so as to avoid being called boring once again.

'Blue would be a good colour for it,' she said, 'and pitch black would be better still. I see no reason why the trains cannot be electrical, and they will be in time. They will be quicker, cleaner, less noisy, and we will not all be living in this hell.'

I was knocked for six by all this. I said, 'In Baytown, where I come from, they do the washing on a Monday.'

'*They*,' she said. 'That is exactly it.'

'We had a part-time slavey to do ours,' I said, adding: 'You object to the work, I suppose?'

'What else is open to me? Sweating at the pickle factory or the rag shop.'

I said, 'You could go into an office and be a typewriter.'

'I don't mind it so much,' she said, ignoring me. 'My father is rather old-fashioned, but a good man, and I will come into his two houses. Then what a difference you'll see.'

'Gas upstairs?' I said.

'Do leave off,' she said. 'Electric light!'

'You are very up-to-date, a modern woman!' I said, for I had heard that expression somewhere.

'I hope to be when I come into the houses; and then I'll be free, too,' she said, at which she gave me a big, sudden smile that was as shocking as if the lion had toppled off the top of the brewery.

'I have heard of free women,' I said, 'but never met one before.'

She was still giving me that really big smile.

I said, 'Shall I tell you something that isn't boring?'

'If you can,' she said, still smiling.

'A man was killed at the shed this week.'

That did for the smile; but it was not boring.

'Killed accidentally?'

'No. If you ask me, somebody crowned him.'

As I said this she carried on with her work, but she must have let her eye linger on the book that was on the table, half underneath the towels. Nothing but a matter of weeks in London, and I was looking for strangeness all about me. I picked up the towels, and my landlady said with a sigh, 'Hawk eyes.' It was *Continuous Engine Brakes* by M. Reynolds. But the important words were written by hand on the first page: 'H. Taylor, April XII 1902.'

'He wasn't here for above two months,' said my landlady, 'and then he . . .'

'What?'

She shrugged.

'You might have told me,' I said.

She said nothing to this; she did not seem greatly distressed by whatever had happened to Henry Taylor.

'I suppose he owes you money,' I said.

'Oh, no. It was a pound down for him as well.'

'What happened to his things?'

'His father came for the box – a gentleman from Dorset.'

I imagined Henry Taylor sitting on the platform of a halt in the Dorset hills with the SM's flowers behind and Rowland Smith walking up. In my mind's eye, I could not make Dorset any different from Yorkshire, and I could not make Henry Taylor any different from myself at Grosmont.

'The worst of it is,' I said, 'I think *he* was done in too – just like Mike.'

'The one who was crowned this week?'

I nodded.

'This is Waterloo,' said my landlady, 'and it is a very bad place. Men are the slaves of the factories and the railways, and the women are the slaves of the men – whether in the homes or the night-houses. There is drunkenness, opium, cramped quarters and all that goes along with it.'

'But you live here.'

'I have no choice, and have my church and my god, Mr Stringer,' she said.

As, by that most unexpected remark, my prospects of making her my girl disappeared, she seemed to become still more beautiful.

'The book was left under the bed,' my landlady went on, and she handed it to me.

'What did you know about Henry Taylor?'

'He was handsome enough.'

I did not like to hear that.

'When did he die?' I said, quite harshly.

'It is not known that he did.'

'When did he go from here, then?'

She was back at the boiler now, poking at the clothes very lazily. 'August.'

'When in August?'

'He was last in this house on the twentieth of August – a Wednesday. I happened to be here the night before, and I heard him leave for work.'

'At what time?'

'Six. Two hours later they sent a man around – a very young man.'

'The call boy.'

She said nothing.

'Do you mean the call boy?'

'I suppose so. He was a boy, and he called.'

'Do you know which way Taylor went to work?'

'Along the river, I think.'

She had gradually turned away from me as she spoke, and I saw she was no longer stirring but simply holding the stick in the boiling water. Then she sniffed mightily, or so I thought, but at the same time she dragged one of my undershirts out of the water and held it in the air with a waterfall coming off it. She could have been crying but it might have been the steam on her face; her eyes, at any rate, were prettier and more full of light and darkness than ever. She let the undershirt fall back and, turning around to face me, said, 'You are like a detective.'

For the first time I felt that I had the upper hand with her. 'You've talked to detectives?' I said.

'Three times,' she said, and then, being sure she was about to cry but hating the thought of it, I felt that this was enough.

I slapped the table with my cap, and said, 'The pharmacy over the road has been telling me, by a dozen adverts all across its front, to "Buy Vianola Soap".'

'And you have finally given in,' she said, smiling somewhat again.

I nodded.

'Now I am going to have a wash.'

'Good,' she said, and with her mystery smile returning we were back on equal terms.

She pushed one of the towels towards me with the book now on top instead of underneath. She reached up to a shelf, took down a bowl and filled it with hot water. I walked upstairs and unwrapped my soap, which was rather on the small side but took away the stink of Nine Elms Loco Shed in an instant. I lay down on the bed and slept for half an hour. When I woke up the sky was a smokier red, and the banging and the crashing were still going on but further out in the distance. I looked at my room – at all the things that Henry Taylor had looked at from the same truckle bed. It was a lonely spot in a crowded place, but when I thought of my landlady downstairs I felt that, whatever lay in store for me, I wouldn't mind for having been here with her for a while.

Chapter Fourteen

Saturday 5 December
continued

I walked down Lower Marsh, and had no trouble: there were too many girls about for that, even though they were lasses of that particular sort – that watchful sort.

The Citadel was a round pub with mighty lanterns dangling over each door (except that one had been smashed off, leaving just the gas pipe, which came down and around like the trunk of an elephant). These you passed underneath to get to a circular bar with mirrors around the top, the bull's eye of the boozer. On the ceiling were paintings of dancing ladies, and there were signs everywhere saying 'Piano Most Nights'. I couldn't see a piano anywhere but I soon learnt that you didn't need one in the Citadel because after a while it just erupted into song, like tinder catching fire.

I took a pint of Red Lion and carried it across to a seat marked 'The Comfortable Corner', although there were no corners anywhere, the place being circular, so this was perhaps a joke. The joxies on the next seat were certainly laughing as I sat down. I had never seen such pretty drunks.

I had bought my pint, thinking my first would also have to be my last, but when I got to the end of it the Citadel seemed quite the place to be, and, sitting there, I began to think once again that progress was being made in my thoughts. But that did not last long, for they all went wrong in the end, like the broken gas pipe: Rose and Hunt were true engine men put to work on a sleepy branch, for which they would have hated the bosses like old boots – and Rowland Smith had been one of the bosses. But then he had also put himself on this balmy branch, and that after having risen to the top of the South Western in what must have been very short order, for he was still a young man.

As to Vincent, I was out with him, but like as not that was only because he knew I was up to the mark for an engine man and might beat him to the regulator. But why could he not relax even for a minute?

Then again, as to the murders . . . were they really anything of the sort? Perhaps Henry Taylor was only lying low, and maybe Mike had fallen on the footplate and hit his head on the handbrake or had some other accident of the sort not unusual around any engine shed.

I started thinking again of Vincent, and when I looked up I had hocussed him out of the air, for he was standing before me with a pewter in his hand. (He's putting on swank, trying to look like an engine man, I thought.) There was a circular sort of fellow next to him, also carrying a pint, and wearing a crushed and twisted black suit. He was shouting, 'Trousers! I say, trousers!' to someone in another part of the pub. I had seen him somewhere before.

'All right there?' said Vincent, over the noise of the other.

So he was talking to me again, and very matey with it.

'This is Mack,' he said, pointing to his pal. 'Saturday Night Mack, I call him.'

Saturday Night Mack was still yelling to someone in the middle of the pub, and it struck me that he was the fellow who'd been holding the brush and being scolded at the Necropolis station.

'Mack!' shouted Vincent, 'pay attention, man!'

He introduced us with words that let me know I was in for more sensation. 'Mack works for the Necropolis. You went into their station on the Red Bastard, didn't you?' Vincent added.

'Thirty-One,' I said, 'yes.'

Vincent sat down in front of me and put his pewter on the table, while Saturday Night Mack carried on shouting across to a gingery bloke.

'Well, you've been a bit bloody silent on the subject, for

Christ's sake,' said Vincent.

'So have you. You've been a bit silent on all subjects, if you ask me.'

'Well, I'm all ears now. Who was Barney's mate for the trip?'

'Mike.'

'Oh crumbs. It knocked me for six when I heard. I was on leave, you know.'

'But who would do that to Mike?' I said.

'Search me,' said Vincent.

'He was a good fellow,' I said.

'Top hole,' said Vincent.

We both took a drink. Talking to this kid?, I thought, was like walking on hot coals.

'Bit of an over-steamer, though,' I said. 'I noticed when I went on that trip with him.'

Vincent left a long pause, giving me plenty of time to regret speaking ill of the dead – it was wanting to sound like a true engine man that had done it, that and the beer – before saying, 'You're bang on, there.'

Just then, Saturday Night Mack stopped shouting about trousers and sat down at our table with three fresh pints of Red Lion on a tray. 'Chatting about that bad business on Monday, are we?' he said, and took a long drink.

'You're on the Necropolis, aren't you?' I said, because I had to get back to that.

Mack nodded.

'What do you do for that lot?'

'Always asking questions, this boy,' said Vincent, wriggling in his seat. 'Always very keen to learn.'

But Mack didn't seem to mind; I fancied he preferred my company to Vincent's, and that Vincent would have liked me to think they were better mates than they really were. 'I put my hand to shifting bodies, humping floral sprays, sweeping up, and a bit of parading on occasion,' he replied.

'So you're one of those silent walking-behind-the-coffin

fellows?' I said. I knew this to be a silly sort of remark even as it came from my lips, but the queer thing was that Mack again did not mind.

'Walking behind? Yes. Silence? No,' he said. 'I *do* talk on the job, you see, otherwise I could never do the words of comfort.' He waved to somebody near the bar, and called out a word I couldn't understand. It was something like 'Norbs!' It could have been that little gingery fellow who hadn't shaved that he was calling to.

'What are the words of comfort?' I asked.

'Bloody hell,' said Vincent, 'we're trying to have a bit of a beano here.'

'It depends if I do a long comfort or a short one,' said Saturday Night Mack, putting the ice on Vincent once again.

'What would be a long one?'

He took a deep breath, and then he was off: 'For no man liveth to himself and no man dieth to himself, for whether we live, we live unto the Lord, and whether we die, we die unto the Lord. Whether we live, therefore, or die, we are the Lord's.'

'I see,' I said. 'And if it's a short one?'

'Chin up,' said Mack, and he caught up his beer and finished it off. 'I mainly do short ones,' he said, standing up, 'and sometimes not even that.' He whacked down his glass and dashed off into a crowd of his friends. A few seconds later he came running back to us. 'Anybody fancy another?'

I tried to give him a tanner but he wasn't having it.

After a bit more shouting and prancing about he came back to us, dragging half his crowd with him, who carried on drinking in the crowd around our table.

'Idiots,' he said, pointing to the crowd. 'Sensible fellows,' he said, pointing to us. The idiots seemed to be more fun, though, so I thought it good of him to stick with us.

'You've got a pretty big set up down at Brookwood,' I said.

'Pretty big,' he said.

'What's the cemetery like?'

'I'll tell you what: steer clear if you believe in spirits.' He took a big belt of his beer, and I could see that he was saturated but it suited him to be like that.

'Mack believes in ghosts,' said Vincent. 'He has these table-top, spirit-talking goes.'

'What happens at these things?' I asked Mack.

'The veil is lifted and I see through to the other side.'

'What's it like?'

'What's it *like*?' he said, and he puffed out his cheeks and made his eyes go big. 'Going back to Brookwood,' he went on, 'you've got four thousand acres, best part of fifty thousand trees. It's the biggest cemetery going, nothing to touch it in the whole Empire, but I'll tell you what,' and here he just grinned.

'What?' I said.

'Business ain't so good at present.'

I liked Mack; despite being a semi-drunk and maybe a rogue, he was a pleasant fellow to chat with.

'Why is business bad?' I asked him.

'When they set it all up, all the graveyards in London were full to bursting, and nobody was allowed to start any new ones. But that was all changed just before our show was started.'

'How did that come about?'

'Act of Parliament.'

'What act?'

'Bloody hell, leave off,' said Vincent. 'Mack's brain is working under two hundred and twenty pounds of pressure as it is.'

'Date of the Act . . .' said Mack, 'can't remember. Name of it . . . that's gone too. Ask me when I'm not DRUNK.'

He said that last word very loud.

'So the Necropolis is in a bad state?' I said.

'Well, now,' said Saturday Night Mack, sitting back, picking up his glass and seeing it was empty, 'there's a fellow does talks on it, a fellow called Stanley, and you can tell what's what in our line by his audiences.'

'I looked in on one of those,' I said.

'Crowded, was it?' said Mack.

'Hardly . . . Listen,' I said – and the questions were coming like winking, thanks to the Red Lion – 'do you know a johnny called Rowland Smith?'

This one had Vincent all ablaze, though saying nothing.

Mack nodded, and it was a job for me to tell whether that meant he knew of my connection with Smith or not. I couldn't believe Vincent wouldn't have told him if they were any sorts of mates at all.

'Really, he's the true Governor,' said Mack. 'He's come over from the South Western to sort us out. Erskine Long's the chairman, and he don't seem to like it, but there it is.'

'So Rowland Smith's all right, is he?'

Mack shrugged. 'His notion is to sell off the land,' he said.

Somebody darted over to Mack and gave him a beer.

'Tell you what,' he said. 'We used to have a Sunday run, and you could pick up the big penny working that turn. Smith's put a stop to it. Nowadays the trip only happens three or four times a week, and that's his decree as well.'

'What's happened to wages?'

'I'm a fifteen-bob-a-week bloke now; it's barely enough to cover my slate in this place.'

I could see very well that it wouldn't be. Saturday Night Mack was a drinking machine, always with a glass in his hand, and he seemed to know everybody in the Citadel. For the next half hour he kept coming and going, whereas I seemed to be trapped at our table with Vincent, hemmed in by the crowd. Some of them were joxies, and they kept lolling right across our table.

'Nice fresh greens,' said Vincent, as one of them rolled against me.

'Want a lady?' she said.

I couldn't believe the softness of her, but I was scared of saying yes, for I had never gone down the road with any girl before, let alone this sort, and I didn't know where she would take me. I thought she might be backed up by an army of blackguards.

'Want a lady?' she said again.

'What for?' I said.

'What for!' said Vincent, and he gave out a sound that was the next best thing to laughing.

'For . . . a while,' said the joxie, who then went off, saying something not very friendly.

'Man,' said Vincent, 'we're down in Waterloo,' and he started shaking his head. I had heard of these girls, who sold what you could not believe would ever be for sale; there were commonly supposed to be some in Scarborough, but I never thought I would see one, leave alone actually be kissed by one.

Vincent lifted his pewter and drank. 'They'll fuck you for a consideration, sir!' he said in a funny voice.

For some reason, thoughts of my landlady were in my head, and I did not like the complication of them. 'Why do you call me sir when you're drunk?' I said to Vincent.

'I have a lot more respect for people when I'm sloshed,' said Vincent, 'and you can make of that what you like.'

I tried to look him straight in the eye but the Citadel had now started to move; it was increasing in speed by the second, until the velocity was something remarkable, but, unlike the Atlantics of Mr Ivatt, it did not go in a straight line.

Chapter Fifteen

Tuesday 8 December

Three days later I was in the shed early, stabbing with the handle of a brush at a mass of ash and mud on the brake block of Thirty-One, when the Governor walked up. He was smiling as usual – well, it was usual when he talked to me.

'Fancy a trip to Brookwood?' he said, and he almost bowed, like a magician about to demonstrate some marvellous phenomenon.

'I'll bloody say,' I said, and I chucked down the brush and rubbed my hands on my trousers, because you're supposed to be clean at all times on the footplate. I then realised I'd made a bloomer with that 'bloody', but the Governor didn't take exception. He was walking down the shed between two lines of Atlantics, galvanising the whole place as he went, sending blokes off wheeling barrows, or scrambling into the pits or doing whatever they should have been doing in the first place. He led me to Twenty-Nine, which was just off-shed, standing in a light rain.

'Hop up,' said the Governor.

I climbed onto the cab, and there was the man with the black beard who fired for the half when he was on spare, and who I now knew to be Clive Castle. There was a good fire in the hole, steam pressure was climbing nicely and the cab was pretty clean, but really only half done, so I decided to finish the job. I reached into the locker for the wire brush, then glanced across at Castle. He looked at me, but gave no friendly nod, of course. But I was becoming bolder with the Nine Elms fellows; I would not eat dog. So I said, very business-like: 'I'm coming out with you on the run.'

No answer. His face was very white, or maybe it was just the blackness of his hair and beard that made me think so. He had something on his mind, all right, something bad, but then they all did all the time. It would have been funny – if I didn't believe that evil was at the back of it.

'Where's Rose?' I said, because I had the idea that only he would let me on for a ride.

'Barney Rose?' said Castle. 'Search me.'

I heard a clatter, and an oil can was placed on the footplate behind me. I could tell by the sound that it was empty. Turning about, I saw Arthur Hunt flashing past on his way to going under the engine with a new oil can. The trip was to be with the big man.

Well, I resolved immediately that he would have no reason to find fault. I climbed down from the cab and scurried off to stores, where I meant to pick up a tin of Brasso, although in fact I came upon one on a workbench halfway there, together with a good clean rag which I also caught up. Returning to the footplate of Twenty-Nine, I began hastily polishing the injector wheels, engine brake, regulator. This was laying on luxury as far as cleaning duties went, but I was determined that Arthur Hunt would think me up to the mark.

Of course, it would happen that I was taking a bit of a breather when Hunt flew up onto the footplate with the new oil can in his hand. He'd been filling the pots underneath, but there wasn't a mark on him – which *was* the mark of a true engine man. Whether this man was a killer, or a friend of killers, he was always perfect about his business, so that I couldn't help but be keen to show him my paces. He wore his usual suit and a tie, and there was a rag folded as neatly as any silk handkerchief in his enormous hands.

I screwed up my courage to a 'Good morning, Mr Hunt,' but of course I needn't have bothered.

The first thing he did was take my Brasso and stow it in the locker, cursing in an under-breath. Then without a word he flung my rag onto the fire, which ate it with a great whump. As he did this I noticed – and I saw to my horror that he had noticed too – that the firehole door ground against coal dust a little as it slid along its runners. Seeing that, while I'd got the handbrake looking like the crown jewels, I'd neglected one of the first footplate tasks, I tried to make amends by reaching once again into the locker for the wire brush, but in doing so I clashed arms with Hunt. I was trying to help, but it looked as though I was attempting to come to blows. He turned and gave me such a look that I shrank down onto the sandbox, where Clive Castle immediately told me I could not sit.

Hunt called over my head to Castle, 'We're ready for off, Clive.' He yanked the whistle, and as he did so a terrified blackbird crouched down in a black puddle next to one of the rails alongside us. Birds, as I supposed, could go anywhere they wanted, so why would they come to this hellish spot?

We pulled away from the shed into a black, wet world. We picked up the funeral set, which looked more than ever like cripples from a bygone age, yet Hunt gave them the kid-glove treatment, buffering up with the lightest kiss of metal on metal. Without a word, Castle climbed down to couple on, and I was alone on the footplate with Hunt. I wondered what secrets those two shared besides the arts of running an engine, and in doing so I glanced across at him. He was staring at his hands, pressing them over and over into his folded cloth as if he was trying to get himself the hands of a pen pusher or a parson. I would not suffer in silence, though. I would uncover all, but by degrees.

'You don't want me on this trip,' I said. 'I've been sent up by the Governor against your wishes.'

No answer to that.

Clive Castle came back up. I asked if there was anything I could do, and he said, 'Keep out of the fucking way.' We crossed out of the yard and started rolling across the viaducts up to Waterloo. The rows of houses were at right angles to the line, with leaning walls of smoke rising above them.

Suddenly there was a great eruption at the fire door, and

I spun about in terror, thinking a gauge glass had exploded in Clive Castle's face, but all that had happened was that he had vomited. No wonder he'd been so white. The stuff was swirling all over the cab floor, and Castle was sitting on the sandbox watching it as we backed into the Necropolis station with a funeral party waiting. Hunt didn't say anything until he'd done Castle's job of putting on the handbrake, then he handed Castle a billy. As Castle wiped his mouth on his coat sleeve and took a drink, Hunt picked up the cab hose that used the water pipes of the injector and sprayed the stuff off the cab, looking like the most enormous skivvy I'd ever seen.

Behind us, the funeral parties – three of them – were waiting to get into the carriages, all solemn and silent but with no tears anywhere. As to their clothes, there was not so much blackness as I expected, and most of the men had made do with black armbands and their ordinary suits. The caskets must have been loaded in double-quick time – they seemed pretty light. A woman – I could not see which one – cried out, 'Oh, I can't believe we shall never see her again!'

Hunt and Castle jumped down from the cab. I leant out and watched them walk along the platform towards the funeral lot, but before they got there they went through one of the doors on the platform, and that was the last I was to see of fireman Castle that day.

Hunt came back a few minutes later alone, with hat off and head bowed as he walked past the mourners. It did not suit him to bow his head, and the effort of doing it helped put him in an even fouler mood than before when he came back to me.

'Get back up there,' he said, for I had climbed down so as to get a better view along the platform.

I went back into the cab as the doors slammed shut along the line of carriages, and Hunt leapt up after me with his coat flying out behind, making him look like a great bat.

'What's up?' I asked.

He didn't answer, but threw open the firehole doors. 'It

needs three more on the right side and six at the front,' he said, 'and a dozen in each back corner.'

'Mr Castle's not been taken too badly, I hope?' I said.

'Never you mind,' said Hunt, and he picked the shovel out of the coal bunker and threw it at me.

I started shovelling. 'If I'm needed to take over from Mr Castle, you might give me a bit of advice. I'm not passed, you know.'

'I'll give you advice,' said Hunt. 'Don't bugger up that fire, or I'll bloody crown you.'

Well, anything was preferable to the treatment I'd been getting on the trip up. Hunt might have telephoned up to Nine Elms and asked for a relief, but if so the Governor would have turned him down. You can't very well relieve a relief, after all; you've got to go down to the next level, which was me.

I wanted the firehole door a bit wider open, but the lever was stiff, and scalding too. I *did* get it open after a while and then I stood and watched, hypnotised, as all the hairs disappeared off the back of my hand. That fire was white and evil, and it struck me for the first time that any engine, however small, travelled around with hell in its belly. I started shovelling, but the fire wanted the shovel out of my hands, and it wanted me in through those fire doors too. I took a step back and started again.

Getting the coal aound the edges of the firehole door was easy enough, but when I started trying to chuck it six foot to the front of the firebox, I couldn't get the right sort of swing with the shovel and the coal, and it just plopped into the box halfway along. The harder I tried, the less far it went, and the blade of my shovel clanged on the top of the firehole at the end of every swing. I thought of my long days at the coal pens, and how I could have used my time there to practise shying, but I hadn't thought there'd be anything to it. Hunt wasn't looking on, or seemed not to be, but was watching the road from his side. I looked ahead from my side, and saw a signal I'd never noticed before. As I looked, it dropped.

'We've got the road,' I said, to let Hunt know that I'd spotted this.

'For Christ's sake,' he said, so I'd probably made another bloomer. 'What's the guard doing?'

I turned and looked the other way, back into the station.

'He's not doing anything,' I said.

I certainly wished he would do something. All the doors were shut, the mourners were on board; I saw no reason for delay.

'Is he going to blow his whistle?' I said.

This was too much for Hunt. He leapt across the cab to my side, shoved me out of the way, and looked at the guard. They shouted something to each other, then Hunt moved back across to his side, tugged the regulator and we were off, beating back along the Necropolis branchline and up towards the thirty-odd roads coming out of the great mouth of Waterloo.

Before long we were clattering across the roads, but eventually we settled onto one of them – I could not have said which one, exactly, having no idea of the route between Waterloo and Brookwood Cemetery – and began approaching a signal gantry that stretched across about twenty roads. On top of the gantry was another jumble of signals and I realised that all my years of reading articles in *The Railway Magazine* counted for naught. There were some big signals, some little signals; some signals had other, smaller, signals underneath them, sometimes doing something different from the one above, sometimes doing the same. Half a dozen lamps were strung up there too: red ones, white ones, fighting the greyness of the wet morning. Of course, I had learnt something of signalling during my time at Grosmont, but up there signals came one at a time and with a good deal of warning.

'Have we got the road?' yelled Hunt over the rattle of Thirty-One.

Now he could see for himself, because our signal – whichever one might happen to *be* ours – would not be the kind that could only be seen from the fireman's side of the cab.

'I said, have we got the fucking road?' Hunt shrieked again.

'How do I know whether we've got it?' I replied.

Hunt rose threw open the fire doors. He lowered his long body and stared straight into the fire, challenging it to hurt him, like a man mastering a vicious dog. He tipped his face up towards the steam gauge. 'We're losing pressure,' he said. 'Fire's caking up. Give it a stir – and double-quick.'

That meant going at it with a fire iron. But which was the one for the job – dart, pricker or paddle? 'I want the dart, don't I?' I said, turning towards the hole in the bunker, from which the crooks of the three long irons jutted.

'You'll have it about your head if you don't look sharp.'

But which was the dart? I couldn't tell from the handles. My head was fairly buzzing as I looked from Hunt to the three handles and back at Hunt, who was just a pair of little eyes now, watching me raise my hands towards the irons. He could have told me which was which but he was making me eat dog. There was nothing for it but to pull hard on one of the three irons, which I did, stumbling immediately backwards in the process, for my tug had caused the whole boiling lot to come clattering out of the hole. I remained on the floor of the cab and shut my eyes, ready for Hunt to do his worst, but when I opened them he was at the fire, stirring the coal with mysterious motions. As he did so he looked across at me, seeming to shudder with hatred at the sight of me. He took the iron from the fire and put it and the other two back in their right place.

'Put another charge of coal at the front of the box,' he said, and by now his loathing was such he could not even meet my eye.

'I can't seem to pitch it to the front.'

'Then you should not be firing,' he said, in a voice so strange and quiet that my legs got soft under me.

'No,' I said, 'I shouldn't be. I'm a bloody cleaner.'

'But you're dead set on the footplate,' he said, in the same

weird way. 'You hold it to be a grand life of freedom or something . . . Now for the last time of asking, have we got the
road?'

Thirty-One was threatening to shake the tears out of me, but
I leant out my side and looked at the gantry again, which
seemed to have sprouted a few more signals since the last time.

'I don't know,' I said. 'I've told you.'

We were chuffing under the gantry now.

'Did we have the road?' I asked him.

'*Did* we?' he said, in his quiet, dangerous way. '*Did* we?
That's one for the hall of fame, that is.' He pulled on the regulator, and I reckoned we were up to fifty miles to the hour,
which was marvellous, except that all my railway dreams
were coming to nothing.

'*Why* have you got your knife into me?' I said. 'You think
I've been brought on for some reason, but I don't know what
it is. You think I'm a company man, but I don't know why I'm
here, and I'll tell you something: I bloody wish I wasn't.' I
wanted to say a lot more but I couldn't hold back the tears
any longer. 'You're a bloody rotter,' I said.

He wasn't listening. He'd started driving and firing the
engine himself, which was like seeing a man riding two
horses at once. He rode the two horses through Clapham
Junction, where there were hundreds of people on the platforms – every one of them alone, nicely out of the rain but
right in the middle of the smoke. We rattled down through
the Southern Division: hundreds of houses on either side
with horses and waggons trapped between them, looking
for a way out of the maze. I had never felt more dismal, and
after Wimbledon I just sat on the sandbox and looked at my
boots.

It must have been half an hour before we came into a new,
wide, blank station – Brookwood – and began some clattering
operations over points on the down side of it. A man came
running out of a signal box in front of us and climbed up to
the cab. Hunt was putting a bit on as he came up; I was still

leaning against the coal bunker with my arms folded, thinking: well, this is the end of all, and it will be a life of butchering for me. I had been of the mind to stick things out at Nine Elms no matter what, to crack the mystery and make the most of my God-given chance to be an engine man. But now my mind was changed. I was going home.

'What's up with this fellow?' said the signalman.

I just turned away from Arthur Hunt and climbed down off the footplate. As I went I could hear him muttering something, after which I caught the guard saying, 'Twenty-one inches of vacuum in his head,' and he started having a bit of a chuckle about that. I had no clue where I was going, and nor did I care.

Hunt uncoupled the engine and then, maybe with the help of the fellow from the signal box, he ran around the coaches on a passing loop so that he was ready to pull the set into the Cemetery itself. I followed the black train in, walking on the track. Anybody watching me plodding behind the carriages might have thought I was part of the procession, except that I had my hands in my pockets and I was wearing my grimy suit with no collar to my shirt. It was easy to keep up, on account of the constant 'five miles an hour' signs.

The cemetery was like the Yorkshire Moors squashed flat: heather, bracken, boggy black soil, with the graves at all angles as if there'd lately been a great explosion of stone. The place was sunk in some long, gloomy dream. Thirty-One, the black carriages and myself were rolling down a single track, raised on a low grass embankment. The cemetery was coming and going between massive trees, three times bigger than the common run of trees and so big they made Thirty-One look like a toy locomotive. The bottoms of their trunks were like giant lizard claws, and the tops of some had been blown off – by lightning, I reckoned. Presently I fell to wondering what the mourners on the train were making of the place: probably thinking they were getting their money's worth because it was all a bit different, just as poor dead Mike had said.

Ahead of me, Hunt had Thirty-One in good order. There was no trace of smoke; he was just pumping out little ghosts of steam every now and again. The nothingness of the steam met the nothingness of the white sky, and it was all certainly very beautiful and strange, but this five-miles-an-hour business, well it was no job for a man, and that was probably where all his evil nature came from.

I followed the train to a station that was a sort of perfect white wooden house with tubs of flowers all around. It was called North Station, and did not look real. There was no fence around it and no road, so you just walked towards it over grass and graves, or came to it on the train. Climbing onto the platform caused no more trouble than stepping onto a box. I walked up and watched from one end of the platform or another – I could not say which, for 'up' and 'down' had no meaning in a place like this. Some of the mourners, and two of the coffins, came off. I noticed a gang of hearty vicars I'd not spotted before, and Thirty-One sat there simmering, with Arthur Hunt inside no doubt doing exactly the same.

One of the coffins, with the mourners tagging along behind, was being taken along a winding track in the grass. I thought at first they were going to march off and put the thing straight into the ground, but then I saw that the coffin men were winding towards a pretty building in the trees that was half house and half chapel. Why that one went there and the other two bodies stayed in the train I did not know.

The doors all along the train were left open, and I stepped up into the rear carriage. There were empty wooden racks here – nothing much more. It reminded me of the stable carriages that came through Grosmont. I opened a door and stepped through into another section of the carriage, and here were more wooden racks, two with coffins on them, flowers wedged into steel brackets, and Saturday Night Mack staring at a page of a magazine. Over his round shoulder I read:

'PRIZE OF AN EIGHT-ROOMED HOUSE: ANYONE CAN WIN IT AND THEN LIVE RENT-FREE FOR LIFE'.

'Bloody hell, where did you come from?' he said, putting down his paper on one of the coffins. It was *Hoity-Toity Bits*.

'The other part,' I said. 'There's nobody in there.'

'Third Class, that is,' said Saturday Night Mack.

I looked down at the pages of *Hoity-Toity Bits*, and read 'QUEER TREASURES OWNED BY KING EDWARD' and 'CURIOUS EFFECTS OF A CRUST OF BREAD'.

'What's this part?'

'Second.'

'What's the difference between third and second?'

'Nothing,' said Mack, and he went back to reading his paper.

'Where's first?' I asked, and he jerked his thumb at a door opposite the one I'd just walked through. 'Anything different about that?'

'Not as I've noticed,' said Mack. He put the paper down again. 'Some differences in the fittings for them as want to look closely, but it's all really just a matter of the number on the door,' he said, and folded his arms.

I sighed – I was still pretty shaken up – and said, 'It's all snob business, really, isn't it?'

'That's bang on, that is,' said Mack, and he looked at me as if I'd just told him something he could never have thought of for himself. I looked down at the new page of his magazine, and read the words 'REMARKABLE FACTS ABOUT BOGUS WINDFALLS'.

We heard a couple of doors bang in other carriages; we were both rocked on our feet slightly, then we were away.

'Where to now, then?' I asked him.

'Church of England part – South Station,' he said, as the cemetery rolled backwards on either side of us.

'So that last one was chapel?'

'Chapel, plus Jewish and Papist – those folks all go together.'

'But the Jews need their own churches of a special sort.'

'Well, it's hard lines, in't it? They can't run to one of those here.'

'I'll bet not many of them come here, then.'

'That's just where you're wrong, mate. A lot of that sort do come here on account of liking to be buried. Well, they don't *like* it, but they prefer it to burning. Who's driving this engine?' he went on, 'Arthur?'

I nodded. 'How did you know?'

'By the smoothness of the running.'

'I was supposed to be on with him – his mate was taken sick –'

'Probably on the pop last night,' said Mack.

'He's chucked me off the footplate.' My questions could have no meaning any more, but I could not stop asking. 'Why exactly is Mr Hunt on the half-link, Mack? And why won't they pass Vincent?' I had heard of a speaking machine they had over at Blackpool, and I imagined I sounded the same, asking questions in a hollow voice, with no hope of answer.

'Don't ask me,' said Mack, 'it's all shed business.'

I looked around the coffin carriage.

'How is it that you're riding in here with the bodies?' I asked him.

'Guard duty,' said Mack. 'A lot of these stiffs are covered in jewels, and there are people in this world with a mind to have such goods away.'

'But they'd have to open the coffins first.'

'Ever heard of a screwdriver?' said Mack, and he gave me a smile that started off little and grew.

Now we were at the second cemetery station, the South Station. It looked exactly like the first, except turned around and put on the other side of the track; and here too there was a little building half-hidden in trees near by.

Mack opened his door and let in a gang of his mates from the Necropolis Company. They took the two coffins away, with Mack lending a hand and the mourners following. I was left alone on the platform. I watched Hunt climb down from

Thirty-One, wiping his hands on the cloth. He strode towards the South Station building and through the door marked 'South Bar', then I hopped off the platform and walked over the track behind the train and out into the cemetery.

I pushed on through the grass and heather. My boots and trousers were soon sopping, and that was fine. I would go back to Grosmont and work in the shop with Dad. I thought of the farmers driving their beasts across the headland to the top of Bay, coming up in the morning with the sun. They brought them into the yard behind the shop for poleaxing by Dad, but they would just as soon bring them to me or whoever was paying out. I would take over the deliveries – running the trap out to Whitby on Wednesdays and Saturdays, and down the steep street to the centre of Bay every morning. But who would be on hand to carry the mallet to stick behind the trap wheels if it should roll back coming up? That's what I had done for Dad, the one bit of work in the butchering line I had regularly performed. Perhaps I would have my own son to do it for me.

I had struck a line of small stone angels: one held a stone star, another a sword, a third an anchor. Behind them was a new-dug grave with black soil and flowers on top, all crushed by the rain, but brightened by it at the same time. Looking up from this I saw a man on a horse; he was pulling a rope that was also held by three men on foot behind. It was a very long rope, and the men were all silently taking it towards a part of the cemetery where the graves gave out.

I could've carried on stumbling all day: one direction is just as good as another when everybody about you is dead. I heard a horse and trap going along the cemetery lanes somewhere, and dripping rain marking time. After the best part of half an hour's wandering I headed back to the South Station, where Thirty-One was still waiting, and for the first time I thought of that engine, which had been the scene of such a disaster for me, as the Red Bastard.

113

Chapter Sixteen

Tuesday 8 December
continued

I climbed back up onto the platform, and through the door labelled 'South Bar' into a light, white, wooden room. The only bit of brick was the fireplace, and there was a good blaze going. There were a few wooden tables with white cloths. Being in that room made you feel it was sunny outside, but when you looked at the windows there was the dripping rain making sad patterns. A barmaid was handing over a jug of something and four glasses to Saturday Night Mack and some of his mates. Mack was leaning with his back to the bar, looking out into the room as if he owned it.

'You're back,' he said. 'Lads,' he went on, turning to his mates, 'here we have Mr Jim Stringer.'

He got another glass, and poured me out a drink from the jug. 'Red Lion,' he said, when we'd both had a good belt of it. 'We bring it up on the train for them. That was our idea, me and the boys. We're off duty as from now so we can take a pint.'

'We can,' said a little gingery fellow, 'and we *do*.'

When I started talking to Mack, most of the Necropolis boys turned away and went into their own bits of chat, all except for this gingery one, who was called Terry and might have been trying to grow a moustache, and might have been the fellow I'd seen Mack shouting across to in the Citadel.

'Hunt was in here, wasn't he?'

Mack nodded. 'Been and gone,' he said.

'Did he say anything about me?'

'You know Arthur,' said Mack. 'Never says much about anything.'

That was a good get-out on his part; quite the diplomat,

was Mack. He didn't want to get you all het up in the way Vincent did.

'What's he doing now?' I asked.

'Oiling up, and other bits of business.'

Yes, I thought, whereas Barney Rose would have been sitting on the sandbox reading his sporting papers.

'Have you done any words of comfort today, Mack?' I asked.

'Not so far. It's a pity, because I do like to keep my hand in.' He filled his glass from the jug, and gave me a refill. 'I'll probably do one or two later on,' he said, settling against the bar again.

'People do get a bit down when they come back from the burials,' said Terry, 'especially if the bar's closed.'

Mack was looking down at my trouser bottoms. 'You're sodden, man. Where've you been?'

'Walking about among the graves.'

'Very nice,' he said.

Then Terry said, 'You need to watch yourself doing that.'

'Why's that?' I said.

'Our chairman was in the habit of taking a quiet saunter among the headstones, and one day it was the end of him.'

Mack looked into the jug, said, 'Oh, me, dear,' and smiled at the barmaid – which was enough to get us another jug of Red Lion.

'What happened to him?' I asked Terry, but it was Mack who answered.

'Came up on the train one afternoon, drifted off for a stroll just like you, tripped and went flying – banged his head on a stone.'

I had that falling feeling inside me: was the monster down here too? 'What was his name?' I said.

'Sir John Rickerby,' said Terry, and it came back to me: he was the only one photographed and not painted on the walls of the Necropolis library.

'So this fellow actually died in the cemetery, did he?'

Mack nodded. 'Quite convenient when you think of it,' he said.

'Do you know what it said on the stone he fell on?' said Terry.

'Now how should I know that?'

'Thy Will Be Done.'

'Thy *Will* Be Done,' said Mack, and he made his eyes go big.

This was all too fast for me. 'How do they know he hit his head?' I asked, and even though I was bound for home, and all was at an end between myself and Nine Elms, I wanted my Lett's diary with me to write down the answers to the questions that would keep coming. 'How do they know someone didn't whack it for him? Did they have detectives up here?'

'I'll say,' said Terry. 'No end of the buggers, because they did have their doubts.'

'What is the world coming to,' said Mack, 'when the Yard is sent in every time some old gent takes a tumble?'

'What sort of a gent was he?' I asked, and I could hear the voice of little Vincent in my head telling me to pipe down.

'He was all right,' said Terry, 'and he loved this place.'

'It's a pretty spot, isn't it?' I said. 'In a queer sort of way.'

Terry nodded. 'In the Smoke, you might go at things a bit harder if you know you've got a bunk-up like this waiting for you.'

'A happy ending guaranteed,' I said.

'That sort of thing. Yes, Rickerby was a nice old bird, but we struck a bigger pill with the next one, a fellow by the name of Erskine Long, who's green as duckweed, if you ask me. Smith's talking him into selling up the whole show – two thousand acres we had here, but it's getting smaller by the minute.'

'I've seen that gent in person,' I said, remembering the little fret kidney I'd spotted talking to Rowland Smith on my first trip to the Necropolis station; he hadn't seemed such a pushover to me.

'Know all the top brass, don't you?' said Mack.

'Was Rickerby in favour of selling up?'

'Dead against,' said Terry, 'which is why he never wanted Smith about the place. But really, he was *put* in the show by the bloody South Western.'

'Why did the South Western Railway want him in?' (I imagined Vincent coming at me again: 'Very curious, this boy.')

'Cor, mate,' said little Terry. 'We've told you that fifty times.' He said 'we', but Mack was now chatting to the barmaid. 'To sell up,' said Terry. 'By contract they're supplying the trains and men, and getting nothing in return on account of business being so bad.'

'Who'd want to buy all this land?'

'Who bloody wouldn't?' muttered Mack, turning back around.

'A good line to be in, hereabouts,' said Terry, 'is building villas for the clerks who've got two quid a week and are bursting to prove it by getting their hands on a bit of garden.'

'Rickerby died just this year, didn't he?'

Mack nodded.

'August sort of time,' he said, before drifting off altogether and striking up bits of chat with his other mates, leaving me with little Terry.

'Mack's a great fellow,' he said, 'and he's a great fellow even with a head full of beer, which is more than you can say for some. But he's always pretty nervy at any talk of the police.'

'Why is that?'

'There's been some little exploits, thieving from bodies, thieving *of* bodies, if it comes to that.'

'They dig them up, do they?'

'That's it – your better class of stiff they might very *well* do. Not that it happens too often, but there's been a spade taken to a few graves recently, here and in other places; some have been made off with, others chucked about for a lark, and Mack's been . . . well, they've said to him: "What do you know?"'

'Who have? The police?'

'No, but the bosses from this show. They've made things quite hot for the lad.'

'Why him, though?'

'Because Mack's Mack, isn't he? There's only one of him.'

Terry caught up his drink, and I said, 'I saw some fellows earlier on. One was on a horse. I'd hardly think stealing bodies was the kind of thing you'd get up to in daylight hours anyway, but . . .'

'They were marking off the poles for selling,' said Terry. 'Face up to it, mate,' he continued, 'they haven't quite managed to make this place a public fad, have they?'

'They've tried, though, haven't they?' I said, thinking of Stanley, the man who gave the address.

'Oh, they've tried,' said Terry. 'They're trying still.'

After a little while, some of the mourners came in looking sorely in need of a pick-up. Mack came back and showed me a sign behind the bar reading 'Spirits Served Here'. He was grinning all round his head at that. Then he told me of ghosts he'd seen at Brookwood, and I wondered whether he'd seen a lot more since they'd had the Red Lion down in the cemetery, and he said, now he came to think of it, yes he had.

I rode back with Mack in the empty coffin carriage. I wasn't much company for him. The fate of Rickerby I'd pushed to the back of my mind, and my own troubles were back at the front. I kept telling Mack I'd stood myself down and that was it, and he kept trying to make out that things could still turn out all right, but then here was a fellow who believed in life after death. Who was firing with Hunt as we rode back to the Necropolis I didn't know, and when we arrived at the station and the mourners were turfed out of the carriages, I scurried along the platform fast, trying not to glance at the cab of Thirty-One. But I couldn't help seeing Hunt standing outside it, too big for his little tank engine, dabbing his hands with that folded cloth of his. I chanced a look his way. He was staring hard at me.

Well, I was so out with everything that I just decided to go to my lodge. This time I found the staircase that led down from the platforms to the courtyard, so I didn't have to use the iron ladder. I walked across the courtyard and under the arch, where I saw the sign reading 'Extramural Interment: An Address'. It was to be held that evening.

As I came out of the Necropolis station it was raining trams and omnibuses. Every window looked black, every face looked troubled; the lights hanging on the front of the shops were too big, swinging too low, and the trains crashing through one after another had the whole place shaking. As I walked, there seemed no solidity in the pavement beneath my feet; my guts were knotted and my head throbbed. I would quit my lodge that very day; I would go straight to King's Cross, and home.

Chapter Seventeen

Tuesday 8 December
continued

I stood at the side wall of Hercules Court looking up at 'Stower's Lime Juice, No Musty Flavour'. I did not now believe that it had no musty flavour. Upon opening the door I saw in the hall a package and a letter, both addressed to me. I could see that the package was from Dad, but the letter was more mysterious. It was from Rowland Smith, and carried yesterday's date. I read it with a galloping heartbeat: he was anxious to speak to me concerning the exploits of the half-link, for, although he did not want to alarm me, he had some grave anxieties on that score. Would I reply directly, giving a time and place to meet? He knew that I, being a young man of good sense out of the common, would regard this as a matter of strictest confidentiality.

Well, I nearly laughed at it. I was in a nightmare without end, for would there not be the greatest danger in talking to him over this? Anyway, it would not come to it: I was going home.

I stood in the hall for a while re-reading the letter, wondering how I could quit my lodge with my landlady not about. I walked up to my room and paced about with the package of Dad's under my arm. There was no coal for a fire. I put my clothes and my *Railway Magazines* into my box, and then took the magazines out again. Why take them back? They were part of my past. I threw them onto the truckle bed.

I looked through the window giving onto the street. There were girls down there as usual, laughing outside the Vianola Soap Pharmacy, and they looked quite a proper lot this time. I wanted a fuck, and I believe I said the word out loud, which I was not in the habit of doing in any circumstances. It seemed a very London answer to agitation. Another one was drink, and all at once there seemed nothing else for it but to walk down the road to the Citadel.

I took three pints before opening the package from Dad, which contained a letter and the latest number of *The Railway Magazine*. In his letter, Dad spoke of a fearful storm the previous month that had sent a schooner crashing through the window of the Bay Hotel – which had happened once before, so it was as if things were going on pretty much as usual up there.

He commended to me a gentlemanly course in all things, hoping I was lacquering my boots and wearing collars on Sundays at least. He reminded me that though he himself was in quite a humble way of business, that I was not of the factory or service class, and should be mindful of that in all my dealings. He said I should speak of having taken 'rooms', and not being in a 'lodge'. He said it was all right to have a bottle of beer in doors, but that he hoped I had not become a frequenter of public houses. For his P.S., he repeated that he had very good memories of Tottenham Court Road and said it was a good spot for a Sunday jaunt.

All in a daze – that letter seemed to have come from a million miles away – I stepped out of the Citadel and walked up the driveway leading from Lower Marsh to the great station. I had been told that you only knew you were at the front of Waterloo because that was where the hansoms waited, but all I saw from my particular corner were high walls, from behind which came muffled cries and the blasting of steam engines, these two noises always coming hand in hand, with moments of silence in between. It reminded me of something, and at first I couldn't think what, but it came to me after a while that it was the little Assembly Rooms in Baytown on a Saturday morning, when they had dancing lessons, and in between the quiet times, when the dancing mistress was talking (which could not be heard from outside), the sound of the piano always came with a great clomping of feet, and it drove me half mad that you could never get either feet or music on their own.

Giving up on making any sense of Waterloo, I came down off the walkway into Westminster Bridge Road. It was dark and cold, and there was a great queue at the ice rink, which was steaming like mad, making extra ice to meet the great demand. The racing trams all carried a huge picture of a man who had improved his kidneys by eating enormous amounts of Hoffa's Vegetable Pills. He had a wide orange face and was grinning like the devil. I turned some corners, and found myself outside the Necropolis station, and there was the sign again: 'Extramural Interment: An Address'. There was no queue for this, but for me there was something mesmerising about the Necropolis show. It was the only spot in London that was not crowded, and I always seemed to have the run of the place.

I walked through the arch and mooched around the lamplit courtyard, which was not quite deserted, for as I walked past a door I heard a muffled voice muttering, 'Plate of inscription, memorial service books, superintendent and assistants, thirty-five shilllings . . . similar without lead coffin, twenty-five shillings . . . Open car, or glass hearse and pair, two broughams and pairs, elm shell-lined swansdown, oak case . . .'

It was a strange speech to hear, for there was never any other voice, no answer to or interruption of these endless, glum particulars.

I drifted back towards the arch. The door in the arch was propped open – to admit those who wanted to hear the address, I supposed. I walked into the wooden vestibule and read the notices there for a while. The biggest was a poster talking up the cemetery: 'The lovely cemetery, situated at Brookwood, is the most complete in all its arrangements, and universally admitted to be the ideal burial ground. It is the biggest in England . . .'

That's right, I thought, and its trains are regularly driven by the biggest pill in England, too. Alongside this were some 'press opinions': 'The privacy and quietude with which the whole business of receiving, conveying and depositing the coffins is effected cannot be too highly commended' – that was one. Another just said, 'Noted for its picturesque scenery.'

Was the Necropolis truly a success or not?

I did not think so, for it was as quiet as the grave at both ends rather than just one. I began walking up the stairs, and, as I climbed, the voice of the strange Mr Stanley – in high force once again – floated down from the fourth floor: 'The lightened and purified system of extramural interment cannot fail to be of interest to all, whether as regards sanitation, morals, convenience or economy.'

But by the time I had reached the doors of the room in which the address was taking place (which also had the secret signs in the wood panels, and an old dusty crest at the back), all this high and mighty stuff had given way to talk in ordinary voices. There were two people in the audience: a man in middle age wearing a salt-and-pepper suit, and an old woman in a sort of sailor's hat. The old woman was very lively though; in fact I'd have laid odds she was saturated.

'But Mr Stanley,' she said, in a voice that sounded put on, 'why are we here?'

Stanley looked at her for a long time, and I looked at him. His suit had given up trying to be black: there were black tints there but also shiny patches of a greenish shade. This fellow is always in mourning for himself, I thought. He was a big, dangling fellow, with sad eyes of a kind of orange colour, and a long yellow face – all in all his looks matched a certain kind of illness that I had read of but could not at the time put a name to.

Stanley glanced in my direction as I entered the room and sat down, but gave no sign of happiness that his audience had suddenly increased.

'We are here,' said Stanley to the woman after a while (and as he spoke the big voice swelled), 'to deliberate nothing less than the furtherance of a city of the dead, a cemetery that will suffice for the absorption of the annual metropolitan mortality, not only for the present generation, or for many years, but for all generations – even until the last trumpet shall sound and the dead arise.'

'Mr Stanley,' said the saturated lady, 'have you ever heard "Brightly Dawns Our Wedding Day" by Mr Sullivan? Oh, it is a most excellent ditty with such a pretty tune. I heard it myself, performed at a Chappell Ballad Concert in St James's Church Hall.'

'What has this to do with extramural interment?' asked the man in the salt-and-pepper suit, looking straight ahead, and not at the high-spirited old lady.

'Mr Stanley, I hold St James's Church Hall to be the very place for the address. It is always packed to the rafters! Here you are rather out of the way. There you will be in the thick of things. Think of it, Mr Stanley – the address on interment following hard upon a zither recital or a pianoforte concert. People will naturally linger on after the one and more than likely flock in for a look at the other.'

Stanley said nothing to this but just slowly began to frown.

'I too have a question,' said the man in the salt-and-pepper suit. 'Shortly before the establishment of the Necropolis and the incorporation of your company, seven commercial cemeteries were created in the suburbs of London.'

'They are of a limited capacity,' said Mr Stanley wearily.

'They are Kensal Green,' said the man, 'West Norwood, Highgate, Nunhead, Abney Park and Brompton and Tower Hamlets, and between them they hold a good many dead. There followed legislation allowing the creation of further burial places in London, and of late the boroughs have been required to supply grave-sites too. You speak of the seventy thousand interred on top of one another in the two hundred square yards of St Martin-in-the-Fields, but no such horror can occur again, and nor need it, for the fact is that wholly adequate provision is now made within the boundaries of the city and the Necropolis is nothing but a vast anachronism.'

I had this fellow down as a rich sort of bloke who had nothing better to do with his time than go around putting a crimp into the dreams of others – and Stanley did not answer him back but merely said, in his ordinary voice: 'Are there any other questions?'

'Mr Stanley,' said the woman, 'when were you last at the cemetery?'

'Some four months ago,' said Stanley. 'Its picturesque beauties were at their height.'

'Did you see the Actor's Acre in bloom?' said the woman. 'I should love to have seen that. There is a part of the cemetery, sir,' she said, leaning over at an unnatural angle in order to address the man in the salt-and-pepper suit, 'reserved for entertainers of one sort or another. I have my name down for a plot there because I am a theatrical myself.'

'I can see that perfectly well, madam,' said the man as he picked up his Derby hat and started walking towards the door.

I followed him out and down the stairs, leaving poor Mr Stanley to the theatrical lady.

I was back in my lodge ten minutes later feeling blue, too tired to think straight, and looking down at all the pretty doxies on Lower Marsh – one under every lamp now. I would go to work in the morning: I might as well get the boot before returning home. A train went over the viaduct and rattled my room, but did not bother the women, who were like the flowers that grow along the railway embankments. I lay back down on my bed and read, in the edition of *The Railway Magazine* that Dad had sent, of some notable railway journeys in Portugal that some bearded fellow had taken, but I put it aside almost immediately. It is a paper for boys, I thought, and I pushed that journal off my truckle bed because I had other business there for the minute.

Chapter Eighteen

Wednesday 9 December – Thursday 17 December

I turned up for work next day all ready to be stood down, but when I booked on, Mr Crook's eyebrows remained in place, and there was no trouble from him. The fires were going into the engines as normal, with the background of happy crashing and men whistling. As usual I walked past a hundred heads that were all looking the other way, and made straight for the Governor's office, which I was sure would on this occasion prove to be my place of execution. However, I came across him before I got there.

Coughing fearfully, he took me to Twenty-Nine and asked me to clean it.

I mumbled, 'I am very sorry to say, Mr Nightingale, that when I was on the ride out yesterday with Mr Hunt, some things passed between us that –'

But the Governor cut me off, saying, 'New trimmings are needed in all pots as well.'

As I worked on that engine, my head was spinning from the complication of everything and the smell of the linseed rags, and that night I was fair on the rocks for a sleep, but after a while the work became a sort of tonic, and I don't believe that Twenty-Nine had ever looked better by the time I'd finished going at her.

I turned in without supper, and without replying to Smith. I wrote out my reply to that very vexing gentleman on the following day, the Friday, taking an age over setting down very little. Every word I could think of seemed highly dangerous. I cursed Smith for putting me to this, and I cursed the half-link for awaking all his suspicions of them in the first place. In the end I said nothing more than that I would be willing to meet him at his lodge if that was quite convenient, but leaving off time and date. Dad would have been horrified, for the usual compliments and pleasant touches were all left off. I was still set on going home, and with the decision made I felt easier: I had no doubt that I would never keep any appointment with Smith.

Things went on as usual at the shed until the Thursday of the following week, 17 December, when Crook, handing me the token, said, 'I was thinking of you today.'

'Good thoughts, I hope, Mr Crook.'

'Not especially,' he said, and took a long drink of tea. 'There's been an event,' he went on, his eyebrows jumping. 'An event touching on your arrival here.'

'Well . . .' I said, 'What?'

'It's not my place to tell you.'

I walked out of Crook's room fast and in a high state of anxiety. The first thing I saw was my handiwork on show for all to see, for there was Twenty-Nine, gleaming, in full steam at the front of the shed and looking somehow like the point of an arrow on a day of marvellous blueness. I saw a fellow inside her feeding the fire irons into their hole. It was Vincent, and he was getting ready for a ride, all right – he must have finally passed up to the half-link.

I began running along the barrow boards, crossing a hundred yards of track in no time, and when I came close I saw the driver was Barney Rose. He was wearing a black armband and lounging against the handbrake reading the *Sportsman's Daily*.

'What's up?' I said.

'A. R. Wisdom is the new amateur billiard champion,' he said.

'No sporting matter too small to be missed,' said Vincent. Then he turned to me and said, 'We've got a special on.'

He meant the funeral of a toff.

'They've put you up, then,' I said.

He nodded, as if too full of happiness to do anything more.

'As from today, I'm a full half-link man.' He had a grin on him like a street knocker – I'd never seen his teeth before.

Then I realised what he'd said. 'Who's dead?' I asked.

Vincent smiled at me. He seemed to have no objection to my questioning this time, but he wasn't answering. Rose was saying to him, 'Have you heard of A. R. Wisdom?' Vincent was at the injectors, looking down from the cab, checking the flow from the exhaust before bringing in the cut off and sending the water into the boiler.

'Who's dead?' I asked again over the rushing of the water and the clanking of the pipe and Barney Rose saying, '*I* never have and that's for certain. All the same, there was a capital attendance at the game.' As he turned over a page I asked my question again, even though I knew very well by now what the answer would be.

Vincent leant down to turn off the injector, then stood up and looked at me. 'Mr Rowland Smith,' he said, sticking out his chin. 'I believe you were acquainted with the gentleman.'

I looked at him as hard as I could, and he did the same to me, but at the last moment I turned away because I fancied he was going to grin.

I thought: if I had replied to Smith earlier he might still be alive.

Rose took out his pipe, sneezed, and said: 'Brilliant innings by Bosanquet yesterday.' Then I heard the Governor walking up, or rather I heard the sound of his cough. He asked me to come down from Twenty-Nine, and I followed him out over the glittering tracks, with Rose and Vincent no doubt staring after us.

There was a newspaper under his arm, and he passed it to me folded in such a way that I had a choice of two articles: 'NEW AMBASSADOR TO AMERICA', I read, 'CORDIAL SPEECHES' – that was the wrong one. The other was under a headline reading, 'IN THE CORONERS' COURTS'. 'In the Camden Court,' I read, 'Mr Laurence Drew conducted an enquiry with reference to the death by fire in his apartment of Mr Rowland

Hubert Smith, aged thirty-nine, of Grenville Mansions, Dartmouth Park . . .'

So there were no letters after his name, and here was the proof. I continued to read:

Mr George Collins, a doorkeeper, said that he had noticed smoke pouring into the lobby at 7 p.m. on Friday 11th of December. On rushing upstairs he determined that the smoke was coming from the apartment of Mr Smith, which was to the rear of the building on the lower floor, but the smoke was too dense and the heat too great for him to enter. After raising the alarm within the building, Mr Collins was able swiftly to alert the fire brigade at Kentish Town, the apartment block being equipped with a telephone. The brigade turned out shortly after, at 7.30 p.m., and they succeeded in dousing the flames at 8.30 p.m., having run their hoses into the garden of the apartments and directed them through the windows of the flat. Mr Smith was found on the remains of his bed, horribly burnt, and quite dead.

Mr Collins stated that he had spoken a few words with the deceased on his arrival at the flat from his business. He had said that he was tired and in need of a good rest, but otherwise seemed to be in the best of spirits. Mr Collins also stated that Mr Smith was a prodigious smoker of cigarettes. He had never seen him without one in his hand. The coroner conjectured that he had lain down on his bed for a brief rest with a cigarette still in his hand, and that this had sadly caused the bed to catch alight. The jury returned a verdict of accidental death.

When I'd finished the article, I told the Governor of the letter I'd received and the one I'd posted two days later, which Smith would have received on the day of his death.

He nodded for a while, and said, 'The police think the fire might have had a bit of help.'

'A bit of help from what?'

The Governor took a box of cigars from his pocket. 'A can of paraffin.'

'That's not in the paper.'

'They don't let on that they know that kind of thing. He was done in,' he said, taking a cigar from the box.

'Will there be a police investigation?'

'There will if I can help it,' he said.

We strolled over the barrow boards, further away from Twenty-Nine. We both looked about to see whether Vincent and Rose were watching us, but Rose had gone underneath and Vincent was at his fire. There were engines coming off-shed all about us, and I had the sensation of many other men turning around on their footplates to keep me in view for as long as possible.

'Smith told me he believed Henry Taylor was murdered,' said the Governor. He lit the cigar, and neither one of us spoke for quite a while. 'He had the idea that you were a bright spark,' he said, blowing smoke.

'I was sent here to be his eyes and ears,' I said quite suddenly.

The Governor nodded once.

'Why didn't he tell me that's what he was about?' I said.

'I expect . . . Because then you would have *known*.'

Crook the gatekeeper was prowling past us. The Governor smoked for a little while longer, looking across to Twenty-Nine, which was doing the same. 'As from this morning,' he said, 'Vincent is firing on the half-link. I couldn't keep him off any longer.'

'Why were you keeping him off to begin with, Mr Nightingale?'

'Because I didn't like him; I was obliged to give him a few firing turns, but I wanted him in the shed as much as possible where I could watch him.'

'He's Hunt's nephew, isn't he?'

The Governor nodded. 'But Taylor and Mike were brought on by myself – well, it was Mr Smith's doing, really. He wanted to change the way things went on here, with any engine man thinking he could get a start for his own grandmother if he wanted. We were worried over what happened to Taylor, and told the investigators so, although we could never prove anything. But we also told them we were set on not going back to how things were. Any new lad coming in would have to be from outside, otherwise . . . well, they'd have won the day, wouldn't they?'

'So that's how I got my start.'

'I expect that now you know, it all seems a bit heartless,' said the Governor after a while.

'I was to be a sort of spy.'

'I was under instructions to watch out for you on-shed,' he said, 'but also to let you see as much as possible of the half-link off-shed, where their tongues might be a bit looser, so that meant getting you on a few trips with them. I knew Mr Smith had it in mind to quiz you, and when Mike got bashed he said it was going to be done directly, but I don't suppose he had the time until he came to write you that note.'

'How could Mr Smith control so much here, Mr Nightingale, after he'd left the South Western?'

'It was his aim always to come back. Our lot were only lending him to the Necropolis, so to speak.'

'Why exactly is Mr Hunt on the half-link?'

The Governor drew on his cigar.

'Because he's a fucking socialist, and you've always got to watch out for those fellows.' He was smoking and smiling at the same time, which made a strange sight. 'Hunt ran the strike here in 1901, so they cut him down to size.'

'Who's they?'

'Who's they? Rowland Smith, giving orders to the District Locomotive Superintendent, with a little help from myself, I don't mind admitting.'

He gave me time to let all this sensational stuff sink in, then he said, 'Now look, the shed's not safe for you and I want you out. There's going to be a bit of a paper war over it, but I can get you a start in any station on the territory.'

'You mean I'll be back portering?' I said.

'Nothing's fixed up,' he said.

One of the Atlantics came out alongside us under steam, sending out a mass of blackness. 'I'll have that bastard,' said the Governor, eyeing the chimney.

Why did I not take the chance to flee? I did not want to go back to portering, but there again I could see the moving shadow coming for me, and present in my mind always was the cemetery, with the railway on hand to take me there on a one-way ride. It was better to be a porter imprisoned in a too-tight, over-decorated waistcoat than to take that trip before my time. But I now somehow knew that all these horrors had always been waiting for me, because becoming an engine man was no mere matter of book learning. Engine men, I could not deny, looked different from me, and they looked different because they had been through just such a thing as this. This was the life of London and the life of men, where threats and fears came, and they had to be stood down.

'I'd rather stick at the job,' I said.

'All right,' said the Governor. 'For now you can, but watch out.' He smoked, watching me for a while with a shrewd look.

'Can I go up with Rose and Vincent today?'

I thought there would be long odds against this, but the Governor just shrugged: 'Don't see what harm you can come to on a jaunt like that – the entire board of the Necropolis is going along from what I've heard. You'll need a ribbon, though.'

He meant a black one. 'I can tear up some rag,' I said.

'I nearly forgot to ask,' he called to me with smoke tumbling from his mouth as I set off for the rag store, '*have* you got any notions about all this business?'

'No,' I called back, because it seemed the best answer at the time. 'I can't think who did for Taylor, Mike and Smith, and,' I added, 'I don't know who murdered Sir John Rickerby of the Necropolis Company either.'

Now it was the Governor's turn for a shock, and I fancied there was greyness mingled in with the redness of his face. 'Oh Christ, let's leave him out of it,' he said.

I walked off to the rag store revolving two thoughts: that Rowland Smith had given me a shot at the footplate, and that I now knew for certain that he had also put me in a very dangerous spot and used me as a spy. I did not give much time to mourning that gentleman.

Chapter Nineteen

Thursday 17 December
continued

I came back from the rag room with a blackish ribbon – or rag, if you were going to be particular – on my arm. The Governor took me up onto the footplate of Twenty-Nine, and there was no trouble as we picked up just two from the funeral set: a passenger carriage and a hearse. As we came into the Necropolis, Rose was half driving, half reading the paper, and every so often exclaiming, 'Oh, my eye,' at some new sporting sensation. Vincent was swanking at his regulator and fire, keeping the pressure at dead on 180 per square inch, which was the right mark for Twenty-Nine. I was staring at them both without minding if they knew it.

We backed into the Necropolis station, where a small crowd waited on the platform, all in fine black coats and toppers. They were all men and looked like a lot of ravens, but one of the ravens had the lined and worried head of Erskine Long, the Necropolis chairman. I watched the coffin come along after the last of the mourners had climbed up. Smith's coffin was as exquisite as his coats. It had panelling, fancy handles and a mass of hothouse flowers on top, and I could tell the Necropolis bearers – not Saturday Night Mack's gang, but a smarter-looking lot – were struggling with the weight of it, even though I guessed there would be little of the man himself left inside. The door marked 'first' was opened to receive the casket.

When I went back onto the footplate, Vincent was at his fire again, and Rose was putting something back in the box under his seat. I had seen him do that before.

Vincent put coal on as I hosed down the cab. After being given the off, Rose settled down to smoking his pipe and driving, both of which he did very badly, knocking ash everywhere and repeatedly relighting his pipe, and jabbing on the vacuum brake instead of brushing it on in the approved way. So we made jerky progress as we passed through the signals and speed limits of the Southern Division.

As we came to the edge of the city, I ran out of jobs to do on the footplate and looked at the passing scenery while a million questions raced through my head. It was a queer business, travelling south of London. The countryside, when it came, was of a very pretty sort, although more comfortable than I was used to, with bright green fields, churches covered in ivy and winding, dusty lanes with tempting inns dotted along the way. But there was no end of building taking place, and you'd get whole streets going up in the middle of fields. You could never quite say that London had finished, and it was vexing because you thought it ought to.

Towards Brookwood, I thought London had really given up the ghost, but then we suddenly rose out of a cutting and I looked down into a wood and saw men with axes and machines steaming away. London, according to the Necropolis idea, could not hold all of its dead, but it could not hold all of its living either, so it had to be ever restless, ever growing.

After a lot of fussing about from Rose, we were into the Necropolis running, bunker-end first, along the single track between the lines of mighty trees. We passed by North Station, which seemed closed up and forgotten like a cricket pavilion in winter. As we approached South Station, however, there was a parson in strange togs waiting on a bench with a pipe in his mouth. Smith must have been church.

The parson stood up as we came closer but did not knock out his pipe until after Rose had struck the buffer bars with his usual bang. I stepped off the footplate and saw the four bearers put the wondrous casket onto their shoulders. They aimed themselves towards the little church that went along with South Station. A moment later the procession was off, with the parson in the lead and the Necropolis board in a semi-march – all save the man at the back, the youngest of the lot, who swished at the tops of the grass with his stick. As they went on, though, they did begin to fall in step in a ramshackle sort of a way, like loose-coupled waggons, and presently they disappeared from view.

It now struck me that I was alone with Barney Rose and Vincent, and at their mercy if they decided to try something. And no sooner had this thought come to me than I heard a crack, like a gunshot, in the bushes, and turned about to see a bony fox racing through the graves. I called up to the pair on the footplate: 'Did you see that?' Looking up, I saw Rose with a bottle of some spirit at his lips. I looked away so as to give this horrible vision a chance to disappear, and when I looked back the bottle had gone.

Vincent was working next to him, putting a bit of oil on the fire-door runners, and for the first time I felt sorry for the fifty-face kid, having to do his best to learn from a semi-drunk. 'He only takes a nip,' he said, looking at me, then added, 'You'd better not split.'

I just stood there dumbfounded.

'Smith's gone,' said Vincent, 'but there's still a lot you can blab to if you're daft enough to try.'

Rose leant forwards and threw the bottle, and cork after it, into the fire, slamming the door immediately after. 'Cat's out of the bag,' Barney Rose said, pushing past Vincent and coming down onto the platform of South Station. As he stood next to me there was a wrong smell about him, and I now realised it had always been there, that it was the reason he'd been looking away from me after the death of Mike.

'You're risking it a bit, aren't you,' Vincent called down to Rose, 'with top brass riding on the train?'

'That's the whole reason for it,' said Rose. 'We've got a carriage-load of swells with us today . . . fellow's got to get his screw somehow.' He turned to me and smiled his usual smile – which now looked different. 'We nearly had White-Chester up,' he went on, 'but he's sent his excuses, or so I've heard. I would've needed a whole other bottle if that gent had shown his face.'

'You'd have been stood down straight away if he'd seen you, though,' I said.

'Leave off,' said Vincent.

'I don't know,' said Rose. 'The Necropolis lot are one thing, but White-Chester likes a drop himself, or so I believe.'

'But he's not driving a train,' I said.

'Well,' said Rose, giving me a queer look, 'in a way he's driving hundreds of them, wouldn't you say?'

He's a socialist like Hunt, I thought, although not so urgent.

Half an hour went by, during which, to my relief, a bloke appeared and started doing odd jobs about the platform, Vincent played with the injector and Rose read his paper, remarking on how the 'men from Marylebone had not persevered with Knight' in Australia but *had* persevered with somebody else against all odds. I just sat on the platform bench thinking how it was not important that Rose was not the right sort. What was important was that I had struck more sadness in a month in London than in all my time in Bay, and there was nothing left for me but to play out my part of the little detective and find out the cause of it all.

The clock on the chapel over in the trees gave ten dings and Rose said, 'Here they all come, minus one' – the one being Smith.

The parson was leading the way once more. He was very cheery, as were they all, really. There was even a smile on the face of Erskine Long, who was directly behind. The same man was at the rear as before, swiping the grass with his stick. Even when they had been walking away from me it had been pretty obvious that he was the youngest, but I now saw that he was the youngest by at least *twenty years*. He was also the only one who did not look mild as milk: you could picture him in olden times, with a sword in his hand.

The four bearers walking behind looked lost without their coffin.

The crowd did not trouble the bar – there was to be some

grand event later at the American Hotel near Waterloo – and boarded the train directly.

'You'll find the ride up a deal smoother than the down run,' said Rose, 'now that I've had my pick-up.'

It was faster and that's for certain. I could not make out the names of any of the stations this time, and we fairly crashed across the points as we aimed for the Necropolis branch. Vincent was putting too much on – the pressure was above 200 – and I couldn't stop myself thinking of him as the friend of the fire, or saying out loud over the crashing of the engine, 'It's my opinion someone put the kybosh on him.' But Vincent just kept putting coal on, and Rose opened the regulator ever wider.

I leant out of Twenty-Nine, and saw the Necropolis station with all the lamps lit, for even though it was only shortly after eleven the light had gone out of the day.

I leapt down as soon as we pulled up because all of a sudden I could not stand to be close to half-link men. As I walked along the platform, I struck the Necropolis toffs climbing from their carriage and talking of some private business. First down was the young one, who I heard saying, 'He was not of our kidney.' He then gave a hand to Erskine Long, who, from his looks, was back to his old fretful self, and was saying, 'But what would you have brought it to, Mr Argent?'

'I should like to have brought it to a vote,' the younger man replied.

Erskine Long put his top hat on his head and said, 'But it has all been carried on with the agreement of the board, has it not?'

'Not precisely, no. I should have said main force was nearer the mark.'

A third gent, who had come out of the carriage and was putting on black gloves, said to the young man: 'But your objection is not to the sales but rather to the –'

Argent nodded once, sharply, at this new fellow. 'Primarily it is to the terms on which the ground has been sold,' he said.

In spite of using my slowest saunter, I had moved some way out of earshot by then, and they were quitting the station in double-quick time, heading for their beano at the American Hotel. Alone on the platform, I thought of how quickly the darkness came down these days, and how quickly the Necropolis packed up. Every day, I thought, is a half day here.

When we got back, Nine Elms was freezing. I went in to see the Governor. His two fires were roaring and there were a couple of Christmas cards on the wall behind him. I wondered who could have sent them, for he was out with every man in the shed.

He was looking at one of the big ledgers he kept on the shelves behind him. For the first time he had his black frock-coat off: there was a red waistcoat underneath, and this, with his white hair and red face, made him look like Father Christmas himself. With Nolan sending sour looks my way, the Governor told me that, provided I kept him informed of any news or events touching mortalities past or present, I could carry on cleaning for the half-link until Christmas, although having given long consideration to the matter, he had decided I was not to go off-shed again. He then asked whether I wanted to take any days for Christmas aside from Christmas Day, on which Nine Elms was closed. This all came out of the blue, and I suddenly had an idea of how I could use the time. I had five days annual allowance of holiday. I asked for Tuesday 22nd to Christmas Eve, and Boxing Day and the 28th too. The 27th was a Sunday so this gave me a good long run for action. The Governor looked surprised – he must have thought I was really going to make a Christmas of it – but he put me down for all these in another one of his books.

As he did so, I asked whether he'd made a note in any of those volumes as to Henry Taylor's last appearance at the shed.

'It wouldn't be in there,' he said, 'and I can't recall it.'

'Would you be able to tell me the last time he went off-shed?'

The Governor frowned a little at this, but after a few seconds he pulled down one of the volumes, searched for a page, ran his finger down a column, and said, 'Wednesday 12 August – to Brookwood.'

'And who was he riding out with on that day?'

The Governor looked down at the page again. 'Arthur Hunt,' he said, 'with Vincent doing a firing turn.' He shut his book with a bang, and said, 'Watch yourself.' He looked at me for a long time and smiled.

In the Governor, at least, I had struck a good man at Nine Elms.

Chapter Twenty

Friday 18 December

On the morning after Smith's funeral, Crook eyed me very closely as I took my token. Walking across the barrow boards towards the shed, I had to stop for one of the two Piano Fronts to come out. Clive Castle was on it. He also gave me a long look, and the only good thing to say was that there was as much curiosity as coldness in it, which I put down to him trying to guess how I would fare with the man who'd brought me on burnt to a cinder.

When the Piano Front had gone past, I saw Vincent and Hunt coming out of the Old Shed talking closely, and I couldn't help but wonder what business had taken them in there.

Then Flannagan was before me: he had one boot in the ash and one on the track, so he was about on a level. He told me, in between a good deal of cursing, to light the fire in Thirty-One because they wanted to find a leak of steam. This was a turn up, and I quite fancied the idea of it, but I said I took my orders from the Governor.

'He's taken sick again,' he said, lurching towards me and putting on a boss, 'so hard lines: Mr Nolan says you'll have your orders from me.'

I followed him up to the engine. 'All the water needed's in the tanks,' he said, and left me to it.

Well, I gave it a go but I still could not throw coal to the front of the box, and the harder I tried, the more my shovel banged against the top of the firehole. I started picking up the lumps and shying them down to the front by hand but even that didn't really come off because they were so heavy. Half an hour later, with bad coal cuts to my hands, I set off to look for kindling, but naturally nobody was helpful because I was the Governor's little favourite and had been Smith's little favourite, and that last gentleman dying didn't seem to have done me any good at all. At the top of the shed I did come across an old ladder, though, which I took back to Thirty-One and began smashing up, feeding the rungs into the firehole. Then I went to the rag store, where a bloke was ripping rags. I said, 'Have you got any soaked in oil?' and he said, 'Fuck off.' So I went over to the oil cans with a wheelbarrow full of rags. The oil cans were upside down in a line in the most freezing part of the shed; there was daylight and cold racing in through holes in the walls all around, piercing me like swords. It was a puzzle why they had the oil in the coldest corner, because when the temperature was below a certain level it would hardly flow. I stood there holding the rags under the oil taps. I knew it wasn't the right way of going about the job, but I doubted anyone would put me straight.

After a while I wheeled my rags back to Thirty-One, and I'd just begun stuffing them in the hole when Arthur Hunt sprang onto the footplate. We stared at each other for a long time. 'Get out of it,' he said, so I started to climb down from the footplate on the other side. 'Not off the engine, you clot,' he said, and there was something about the way he spoke that made me look at his face again, but there was nothing there except the usual fierceness.

His long body suddenly folded, and he was looking through the firehole. 'What's that in there?' he said.

'A ladder,' I said.

He nodded; he didn't seem to think it was so out of the way. 'All right,' he said. 'Go to the stores and get a tin of kerosene. Tell them you've been sent by Lord Rosebury.'

In the stores, they were very surprised to hear me come out with it but Lord Rosebury did the trick, and they gave me the stuff in double-quick time. I fairly ran back – for this turn up had put me in a fever of excitement. Hunt was winding the rags around bits of wood, and shoving them through the fire-hole door. When he'd done this, he took out a match, lit it, and held the flame between our two faces. He turned and dropped the match in the hole, and the fire started straight off with a soft rolling roar. 'One match,' he said, turning back to face me, 'gives you five hundred horses. Not such a bad exchange, is it?'

Then, for a marvellous moment, he smiled, and my whole dream of high speed seemed to come alive. 'A life on the footplate is the best sort, isn't it?' I ventured, because although I was somewhat more doubtful on that score than I had been before, I did still hold it to be true.

'An engine driver,' said Arthur Hunt, 'is an Adonis in every way: a first-class man in mind and body, and it is no wonder that he commands the respect of his fellows as a result.'

I nodded; this really was a bit of all right.

'But a driver is also a piece of dirt beneath the chariot wheels of the big man,' continued Hunt, becoming fierce once more. 'It's, "On that engine or you'll be up the bloody road in two minutes." You're hanging out to get your air, you're choking to bloody death, everything's red hot, you've got wind, rain, fog, broken rails –' He broke off here and, looking back into the firehole, said, 'You need to put a bit more on at the front.'

'Oh, but how?' I said.

There and then he showed me how to swing a shovel. He showed me how the common sort of fireman did it, then how the better sort went about the job. The thing was to let your bottom hand slide on the handle, and not to *try*, so I tried very hard at not trying but it didn't really come off, so Hunt said, 'Imagine you're chucking the lumps at White-Chester – aim straight for the bollocks.' That didn't really do it either, but he made out I was improving. He told me that any fireman will be chucking coal for years on end before being passed for driving, and that you'd finish up a cripple unless you kept your movements to a minimum.

I was just wondering why he had stopped putting me on ice when he said, 'We have a mutual improvement class on

Monday evening at eight o'clock. Would you come along?'

'Who will be there?' I said, after a pause.

'Besides myself?' said Hunt, and he was back to his dead voice now. 'Besides myself there will be Vincent, Mr Rose . . . Mr Nolan and Mr Flannagan will come along too, I should think.'

'Mr Flannagan?' I exclaimed.

'He is all for improvement,' said Hunt.

Well, I thought, there's a lot of scope for it with him.

'You are not to let on to anyone about it,' he said.

'Where does it happen, Mr Hunt?'

'In the office at the back of the Old Shed.'

'Of course,' I said. 'Thank you very much, Mr Hunt.'

I tried to smile at him, and he tried to smile back.

Chapter Twenty-One

Saturday 19 December – Sunday 20 December

'How is the engine-driving life?' asked my landlady, who was at her boiler.

'Fine,' I said.

She stirred my clothes into the mixture. 'Except that you are not driving engines,' she said.

She never ceased to remind me of that.

'And you do not sound as keen on whatever it is you are doing as you were before.'

'There was another murder,' I said, so as to get at her.

'My goodness,' she said. But she didn't seem very interested, and nor did she turn around; she was in a devilish strop, and I was beginning to think I should have passed by her kitchen and gone straight to the Citadel this Saturday night, the one place I could be sure of putting aside thoughts of Arthur Hunt's strange behaviour and the mutual improvement class on the Monday to come, where I would be at the mercy – in a dark and deserted shed full of crippled locomotives – of all the many enemies I had managed to make in such a short time at Nine Elms.

'A man who used to be a director of the London and South Western was burned to death in his flat,' I said, because her behaviour did not put me in the mood to mollycoddle.

'And was it an accident?' she asked, still with her back to me, and now scraping soap into the boiler.

'I don't think so,' I said.

I wanted to give it all to her straight to see how the ordinary sort of person might react. Then I started with my questions, which were the one bit of power I had in London. 'When Henry Taylor lodged here, did anyone ever come calling for him?'

'One man came calling.'

'What did he look like?'

'I only remember one thing about him.'

'What?'

'Teeth.'

Mike, I thought.

'It is why no one will lodge here,' she said, 'because they know what happened.'

'*I* lodge here,' I said.

'But you didn't know. I haven't had any luck with my notices, in any event.'

I thought of the one she had given me, which I had quite forgotten to do anything about. My landlady washed our clothes in silence, and I fell into my habit of reading the names on the tins on the mantelpiece: Bird's Eye Custard, Marigold Flake, somebody's candied peel, Goddard's Plate Powder, raisins, currants.

'What's wrong?' I said eventually, and not in a very friendly way, either.

'You come in here,' she said, still not turning around, 'and all you do is tell me about your horrible rattling trains, and men crowning each other and burning each other, and you keep coming back to the boy who was here, who I only saw half a dozen times, and you make me feel awful about taking his money in advance, and keeping his book. You shouldn't be in this lodge if you don't like it.'

'I didn't say I didn't like it.'

'And you complain about the water on the floor.'

'That's gone,' I said. 'There hasn't been any water on the floor for some time now.'

'That's only because it hasn't been raining so much,' she said. 'It's been cold but it hasn't been *raining*.'

'Well,' I said, 'I am very sorry about all that. I will be going now.'

I walked towards the door; I was in very low water, for a man ought not to be turning his back on a face like hers.

'At the church . . .' she called after me.

'What church?' I said. I had forgotten that she was keen on religion, and if the subject gave me hopes of continuing in her company, then I was all in favour.

'All Saints . . . where they've put up a scheme to help the ladies of the night-houses.'

'The fallen women, you mean?'

'They are *not* fallen,' she shouted. 'It is the men who come to them who are fallen.'

I nodded, remembering a little bit of Bible class: 'Well, everybody is fallen, anyway,' I said.

She was now looking at me in amazement for some reason. 'Oh, you're not at all interested in this,' she said.

'I certainly am,' I said, and the beautiful looks of her – she really was an eye-opener – and the thought of her going to waste in this kitchen with its empty tins and the soap works towering over her garden, which was no garden at all, made me walk towards her and put my hands on her shoulders.

Of course, I took my hands down quickly enough when I realised what I had done, but she hadn't seemed to mind, and it was with the strangest mix of sadness and happiness that I listened to her woes.

'Well, it is the ladies who are to be involved,' she said, more calmly, 'and I do mean the *ladies*. Oh, they all have their own broughams – and one of them a motor brougham – and three hundred pounds a year to do nothing with, and all I wanted to do was help in some small way, really nothing more than be on hand. I told them that I would make tea, I would make beds, but it is not to be. My face doesn't fit because they think I'm a skivvy, but it's just that our skivvy is taken sick, and has been for quite some time, and if you're not the right class in that place then the Christian religion goes *right out of the window*, Mr Stringer, I promise you it does.'

'I'd say you were in the wrong church.'

'Would you?' she said, and she almost smiled. 'Are you church, Mr Stringer, or chapel?'

'I think chapel is more modern,' I said, because I knew she

liked to be up-to-date, and it was also a way of not having to say I was neither.

'You're right,' she said, and then, although she was not quite crying, she gave a mighty sniff, so I handed her my undershirt, which was on the table waiting to be washed.

'Why are you giving me this?'

'So that you can blow your nose on it.'

'But it's your undershirt.'

'Would you like to come on a jaunt with me tomorrow?' I said. My plan was to cheer her up. And to spoon with her as well.

'Of course I wouldn't. Well, I *couldn't*. Anyway, where would we go?'

'I'd like to go on the Underground Railway,' I said. 'I've read a great deal touching on it but never seen it, and I think that, since I've been down here for so many weeks, it's high time I did.'

'It's electric in parts,' she said. She was always ardent for electricity. 'And would it be quite all right if my friend Mary Allington came along with us?' she added.

This was a blow, but, since I had gained so much ground, was only to be counted as a small one. 'I would be delighted,' I said.

'Because otherwise it would look as though I was your girl, wouldn't it?' She smiled, and all thoughts of the Old Shed, and how it was the perfect place to jack somebody in, flew from my mind for the time being, for this was London: a place of constant change.

The next day my landlady knocked on my door at ten o'clock and said, 'All set?' She seemed very keen to get on. She had put on a blue coat and a very effective hat, and I thought: all this for me. It was very hard to believe. I had on my best cap, best suit and collar, and I had plastered my boots with the Nuggets *and* the Melton Cream, so that they quite out-did my best suit, which was actually falling apart.

We waited for Mary Allington outside the front door of Hercules Court. It was a middling sort of day: quite grey and quite cold, but it was the two of us against the weather. The air was full of church bells and trains. The Citadel was going – it went around the clock, after all – but it was quiet, and the noise was low. At ten o'clock it was like a candle that had burned right down.

By ten after ten there was still no sign of Mary Allington, and my landlady expressed the opinion that she probably wasn't going to turn up.

I said, 'Well, where does that leave us?'

'There's no harm us going as friends. We were meant to be a crowd, and it's hardly your fault that it's ended up being just the two of us.'

So we set off, and I wondered whether Mary Allington was any more real than the skivvy my landlady had spoken of. In truth, I was a little put out that there was no other with us. We were all set for spooning, but I had no more idea of how to go about it than I did of how to drive the express to Bournemouth. I would have to watch her carefully, to read the signals. I paid her a compliment on her hat, and she gave me a perplexing look, so that I thought buttery of this sort was perhaps not the way.

We walked first into Waterloo – the first time I had been inside, I reflected in amazement. There was an army band playing and a Christmas tree going up. It looked better inside than out, with trains waiting in a neat row like horses in a stall; and it was very crowded, but with a Sunday lot – excursioners and shooting parties and so on. There were two of the Jubilees in, and any number of T9s, but I kept all that to myself. We both had a ham sandwich and a lemonade by way of breakfast, and tried to go down onto the Waterloo and City line to reach the Bank by Underground. The gates were locked, though, as it was closed on Sundays. As we came back up I could not resist telling my landlady that the Waterloo and City Line was run by the London and South

Western Railway, who also supplied the trains for the London Necropolis and Mausoleum Company, and she said, 'I can't keep up with all these names.'

We walked over the river, going slowly, watching the boats, then we struck the District Railway at Charing Cross, but my landlady said that was no good for a first ride because the trains were not electric. We came to Tottenham Court Road after a while, and I told her it was my dad's favourite spot when he'd been in London. Being all pubs, dining rooms and doxies, and very bright and tinkly, it was hard to imagine him there. Or maybe he'd been different when young, more like me, in fact. It was the first time I'd had that thought.

We stood about looking for motor cars, and two or three did come by. My landlady said they looked very strange, and I said you could supply the horse in your imagination. We also saw a motorcycle with a man on the front and a lady on the back, and my landlady said, 'I should like to ride on one of those.'

I said, 'Well, then, you'll have to find yourself a young fellow who has one.'

'Why should I not have one of my own?' she said.

I told her I had never seen a woman on a motorcycle before, and she said, 'I daresay you've never seen a *motorcycle* before.' I said I certainly had, and she said, quite fiercely, 'Where?' I said on a railway waggon in a siding at Whitby, and she said, 'In a *siding*!' and shook her head.

We walked through the front of what looked like a shop, and we were in the Central London Railway station for Tottenham Court Road. All tickets were 2*d*. As we rode down in the elevator my landlady had an even livelier look than usual in her eyes, and then I realised that all the half dozen fellows in there with us had the same moustache.

On the platform, you couldn't see the wall for advertisements and maps. I learnt from one of the maps that the Central went in a nearly straight line from a place called Wood Lane to a place called Bank – not *a* bank or *the* bank, but just Bank.

I was just going to ask my landlady about this – which I knew would involve the risk of a pretty sharp reply – when I saw that she was enquiring of a fellow in a uniform whether the electricity was Mr Edison's. He didn't seem to understand the question but he didn't mind being asked it by her. I could tell he was thinking that we were a handsome couple, and that I was a fellow with more luck than he deserved.

There were no timetables of any sort, just signs saying 'Trains arrive every few minutes', and certainly we only waited ninety seconds or so before one came in. We liked the coaches, which my landlady said were like little villas. It was a funny arrangement, though: a loco at the front and one at the back, but they were just electrical boxes on wheels. When they moved there came a buzzing noise that just went on and on. I wanted them to breathe. As we buzzed towards our destination of Notting Hill, I said, 'They often have steam locomotives along here, you know.' She asked why, and I said, 'To rescue the electrics!'

'No!' she gasped. She would not hear of it. She said that, even though it was very good, it was very rattly, and I said that was because the track lengths were too short. She said that she'd read of draughtsmen in a spot called Cheapside who'd been drawing wonky lines ever since it was built, and then she asked: 'Why can they not have tyres like the motor cars?' and I couldn't think of a good answer.

We came to Notting Hill, from where we walked to another station which also turned out to be called Notting Hill, and there took a Metropolitan train to Brompton, where we changed for West Kensington. This was all by steam, and the lines mainly went through brick valleys between the houses, although some of the valleys had roofs. All parts were very smoky, and I couldn't see why they bothered with windows in the carriages since, if you opened one, you'd be choked to death.

'How can this work?' I asked my landlady, 'Steam engines underground?'

She said, 'It can't. It will all be electric soon.'

That was one up for her, but I didn't care for these little locomotives in any case. 'You wouldn't get me driving one of these,' I said. 'It would be like being a dog always on the leash.'

My landlady told me not to be swanky.

I asked where we were going, and she said, 'Timbuctoo.'

It was a mystery tour, but as we rolled in to West Kensington my landlady told me to take a look out of the window, whereupon I saw a huge wheel, three hundred foot high, turning in the sky, with cabins for people to sit in.

'Whatever next?' I said, sitting back down, closer to her than I had been before.

We couldn't ride on the wheel because it was a guinea even for second class. It was like the Necropolis Railway in that there was little difference between second and first except the number on the door. We noticed that both classes were packed with johnnies, and I ventured to say, 'But I've got the prettiest girl of all.' But when I looked at my landlady she seemed not to have heard, which I was glad about.

Underneath the wheel was an Empire exhibition of some sort, with elephants that you could see for free. We had a look at those while drinking ginger beer, then we walked through a pretty Japanese garden decorated with lanterns that was alongside the exhibition, and so returned to the District Railway. As we stepped into our carriage it was dark, and the wheel was still turning above the station with lights burning in every cabin, and the sky around seemed not black but very dark blue.

We were back at Hercules Court for five-thirty. I asked whether she would like to come along to the Citadel. I told her about the mirrors with the electric lights like bunches of grapes, but could not persuade her. I said, could I go and get some bottled beer, and we could continue talking in the kitchen, so she made tea while I did that. The fire was going when I came back, and her hair was somehow different and even more fetching. When I finished my beer she just came

154

over and sat on my knee, and I kissed her until she had to return to her father. As she rose to her feet I think I made a pretty good show of looking as if I had done that sort of thing a hundred times before.

But when she'd gone it was as if I'd always been alone in the lodge, and had never had anything in my thoughts but the half-link and the mutual improvement class they had arranged for me.

Chapter Twenty-Two

Monday 21 December

At five to eight in the evening, I clocked off, not at all liking the way Crook took the token from me, looked at his clock, and followed his note of the time with a full stop stabbed into his ledger with a force fit to break his nib. Then, instead of leaving the yard, I walked back into it, heading for the blind house that guarded the Old Shed, stepping over half of the twenty-three roads with my boots going into shaking puddles between the tracks and the rain blasting across my face. As I approached the mutual improvement class, I thought of that left-behind house as nothing more than an enormous, infernal well-head, where, once through the door, you would roll over in air and plummet instantly to the bottom of a mile-deep black hole.

The Old Shed itself was more fearful still, but if you are destined to shine there are some things that you must do, and you always know what they are. I had thought of splitting to the Governor, but in that case all the half thought of me would be true, so the matter could not be handled like that. I had to find out their programme.

It was eight o'clock when I entered the Old Shed. I walked into that locomotive graveyard holding a bull's-eye lantern. The rain didn't stop hitting me when I stepped under the roof of the shed, but just whirled about the broken engines in a strange way. Who was the man who came over and wrote the numbers in chalk on the boilers and buffer beams, and why did he do it? How could there be improvement of any sort in this place? But there was one thing that gleamed, and I glimpsed it on a pile of ash straightaway. Picking the thing up, I saw that it was the weighty brass handle of an engine brake, brought to a beautiful finish, but for no reason. Well,

157

it would come in handy if I had to crown somebody. I slid it into my coat pocket, where it fitted snugly from wrist to elbow, and walked on. At the top of the shed I struck some wooden lean-tos that were mainly smashed, but there was one brick building a little more solid than the others; it even had a door. I lifted the latch and walked in. There was a table, and I put my lantern down upon this, from where it shone onto a wooden model showing the workings of the motion of a locomotive. I turned the lamp and saw a chimney breast of crumbling black bricks, then some dusty bookshelves. I walked closer to these with my lamp in my hand. They had *Continuous Engine Brakes* by Reynolds, of course – about a dozen editions of it. I saw also *Power in Motion*, *Fuel: Its Combustion and Economy* and *The Correct Use of Steam*, along with books that seemed to have no connection with railways – *Well Digging, Boring and Pump Work*, *Practical Organ Building* – and others even further off the mark, such as *Fabian Essays* by George Bernard Shaw, *King Lear* by Shakespeare, and the works of Dickens.

Turning back to the table, I spotted two candle ends. I lit these from my lantern, causing enormous posters on the walls to leap out at me: 'Every Member Shall Obey the Chairman', I read; 'No Member Shall Ridicule Another On Account of Lack of Knowledge'; 'Smoke Is Waste'. On the table I also saw papers headed 'A. S. L. E. & F.' – this was the name of the union. They had it in some sheds and not in others – I didn't think it had got into Nine Elms. I picked up one of the papers and shone my light on to it: 'Fellow Members,' it began, 'It is my most painful duty to inform you that our worthy and respected General Secretary passed away from this mortal flesh at about 2 p.m., 20th September 1901 . . .'

Just as I was putting the paper down, I heard a mighty clang, and all the breath stopped on my lips. I walked towards the door, and there came another clang, then a third and a fourth, like a bell ringing in an abandoned church. I came out of the brick hut and shone my lamp down one of the middle roads. Nothing but a line of broken locos on either side of the beam, but the clanging carried on. I walked a little further across the top of the shed, and tried my lamp down another line. Nothing again but the noise. It was getting louder, and the clangs were becoming more frequent.

I tried yet a third road, and there they were: the men of the half-link, with a couple of others besides, were approaching. They were little more than shadows behind their lamps, but I was able to make out that the smallest of them, Vincent, was carrying a metal bar of his own, with which he was striking the broken engines as he advanced in a line with his fellows. As I watched, a gust coming through a hole in the wall pulled all their coats to the right.

I turned back towards the little room, and stood at the door, listening to the banging of Vincent's metal, which made different sounds, like slow, monstrous music, according to whether it was striking an old boiler or something solid such as a pair of buffers, but which was becoming more deafening by the second, all the same. It was as though a slow train crash was happening all around me.

Arthur Hunt and his little gang were all out to get me, and it made no difference that Rowland Smith had died. They knew of the note he had written to me, and of the one I had written back. They knew I knew they had done for Henry Taylor and Mike: Taylor was killed because he was Rowland Smith's man, and had done something to rile one or all of them, and Mike knew what had happened to Henry Taylor so he had to go too. Then they had got round to the source of all their troubles, which was Smith himself, and they were certain I knew what they had done: they had taken paraffin from Nine Elms and they had burned him in his own flat. This explained all, and as for Sir John Rickerby . . . well, that old gent could be put out of the picture, for he was an old crock who had fallen over at Brookwood and there was an end to it.

I moved across the back of the shed, away from the road

down which the half-link was coming, and somehow I struck my lantern against something. The buffer of a locomotive? I couldn't see. I couldn't see anything, for my part of the shed was in darkness now, which was the way it was always meant to be. Among the fearful banging there came a cry: 'There he is!' And at that, there was not a particle of fear left in me, but just the need to run. I flung down the useless lantern and hared straight into a metal wall. I had struck the side of an engine, and done so head first. My mouth was all blood, and I spat and spat, and still it came.

The clattering was everywhere, now, and in among it were cries I couldn't make out. I wanted more light and less noise. I whirled about and darted forwards again, this time with my hands out before me, but they struck an engine soon enough. I turned again, turning about and about, trying to finish so that I was facing the black mouth of the shed where the rain and the night waited. But whenever I moved forwards I touched an engine. The whole shed seemed to have been picked up and turned about, so that the locomotives were set across my path to the entrance. But that couldn't be – I had simply faced the wrong direction twice.

The half-link were spreading out; I could see the flashes from their lamps, and the banging . . . It seemed they were all at it, and I knew this was how they did their murders: as though they were playing a game. I thought I would go distracted with funk, yet I wheeled about for the third time and began to make my run.

I ran hard with my hands out, and as I ran I realised that the banging had stopped, but that that was not good. At any moment the stick would be smashed into my face. No, some sixty tonner would fly forwards to check me, and what good would my brake handle be against either? The banging of the half-link men and their strange cries had stopped, and everybody, it seemed, was waiting for my smash. I ran and I ran, with my arms out to the side of me now, skimming two rows of engines, keeping them in their place, parallel with my running and not against me. I came out of the shed into the freedom of the rainy night, with the fires and the lamps of the yard. That wasn't a safe place for me either, though, so I kept on running.

Chapter Twenty-Three

Thursday 24 December

The day after the mutual improvement class that never was, I lay low in my room, reading the notes in my Lett's diary and waiting, revolving in my mind the Christmas plan I had made in the Governor's room after Smith's funeral. My engine brake handle was at all times on the mantelshelf. I didn't fancy even walking in Lower Marsh, mainly because it had suddenly come to me that there was nothing keeping the half-link in Nine Elms. I had no doubt that they had meant to put the kybosh on me and would do so again at the first chance they got. Down there, among the wild, big-booted fellows, they could twist me in broad daylight.

On Christmas Eve, my landlady unexpectedly appeared with a small cake, which I thought proved she was my girl, although it was a shame for her to have chosen such a milksop. We ate the cake in the kitchen before a straggly fire, with the washing – which she said she was anxious to get out of the way – boiling merrily behind her. There was some holly resting on the tins on the mantelpiece. She told me she had been distributing notices about her spare room all around Waterloo, and that the terms were now being advertised as '*extremely* moderate', and it was down to *half* a minute from the station. We finished the cake and I opened a bottle of beer. She stood up and walked over to the chimney piece. There was an envelope alongside the tins and holly; she stared at it for a while, then caught it up and gave it to me. On the front it said: 'Mr Stringer'.

'Is it for me?' I said, and she rolled her eyes to heaven.

It was a Christmas card showing a signal man in his signal box. He was being brought a hot punch or some like drink by a little girl, and there was snow all around. Inside, the card said 'With fond wishes for a merry Christmas', underneath which my landlady had written, 'Merry Christmas, Mr Stringer', and signed it with her name, which was Lydia. I was quite struck dumb for a moment; I began to say that I would keep this for ever, and to apologise for not having got her a card, but she would not let me speak, and instead asked me what the biggest difference was between London and Bay.

I said no stars in the sky in London, and she liked that, I could tell. She asked – I fancied a little anxiously – whether I would like to go back to Yorkshire, and in doing so she hit on the very thing I'd been thinking of as the only thing to do if my last plan failed.

'I would go,' I said, 'if you would come with me.'

When the words were out I could not believe I had said them.

My landlady stood up and said, 'Oh', and I made to stand up too, and all was confusion for a second. Presently, though, we were both back sitting down, and she said, in a curious tone, 'So you're half on a *half*-link?'

I said that that was it exactly, and explained as best I could about links, of which there were many, and half links, of which there was only one. I added that I might soon be leaving it.

'Maybe your half-link can join up with another half link and become a whole link?' she said. She didn't know very much about railways, but she looked very good, and there ought to have been some way of doing something about it, especially since this was Christmas. But after only a moment or two of spooning, she went off to her father's place, from where she would be going on to church.

Afterwards, I could not return to my room; those moments with my landlady had galvanised me into acting in a more manly way. I had a pound in my pocket book and some coppers besides. I would brave the street, with a pint at the Citadel as my prize.

It was a cold but clear night and I actually spied two or three stars in the sky, which was a lot for London. I thought: I can see them because it's Christmas. And there were no low types in the street, and I thought that in this case the reverse was true: they had been removed from my sight *because* it was Christmas.

The Citadel was full of orange light, galloping piano music – 'Hold Your Hand Out, You Naughty Boy' – and advertisements for beef, plum pudding and special beers. Everybody was already having a jolly time of it, and I thought: if everybody is saturated now, what will they be like by the end of the evening? But it was amazing how some people in London could keep it up. There weren't any Christmas decorations as such that I could see, but with the fancy white electric lights, the big rippling fire and red-faced people, there might have been a thousand.

I walked with my beer towards the Comfortable Corner, but there was a man already there with a small glass. He was very large and sad, and was talking to himself in an underbreath. It was Stanley, the man who gave the address at the Necropolis in favour of extra manure, or whatever it was. As a barmaid came up to take the glass, he looked up, and his golden eyes flooded with sadness. The cause was lost, by the looks of him. Then he stood to hunt in his pockets for money and I went off to hunt for a seat in another part of the pub, but, not finding one, drunk two pints standing up.

I walked out of the Citadel at nine o'clock. Three little girls were hopping and twirling next to a barrel organ playing a Christmas tune. There was a goods train going over the viaduct, and the driver had slowed down to a sauntering pace as though he too was watching the dance.

I walked to the music hall on Westminster Bridge Road, and paid 3d to go into the stalls and see some Christmas joys, or something of the kind. Inside the theatre, all the gas lights were seething and shaking, and there was ivy on most of them. The roof was pink and blue – it seemed to sag like the roof of a tent – and there were posters everywhere announcing 'A Bioscope: The Latest Events from All Around the

World'. I knew the bioscope would come on at the end; it was what I really wanted to see because it was up-to-date, and I would be able to tell my landlady all about it.

Meanwhile, an old man in a long coat was standing on the stage, with a painting of a Christmassy street behind him, looking at the audience. There were not a lot in, but the man clapped his hands anyway, as though delighted with the crowd he saw. A puff of white powder flew up from his gloves, and the old man watched it rise with big round eyes. Then the lights changed and the Christmassy street was instantly gone – which was the best bit of all – and a ventriloquist was sitting on stage with his doll and a kind of desert behind the two of them. They both looked exhausted. The ventriloquist started talking – shouting, really – about beating the Boers, and the doll would not take its eyes off me. After a little while this started to get me down, so I turned my head away, at which moment I spotted, no more than half a dozen seats along, Saturday Night Mack, watching the doll and the ventriloquist with very close attention, with his feet on the seat in front, and a bottle of beer in his hand.

'You're not supposed to move your lips!' he shouted at the ventriloquist, after a while. The ventriloquist was telling the doll about 'the boys of the old militia', and Mack carried on drinking and watching. Then came the end of the turn, when the dummy asked us all to 'kindly rise and give a toast to his Majesty the King', at which Mack didn't stand but shouted, 'Kindly leave off, will you?'

I moved along the row of seats towards him. By the time I got to him they were changing the scenery on the stage, and he was having a fight with the chucker-out.

Five minutes later, Mack was telling me how he'd given the other fellow quite a pasting, but he was outside the music hall all the same, and so was I, with no hopes of seeing the bioscope. Mack's black suit had got pretty dusty in his set-to with the chucker-out, and his hat was no longer with him. Over the road was a butcher's shop. The outside gas mantels were all burning, but a line of white turkeys hanging above the window was gradually disappearing as men in aprons walked out of the shop and took them back in. It was almost ten; my dad's place would have been closed long before.

'What I'm looking out for just now,' said Mack as we watched the men work, 'is some nice fresh greens.'

Next to the butcher's was a pub – just a hot little room, really, that was more crowded than it should have been because of a piano and a big wobbling Christmas tree with tapers all lit. It was called the Kingdom of Italy. As Mack walked in ahead of me, the piano started playing on its own. He stood us both what he called 'brain dusters', and all I could say is that they came in very small glasses, which was just as well. There were some pretty women in there, which brought Mack back to talking of fresh greens, green gowns and so on, by which he meant the ladies of the night-houses and the kinds of business that could be conducted with them, and all this made me feel quite hot. After Mack had got us both a couple more brain dusters, I said I was drowning in mysteries. He said 'Give me one, mate.'

Mack was not like anybody I'd met before. He was a man of the world – a man of the London world, I mean – and I was always surprised that he would hear me out. Anyway, I told him that on my first day in London, the clock on King's Cross had been ahead of the one on St Pancras, that it had said five after three, and the clock on St Pancras had said five to, and Mack said, 'I spotted that myself when I was in that neck of the woods the other day.'

I said, 'It's a bad business, ain't it?'

Mack didn't seem too vexed over it, but said, 'I expect the Midland had it right . . . Them's the jockeys for me.'

I couldn't tell whether he was talking here of the Midland Railway or the two pretty monkeys in the corner that he was giving the over-eye. They were a pair of spankers, I had to admit, and I helped myself to another look at them.

'Anyway,' said Mack, 'how do you know the King's Cross clock was the one that was ahead?'

'What do you mean?'

'How do you know it wasn't behind?'

'Because it said five after.'

'I know that.'

'And the other said five to.'

'Yes, but how do you know that King's Cross wasn't so far ahead that it was catching the other up?' Mack saw off his brain duster, and called for two more.

I said, 'Catching the other up from behind, sort of thing?'

'Course. You can't catch something up from in front, now, can you?'

'You might have put your finger on it,' I said. 'Listen: how long do you think it would take a clock that was losing, let's suppose, a minute every hour to get so far behind another clock keeping good time that it would start getting ahead of it?'

'I don't know,' said Mack, who began telling me of a little spot in Waterloo where there were 'some girls who take a real pride in their work. There's a low lot round about, mind you, and you must take care or you'll be ripped, but the place itself is fine.'

As he took out his pocket book to buy us two more brain dusters – Mack was certainly in funds this Christmas – he said I should give this place a go; that he would be along there himself, only he had his eye on the one in the corner who was kissing her cigarette as she smoked it and looking at Mack very slyly all the time. I have better looks than Mack, I thought, but he has more of something else. More of London.

I said I would be kept from going to a place like that by thoughts of my best girl, meaning my landlady, and Mack said, 'You have your meat and veg, and your greens are on the side.'

'Mack,' I said, as he bought a third lot of drinks for us, 'do you ever wonder about what happened to Henry Taylor,

Mike and Rowland Smith?'

Mack might have been out of his nut but he managed to give me a pretty straight look. 'Accidents,' he said. 'It's a dangerous business being on the railways.'

'But Smith was in his flat.'

'It's a dangerous business being at *home* in this modern world. Now off you go to your cunny house.' And he dragged himself off towards the doxy with the cigarette.

You have your meat and your veg and the greens are on the side. Saturday Night Mack had a way of making everything seem simple. Of course, standing against what he said was the Christmas card from my landlady.

The place was bang up against a viaduct at the bottom right hand of a stubby, blank street in Waterloo called Signal Street. I was all of a jump as I looked at this spot for I knew it held trouble in some way. Might Mack have sent me into the arms of the half-link? I tried to tell myself to turn back, but those brain dusters and my exploits with my landlady had stoked a fire that would not be put out, so I walked towards the viaduct. Nearly the whole of the bottom of Signal Street was blocked off by it, as if someone had thought: I want to put an end to this now. Well, not quite, because the arch of the viaduct started on the left side of the street so there was a gap in that corner.

I walked past two brown doors with no name and no number. The third door looked no different, but when I knocked, a broken voice shouted, 'Come in.' Feeling half excited, half doomed, I opened the door.

It was a big room, almost destroyed, with a fire that was too small. An old lady sitting at a table said, 'Merry Christmas, sir'; she sounded like the ventriloquist's doll.

'Yes,' I said, fairly shaking from nerves.

'You want to see a young lady?'

I nodded.

'You can be manualised at five shilling,' she said.

'Very well,' I said, and then I thought again, and said, 'By whom?' because I did not want to be touched by this mutton dressed as ewe.

'Jacqueline is presently available – she is our top indoor girl.'

It was when I took out my pocket book that I became sober. I broke into my pound to give the woman five shillings but that wasn't the end of it – there were certain extras for the old lady that came out at another shilling. We went up the stairs, and a train came up so noisily I thought it would burst through the wall, but of course it was only heading for the viaduct. A door was opened for me, and this time the room was too small and the fire was too big. There was a girl inside in a blue skirt but nothing on top. She had short hair and shiny eyes of the sort I like, and was half sitting, half lying on her bed. She reminded me of a mermaid, except for the short hair and the plain fact that she was sweating with a bad cold.

'Have you paid your money?' she said, as I walked in.

'I gave it to the old woman downstairs,' I said. 'She's the one who takes the money, isn't she?'

'You've got her in one,' said Jacqueline. 'What have you paid for?'

'Manualising,' I said.

'At what price?' She picked up a little towel from the stool by the bed.

'Five shillings.' There seemed to be something wrong with the system, for I could have said anything. 'How are you?' I said, to put things off.

'Oh, fairly blue,' she replied, and she walked up and started undoing my trousers. 'Are you a railway man?' she asked.

'Yes,' I said, and I thought guiltily of the driver Hughes of the Great Western Railway, at home with his wife and many children, at home in *The Railway Magazine*.

'Several of my gentlemen are on the railways,' she said, 'and one is very high up on the South Western.'

'What is his name?' We were on the bed by now, and my trousers were over the stool.

'Now, I'm not going to tell you that, am I?'

I was always more comfortable asking questions though. 'Is it a fellow called White-Chester?'

There was a very, very long pause while she started with her manualising. 'No,' she said eventually.

As she carried on with her work, I thought of my father and felt bad. Then I thought of my landlady and felt much worse. My thoughts were anywhere but where they should have been and now, strange to say, they settled on White-Chester himself, and I wondered about his name. What did it mean? It brought to mind a man – very like a circus strongman – who was in the habit of showing off his chest, which would have been very muscular but also, and more to the point, very white.

'I can't bring anything about,' said Jacqueline after a while. 'Do you want to try a suck?'

'All right,' I said.

'It'll be another sixpence.'

With a heavy heart I counted out the coppers for this. She blew her nose very hard, and then rolled around on the bed so that I was looking down on her hair. Better than her mouth was the feel of her breasts, which was almost like nothing at all. Still nothing happened, and, the effects of the drink having completely worn off, I said thank you, but could she stop, which she immediately did, saying, 'You're slow as a wet week.'

I walked downstairs, past the woman with the voice, which I didn't hear this time, and out through the front door of the night-house. Church bells were ringing for the midnight services, and cabs were racing across the mouth of the street on their way to happy places far beyond my reach. The night-girl had been feeling blue, and her blues were catching. Looking again towards the mouth of Signal Street, I saw a Christmas crowd walking across it – church-goers, I was certain. The youngest and oldest were at the rear: a man so bent over that I marvelled at the way his stove-pipe hat remained on his head, and beside him a beautiful woman.

Well, it was my landlady, of course.

Her father looked a very infirm gentleman indeed but she seemed happy, talking with wide gestures, loud exclamations and laughter. Whether the old man was laughing back I could not have said, for he was shaking all the time in any case. I could not let her see me, and I was glad of the darkness around the night-house. My dad wasn't church and he wasn't chapel, but as my landlady and her father gradually disappeared from view, I wished he had been one or the other because then I might not have been where I was presently standing, pressed into that black corner between the night-house and the sleeping viaduct, feeling cold, powerfully ashamed and six shillings and sixpence to the worse.

As I began to walk out of Signal Street, a fellow walked into it along the same pavement. He was small and wide and had a beard; he looked quite well set-up, but I knew there was something wrong. I wanted the brake handle about me. Seeing that we were on a collision course, I moved to my left, but on seeing me do this he moved to his right, so that we were still destined to meet in a smash, but I did not care. I tried moving the other way at the last, but so did he. Finally he walked into me, and I swung a punch at him directly. All the built-up fury of the past weeks went into that swing, but he stepped away from it easily, saying in a put-upon voice, 'Let a fellow by, would you.'

He continued on his way, and I watched after him as he gradually started to run, streaking finally through the one exit from the top of Signal Street, that one bit of viaduct arch.

I had Signal Street to myself once again, but the man had done his work, because when I checked over my jacket my pocket book had gone, and with it the ten shilling note I'd had left over. It was fair payment for what I had done, I thought, which left me about square with my landlady and my conscience.

When I returned to my lodge half an hour later, through frosty streets full of racing cabs and the broken-down human remnants of Christmas Eve, there was a package from Dad containing a letter from him and a Christmas card that had been sent to the two of us from Captain Fairclough. There was no note inside the card, just the letter 'F', and, using this 'F', my father had leapt to all sorts of conclusions: that we were much in Captain Fairclough's thoughts, that Captain Fairclough wished me success in my railway work, that the trade of butchery was not to be so looked down on after all. In his letter, Dad also said he had found Christmas very hard on his own. He now had thoughts of retirement, and asked whether I would like to have the shop. He was sure I would say no, such was my keenness on my present employment, but could not help thinking it was a shame that, once established in business, a family should go back to the common run of wage slaving. I thought of my landlady: she would never come with me to Bay for it would mean leaving behind her father.

I was all done up. I climbed into my truckle bed and slept soundly for a while, but woke at around four, when something made me walk over to the back window and look out into the yard. It was full of steam, swirling and somersaulting, coming in from the soap works, pouring silently over the wall on either side of the lamp and mixing with falling snow. I walked over to the mantelshelf and looked at the Lett's diary, at the facts as I understood them.

I stared again at the gas lamp, the only thing steady against the steam and the snow, and then in my mind's eye there came a picture of a locomotive revolving on one of the turntables at Nine Elms; I thought of Hunt telling me that 'an engine man is an Adonis in mind and body', and saw the Governor reaching for those tall books of his, and close upon this, in the silence of that night with no trains, there came to me again the idea that my notion was a pretty good one. Certainly it was my last and best hope of saving my job, my hopes of making my landlady my girl, perhaps even saving my life, such as it was.

And Christmas Day was the time to try it.

Chapter Twenty-Four

Friday 25 December

On Christmas Day, the snow lay thinly, making the world black and white. The trains were still not running, so that the mighty viaduct of Lower Marsh just looked like a giant waste of brick.

I walked over the road to the dining rooms and had a late breakfast at the table nearest the fire, which I had never been able to get to on any previous occasion. There were two policemen in there besides myself, and I waited until they'd cleared off before I came out of the dining rooms. I ran to the viaduct, climbed the metal ladder that was fixed to the side, and in a trice I was on the tracks. Then, with a heart beating fast for fear of meeting railway police, I walked into Waterloo, which was locked at all of its normal public entrances, so there was not a soul to be seen.

I could not believe that at least one of the men who worked there – either in building the new platforms or serving those already existing – had not come back on this special day just so as to have the place to himself for a little while, but the station was different not just on account of its quietness: the snow on the glass roofs had changed the light. As I looked at all the silent signs, swinging in the cold air – 'Refreshments', 'Lost Property', 'Station Master's Office' – I felt as though I had entered into a secret with the station, and would never look at it in the same way again.

All down Platform Four was a line of handcarts; I walked along beside it, and when I got to the end I looked out to see all the signals were at stop, which checked me for a second, but I leapt down nonetheless. Soon I was marching as if to Bournemouth, with no sound in my ears but the crunching of my boots in the snow and all the crows of London, or so it seemed. Every time I passed a sign saying 'Beware of Trains!' I laughed inside, for the men who had written those had forgotten about Christmas Day.

I turned left after a while, and hit the spot where the Necropolis branch went off the main line, then I walked along it towards the Necropolis station, so I had come in a big upside-down 'V'.

The Necropolis was as dead as one of the bodies they sent out to Brookwood, but Twenty-Nine was there, though for some reason, with the funeral set coupled behind, as black and blind as the station itself. Making my second ladder-climb of the day – down, this time – I entered the empty courtyard. This I crossed before going under the arch to the main gates, which were locked as I had expected. But I was on the inside of them.

I turned the handle of the door in the arch and it was open – probably it was always open, because they didn't bargain on anybody braving the tracks, but they too had forgotten about the one day when the world has a rest from trains.

I opened the door and stepped inside the heart of the Necropolis station and outside the law. Well, if I was pulled in, nothing that any court could do would be worse than what the half-link had in mind.

I climbed the stairs to the top two rooms: the one in which Mr Stanley gave his addresses and the Necropolis library. I entered the latter, making straight for the volumes marked in gold 'Necropolis Minute Book 1902' and 'Necropolis Minute Book 1903', which I laid on the floor, putting my own Lett's diary alongside. All the hatred that came from the half was tangled up with Smith, and I thought it might be tangled up with the Necropolis too. The books in the Governor's room had put me in mind of the books here, which were at least ones I could think of a way of looking at. There might be something in them that would illuminate all.

Beyond the windows was nothing but greyness and the beginning of more snow. I had had the best of the day on my trek from Waterloo, and now I had to work fast because I did not want to put on the electric light. The first page of the first volume began: 'On Monday the sixth day of January, at a meeting of the Directors . . .' This was followed by the names of the directors, half a dozen in all, and I recognised 'Sir John Rickerby, Chairman', Erskine Long, and the name Argent – he was the tough-looking fellow I'd seen on the train at Smith's funeral, and was down in the book as 'Major Argent'. Beneath was written: 'The minutes of the last meeting were read and declared to be correct,' and then came notes as to business such as: 'The secretary reported that the tenant of the bungalow New Copse, viz Samuel Welch, had become a bankrupt and it was ordered that he be served with a notice to quit . . . '; 'It was resolved that the request of the Woking Golf Club for a small alteration of the boundary on the south side could not be agreed to . . . '; 'In the matter of the payment over to the Company by the South Western Railway Company of the compensation for the removal of the offices, Messrs Long and Simmons are authorised to assist.'

The Necropolis station had been moved from York Street to its present, smaller site only two years before, which I took to be another sign of the decline in its business. But as I turned the stiff pages of the great book, I at first found very little – aside from some regretful remarks on the poor health of Sir John Rickerby – to cast light on the various riddles before me, and I became quite tired of reading of the minutes being 'read and declared to be correct', wishing that just once they might have been read and declared to be *in*correct.

I turned to the second volume and, in the minutes of the meeting held on Monday 6 July of that year, read: 'It was moved, seconded and carried unanimously that Rowland Smith Esquire be hereby appointed Agent of the Company.' There was then some difficult stuff over the next few lines as to what Smith was being brought on to do, and it boiled down to this: making economies.

He had set about his work quickly, for in the minutes of the next meeting, held on Tuesday 4 August, I read for the first time of cemetery lands being sold: 'It was ordered that the seal of the Company be affixed to the conveyance of sixty-four rods at Brookwood to Mr P. Everett (builder) for £200 . . .' and 'seventy-eight and a half rods to Mr Humphrey Warden (builder) for £220.' In all, there were above half a dozen sales reported in that month alone.

At the meeting of Thursday 3 September, the death of Sir John Rickerby on Wednesday 12 August, at Brookwood, was recorded, the directors expressing their deep sorrow and regret that he had been unable to enjoy the years of well-earned repose that would have been so amply merited by his long service to the company, and so on. Later in September there was a further meeting – this one of a special sort – at which it was 'moved, seconded and carried unanimously that Mr Erskine Long be elected Chairman of the Company.'

The smoothness of these words at first prevented me from seeing the sensational fact, but it came to me after half a minute: 12 August, the date on which Sir John Rickerby had stumbled at Brookwood, was also the date on which Henry Taylor had ridden out to the cemetery with Arthur Hunt and Vincent.

I scribbled in the back pages of my diary. All doubts were gone now. In high excitement I turned to the pages recording the meeting of Monday 5 October. Further sales were recorded, and my eye got another jolt by news of the biggest sale of the lot: 'It was ordered that the seal of the Company be affixed to the conveyance of 300 rods to Mr Roger White-Chester (Company Director) for £650.' In the minutes of the meeting held on Monday 9 November, more sales were recorded – little else but these, in fact. All the sales so far amounted to but a tiny amount of the whole cemetery, but still, Smith was going at a fair lick. I turned to the minutes of the December meeting, the last in the volume, which occurred on Friday 4th, and here, among details of further sales, I came upon a queer little remark. 'The Secretary read a letter dated 2nd inst from Mr Adrian Stanley, and it was voted to decline the request therein.'

This set off a kind of echo in my head, and I flipped rapidly back through the pages until I landed once again on the first page of the minutes of the 9 November meeting, and there it was again, almost word for word: 'The Secretary read a letter dated 3rd inst from Mr Adrian Stanley, and it was voted to decline the request therein.' I went back further, to the minutes of the meeting held on 4 August. There again it was written that Mr Stanley had made a request, and that it had been declined.

I picked up my own diary and made marks against dates as to the events that concerned me. What it totted up to was this: Stanley, the funny little fellow who gave the address, made a request to the directors at the meeting that took place early in August. The request was declined, and Sir John Rickerby died on 12 August at Brookwood; Henry Taylor was there, and he was first noticed missing from Nine Elms later in the same month.

Stanley made another request of the directors at the meeting that took place in early November. The request was again declined, and Mike came to grief on 30 November. Stanley made a third request at the meeting held in early December, and was once more turned down. Smith was burned at his flat on 11 December. In September and October there had been no suspicious deaths, and no requests from Stanley either.

But what of it?

I had no notion of whether Stanley had actually been at any of the possible murder sites, whereas I had now learnt that Arthur Hunt and Vincent had been in Brookwood on the day of Sir John Rickerby's death. Hunt and Rose, I also knew, had certainly been at Nine Elms when someone put the kybosh on Mike, and close at hand to the Jubilee he'd been riding on to boot. These were big black marks against the half-link to set alongside all the others, including hatred of Mike and

Rowland Smith. But now Stanley, that strange-eyed jack-in-a-pulpit, was in the picture too, and as I sat there in the gloom of the Necropolis library, the idea of little Stanley being the one seemed to grow more horrible by the second, for it might mean that Arthur Hunt, who had driven expresses and was most definitely a fellow of the right sort, really had got over his suspicions that I was Smith's man, and had brought the rest of the half-link around to the same way of thinking, only for me to throw his offer of friendship and instruction in all footplate arts straight back into his face.

But then why had Vincent been banging his stick in that way on walking towards me through the Old Shed? Why had they come at me in that death march?

I used what remained of the light to fly back through the book looking for any other mentions of Stanley that I had missed. I came upon just one, during the June meeting: the Secretary had been requested to ask Mr Stanley to consider giving his Tuesday address on alternate weeks only, 'it having come to the attention of the Directors that the audience frequently consists of one or two people, and sometimes fewer' – but this, I knew, had not come about; the address had remained weekly.

I closed the book for 1903, and returned it to the shelf. I then stood before the fireplace and looked up at the pictures on the chimney breast, searching for some sign of curiosity in the faces of the Necropolis chairmen, but all that happened was that the clock ticked and the darkness grew.

Ten minutes later I was back on the tracks. The trains had not yet started up again but the lamps were on, showing me that the snow had been replaced by rain, which was coming down slowly. I could have gone into Waterloo in any old way but I marched in on the 'up' side so as to be quite correct, and to keep a little bit of order at least in my life. As I ran back along the great viaduct of Lower Marsh, I thought: I have solved nothing; all that has happened is that I have gone deeper into the mystery. I neared the ladder that would take me down to my lodge, and stopped. I was level with the roofs, and all about were the sleeping, streaming chimney pots, but there was a great clanging from somewhere.

It was only the work of a second to identify the cause and, sure enough, as I walked across to the ladder, the thing was shuddering in time with the clangs. I looked down and there was the human bell, chiming away. I thought: yes, people do like to hit metal with metal; there isn't necessarily any harm in it.

He was shocked to see me, because this was *his* ladder, after all, but he moved aside for me very meekly. I should have given him a 'Happy Christmas' as I climbed down, and would have done so had there not been so much on my mind and so much more to put in my diary, chiefly concerning Mr Stanley.

Chapter Twenty-Five

Friday 25 December – Tuesday 29 December

At midnight the trains started up, and it was as though the world started turning again, although I just kicked my heels in the lodge for the next three days, my only excursions being across the road to the dining rooms. What requests had Stanley made? What, if anything at all, did they have to do with the deaths that came hard upon those meetings to which the requests had been put? And were the questions in some way connected to the men of the half-link? There was only one way to find out, and that was to wait for the following Tuesday and ask.

At six in the evening on 28 December, the Monday, I walked from Hercules Court to the Necropolis station – by the usual route, this time – and there I saw the poster on the board propped outside the front: 'Extramural Interment: An Address'. It was to happen the next day at 8 p.m. Who wants to hear of cemetery schemes at Christmas? I thought, as I scurried back to my lodge, but it did not matter. I would be there, for one.

The Tuesday ought to have been the day I went back to work, but I did not return, for fear of more meetings with the half-link, and I kept to my room at nine o'clock when there came an awful pounding on the front door of the lodge, in which I had been alone, with no sight of my land-lady, since Christmas Eve. The call boy had been sent. He was certainly a great hand at knocking, and it was queer to think that the sound would have once represented to me the greatest nightmare of all.

I took two pints at the Citadel before setting off to the address. They were meant to boost me, like the engine brake handle that was in my coat sleeve once again. It was just before eight, and the rain was coming down hard on my best suit as I walked once again to the Necropolis station. As I came within sight of the place, a black funeral van came swirling out through the gates and away – light and fast and free, having, I guessed, left a body behind. The traps and cabs were all rattling past at a great rate, and throwing out mud onto my suit as they went.

Passing Mr Stanley's sign, I walked through the gates and stood looking into the courtyard, lit by its gas jets, some trembling high up on the walls, some low down, like fireflies that had settled themselves in any old way. I turned towards the door in the arch and saw the board where the forthcoming funerals were posted up. Underneath large black letters spelling out 'In Memoriam' were the details of the burials at Brookwood on the following day – the last ones of the year, I supposed – of a Mrs Lampard and a Mrs Davidson-Hill. Both were to ride out in 'first', as were their mourners, and it struck me that this was why Twenty-Nine had been standing ready on Christmas Day.

I climbed the stairs, passing the trapped flowers, and walked through the double doors on the fourth floor marked 'Address'. Mr Stanley was there under an electric light, sitting at a table upon which were some papers, his bowler hat, a tumbler and a glass jug of water. His big head was dangling down and there was a gap in the black hair on the top of it – but it was not as if his hair had fallen out; it was just as though some of it had been worn away as part of the overall sadness of his life. Before him was a cluster of chairs – every one empty. There was a palm in the corner this time, fluttering in the wind and rain that was flying in through an open window. Stanley looked up as I entered, and I saw the long brown face and wide golden eyes. I took a chair at the front.

Stanley sat still for the next ten minutes while he waited, or pretended to wait, for a crowd to come in. I sat there and did the same, looking, I hoped, like a man without a care; but it was only those two pints and the brake handle that enabled me to pull it off. (I'll take two more besides, I thought, when this business is over.)

It was ten minutes, then, as I say, before I called out: 'Will you carry on with the meeting?'

Stanley made no answer, but rose to his feet and immediately commenced booming in that very unexpected voice: 'As it is appointed unto "all men once to die,"' he began, 'the subject of interment is one of universal interest.'

He looked at all the empty chairs for a while, and I looked at him, gladder than ever of the Red Lion inside me.

'It comes home to every human breast, not only with a solemn but an emphatic closeness,' Stanley continued in his surging voice. 'Whatever, or whosoever, the head of a family in this vast population of London may be – whether high or low, rich or poor, young or old – he knows that sooner or later himself, his wife, his children, his domestics, his associates, must each in rotation pay the great debt of nature and descend into the silent mansions of the tomb.'

He paused here, seeming to shrink rapidly as he did so, and when he next spoke it was in that fast, pernickety mutter he came out with when not speechifying; this mingled with the clattering of the jug against the glass as he poured himself some water.

'These words were written by the founder of our Necropolis Movement some sixty years ago.'

(Stanley might have given out a name for this founder, but I had not caught it.) 'In the same year he also wrote the following . . .' He breathed in and came out with the big voice again: 'Within numerous and loathsome decomposing troughs, for centuries past in the heart of the capital of a great Christian nation, the most depraved system of sepulture has existed that has ever disgraced the annals of civilisation.'

As Stanley spoke he would rotate a few degrees in one direction then back, his whole huge body – too big for any work it was ever called on to do – rocking gently as he came to rest facing one way or the other. He reminded me of some seaside automaton that I had seen, but his eyes were alive – as beautiful and sad as any woman's.

He took a short drink, put the glass down hard. 'Our founder calculated,' Stanley went on, resuming his rocking, 'that within the first thirty years of his life, one and a half million corpses had been partly inhumed, partly entombed, within the metropolis. During that time the amount of poisonous gases evolved from putrefaction into the civic atmosphere, beyond that absorbed by the soil, exceeded seventy-five million cubic feet. And further, this system, which whether as regards public health, public morals or public decency, is the most gigantic abuse that has ever –'

'You needn't continue with the full address for my sake,' I said.

Stanley stopped and looked at the blackness beyond the windows for a while; then he took a step towards me. 'The address, once begun,' he said, using his ordinary, smaller voice and facing towards the windows, 'has never been abandoned for any reason.' He shifted his head slightly so that he was looking at me from the sides of his eyes, and all of a sudden he looked like a slugger. 'The first Mr Gladstone, when he came to hear the Tuesday Address, said that he had never heard the case for extramural inhumation put with such eloquence since the days of our founder.'

'That is something,' I said, and I thought: he's off his onion.

'He is reputed to have written a letter to the board,' said Mr Stanley, still not looking at me, 'but they have never seen fit to give it any very wide circulation.'

'Where is the founder today?' I said after a while, as though the fellow had been a great pal of the two of us.

Mr Stanley's eyes flickered and then he put them on mine for the first time. 'He has gone beyond this world.' He continued to stare in a most unnerving way.

'You mean that he is in Surrey, I assume . . . in Brookwood . . . that he is dead?'

Mr Stanley gave me a sharp nod, then his eyes left mine,

and I felt very relieved.

'So they have you to speak up for the Necropolis, and speak this dead man's speeches?' I said after some little while.

With no expression in his voice or face, Mr Stanley, looking now slightly to my left, said, 'At a rate of nine shillings per address, fifteen shillings and travelling expenses for any address that takes place outside London.'

He turned around, and picked up the jug again. He filled the glass with his wide, shaking hands, and drank the water.

'Is there much call for addresses outside London?'

'There is no call for it *whatsoever*.' And he switched his eyes back onto mine; I did not like it.

'And within this city the interest is not great?'

'Not great.' Still the eyes were upon mine; and he had not put the jug down. 'You are speaking to one who has performed very great service on behalf of this company,' he said.

'You were speaking of all those poisonous gases.'

'Our founder did.'

'But since his time, very shortly after the creation of the Necropolis, I think, there was an act of some sort.'

'There have been many acts.'

Still the eyes; his eyes were like fires.

'No, I mean an *act* – an Act of Parliament allowing the creation of cemeteries inside the city.'

As I spoke, he looked down at the jug. It was a well-made, big thing, but it looked small in his hands. 'That has been one of the acts, yes,' he said, looking up again, 'and yet somehow a hopeful spirit is maintained.'

Still staring at me, he now rapidly stood, and I thought: the death of Sir John Rickerby is where it starts; all else follows from that. With my right hand I felt the heaviness of the brake handle under my sleeve.

'It is by written contract that addresses are supplied,' said Stanley, stepping out from behind his table and beginning to pace before it. 'Do not think that any individual, let alone

187

a barrister of twenty years' call, would be so blind as to get into this sort of work without making stipulations pertaining to, for example, the minimum number of addresses to be given over any given period. Naturally there are to be more in winter than summer. The call for the addresses is greater in winter if only because the rooms in which it is given are –'

And here he stopped his pacing.

'The rooms are what?' I said.

'Warm,' said Stanley, and then he was off again, pacing back and forth.

'But you just speak for money,' I said. 'You have no personal interest in any of what you say.'

'Intramural burial is a grievous wrong, and one particular aspect of the company's operations is of special interest.'

'Which is what?'

His eyes were on me again; they were not like fires, I decided, but like flowers.

'Trains.' He took another step towards me.

'Trains?' I said. 'Oh, they're a bit of all right, aren't they? Quite exciting, you know.'

Stanley nodded. 'As a means of conveyance for the dead, yes.'

'I am on the railways myself, on the London and South Western Railway, to be exact. I clean the funeral engines.'

'I know,' he said.

His eyes stopped dancing and went dead. He seemed to be in the grip of a fever; he was sweating freely – and this with the coldness of the night coming through the open window.

'It is written in the minutes of the Necropolis that you sent requests to the directors at their meetings of August, November and December.'

He was looking down at the jug again; he was very intent on the place where the handle joined the body. Then he looked up to me and his eyes were full of orange flame.

'What was your request?' I asked, letting the brake handle slide a little way into my palm.

'I asked for an increase in pay.'

As he swung the water jug, I said, 'You're off your onion,' and the water and the glass exploded against my head as he said in his fast voice: 'I did not receive it on the first occasion, and nor did I receive it on the second or the third, by which time the company's indebtedness to myself for services provided had . . . oh, it had not decreased, oh, it had most certainly not *decreased*, and yet I was to be content merely with the restoration of the Tuesday Address as a weekly –'

I had sunk to the ground as Stanley raved, and that wasn't the end of the matter. I was sinking through the floor as my murderer spoke, and the blood in my eyes turned into the red flowers among those that the board of the North Eastern gave T. T. Crystal for his shows. No, the *certificates*. They gave him certificates for the flowers that were everywhere. You couldn't see out of the waiting room for them, and you couldn't properly see out of the signal box either – they were dangerous, those gardenias.

On the platform you can see very well, though – the hills of Eskdale rising and rising, and here is the bird train coming down from Whitby at half-past eleven on a summer Saturday morning: 137, that silly little dock shunter that would have been better off banging cod waggons about at West Cliff, two waggons full of pigeons, and my old favourite, Mr Saul Whittaker, the pigeon conveyer, who tells no end of yarns, and is semi-drunk at all times.

Number 137 stops, and this time there is a flat-bed truck tagging along behind, with something under a tarp. In the first pigeon waggon, Mr Saul Whittaker rolls open the door and slides down onto the platform like a heap of brown sand. 'Bugger me!' he says – I don't know why, maybe it's the smell of Crystal's blooms hitting him – and then, squatting down against the truck, sweating Old Six and breathing hard, he says, 'Sporting challenge, lad?'

'I'm on for any mortal thing,' I say, while pulling the baskets for Grosmont out of the vans. I set them up in a dead straight line along the platform, having a look onto the footplate as I move towards the

'up' end. All is too dark inside, the firehole door being closed: just two pairs of boots, maybe, one fellow singing a Moody and Sankey hymn in a little voice.

'Ow do,' I say, but nothing comes back, and the singing doesn't even stop.

Behind me the station clock goes clunk, which is twenty-seven past eleven, which is no good because it is Whittaker's watch that counts, and this he is holding high in the air while tipping his head backwards, looking about ready to sneeze. The silence carries on as I watch old Father Whittaker, whose thin red head is tipping ever backwards . . .

'Go!' he shouts.

'Hold on, you rotter!' I shout back, but I'm pelting along that platform in any case, lifting the lids, with the birds flapping and crashing straight up into the air like bombs going off behind me. At the end of the line I stop, gasping in front of Whittaker and his watch, with the birds in a cloud above us. He's nodding, grinning all around his head, and I am blowing my nose on my sleeve, even though it is a North Eastern Railway coat and I'm proud to wear it. I've let the birds go within one minute. The two of us look up and see them, still hanging over the platform like a Piccadilly Circus in the sky. As we watch they make a bigger circle, turning fast before beginning to go off in all directions like sparks from a catherine wheel at a bonfire carnival.

I start to load the boxes, and when I've finished Whittaker seems to be sucked rapidly backwards into his van; he doesn't exactly stand up. I move along to the back waggon, where I see, underneath the tarpaulin, the shafts of a yellow gig rocking on its blocks in the sunlight. As 137 starts barking and pulling away from Grosmont, I say goodbye to that old gig, because very soon there will be no more of its kind. I am seventeen years old, and it is a very special time.

High-speed is coming.

But then I somehow moved my head again. There was a shortage of secondary air; people were appearing and disappearing at a great rate all around Nine Elms, and I was dragging my feet, which sounded like rain. But then I had to go on a railway journey in Portugal to meet a man who wrote an article in *The Railway Magazine*, and if only the wind had died down I might have been in with a chance. I was staring into the firebox on Thirty-One, closing my eyes but it was still light. Every time I closed my eyes the music hall began, for I had that damn firebox leaping in my head.

I wanted three more on the right side, three more on the night side. 'It's Welsh coal,' said a voice in my head: 'damned slow to ignite.' The voice went and I found that half of my face was my face and the other half was joined on to something else. When I tried to move, my mouth was dragged into a kind of smile. All was darkness and there was again a shortage of secondary air. I moved my hand up and something at the same time hard and soft came quickly down upon it. I lifted my hand again but not so high, then higher again and the thing came down swiftly once more. So I slid one of my hands up towards the half of my face that was still there, moving my fingers until they touched a rock, which was what joined me to the hard and soft. The voice came back again and this time gave me three words in the softness and the darkness: dart, pricker, paddle. Well, they were the fire irons to be found on any engine. I was grateful for the words because I liked them, but did not know why they had been given to me.

In a funny sort of way I went back to sleep and in a funny sort of way I woke up – I did both, I mean, without really doing either. All was the same as before, but I was being shaken in a way that I had been shaken before.

'I am on a train,' I said, and I realised that the whispering voice had been mine all along. The rest of it came to me quickly: I was now in Mrs Davidson-Hill's coffin, or Mrs Lampard's, and heading for the grave of the one or the other in Brookwood, and when this knowledge came to me I found I could not suck in enough air to keep alive, and sweat began rolling off me in an instant. I jerked and there was a tearing in the rock, and a great boiling of the blood underneath it. I thrashed at the solid darkness, only I could not thrash. And yet I was not blind, at least, for there was a very thin line of light going all around me like a halo, happily around and around and around like a song being sung. The sight calmed me somewhat, and I started on smaller breaths, which seemed to serve, and with them came a return to the state of semi-sleep into which I let myself go gladly, until I heard my own voice speaking. 'First class,' it said, and I felt the water from my mouth that those two words had produced trickling across my cheek towards the rock, where I stopped being able to feel it.

First class. Saturday Night Mack could be standing guard over me. For a second I could not recall whether he was a bad man or a good man, and then it came to me that he was good, that he was off the hook like the men of the half-link. If I carried on living they could be my friends and my landlady could be my best girl, for this all made my mistake in visiting the night-house seem a very small matter. It was the sort of thing a fellow might do because he was alive, and being alive was good.

I slid my hand under my coat and into my waistcoat pocket. My landlady's advertisement was in there. I wanted to go back to the summer pictures of Grosmont in my head, but Saul Whittaker had gone, and the whole of the North Eastern Railway with him. I was alive until I died, and stuck with it.

The journey to the Necropolis – and the hole in the ground waiting for me there – was one of forty minutes, and I must have had most of those. My one hope was Saturday Night Mack. I slid the advertisement from my pocket, then through the crack of light, and waited. But as the minutes passed a terrible picture came before my mind's eye: of Saturday Night Mack reading *Hoity Toity Bits* with the paper so close up to his face that all was quite blocked out but 'PRIZE OF AN EIGHT-ROOMED HOUSE: ANYONE CAN WIN IT AND LIVE RENT-FREE FOR LIFE'.

I felt myself sinking into the softness of the velvet, and

becoming rather velvety myself. My head was going away again and I did not mind. I seemed only to be able to breathe out, as though in small soft gasps. I felt a change in the heartbeat of the train, and we came to a stop, and it seemed as though I too had come to a stop. I did not breathe, and I could not tell what was me and what was not me in the world of the coffin.

The train started again, but I was beyond thinking why, or wondering which signal had halted us. Was it the trains that were scared of the horses or the horses that were scared of the trains? The question kept going round and around, and I could not answer it, and it did not matter. There was a train somewhere, far away on the cliffs, but I was down on the beach with a crazy person and the tide coming in. Sometimes I was under it and sometimes on top, but the crazy person it did not affect. After a while I began to be more under it than on top, and I seemed to become uncoupled from the train because it went on its own way, and the question stopped being a question but became just words, before long becoming only sounds, after a while becoming not even that.

The noises slowly returned, becoming words again, but this time they were the words of Saturday Night Mack, muttered between panting breaths, 'Diamonds . . . diamonds . . . big as beans!' he was gasping, but then in a different voice, a worried whisper, he said, 'Half a mo,' and it was with the wrenching cry of a rooster and a great upward surging feeling that I seemed to shoot out of the coffin when the lid came off.

In fact, it was not at all like that: I remained exactly where I was, stuck by blood, watching Saturday Night Mack with his screwdriver in his hand swerve and fall across me before rolling away onto the carriage floor.

The head of Mack came back up after a while, and looked very ill indeed. 'No diamonds,' I said, but I believe it did not sound like that to Mack because of the way that my mouth was.

Chapter Twenty-Six

Wednesday 30 December 1903 –
Monday 4 January 1904

I was in a green ward so full of plants it was like a garden. There were three pillars in amongst the plants which in fact were chimneys with firesides front and back. Ladies in white walked between the plants carrying medicines, and the ladies were so beautiful they made the medicines look precious. Other people moved around on wheels, and everybody kept quiet most of the time, but it somehow came to me that I was in St Thomas's Hospital, which was where the London and South Western always took their accident cases if they could. I was in Purvis Ward, called after the sister, Elizabeth Purvis, but which of the beauties she was I could not say, although again it came to me that she had arranged for this ward to have the biggest of the hospital Christmas trees, and that there had been presents from it.

Over my head was an electric light that moved – all for me. All the time beneath my bandages there seemed to be distant violins, which in the middle of the afternoon and the middle of the morning would fade to almost nothing, but at meal times were joined by louder instruments, drums, and the sight of everybody moving much more. But I did not eat for two days.

The side of my head was all sewn, and painted with carbolic. A man came several times to see it. He was called Dr Stone, and I did not like his name in case he hit me over the head with it. Once he came and lifted the gauze and said, 'We had a marathon of sewing with you, Mr Stringer.' There had been so much, they had given me ether – of which I remembered a thing that was rubber with metal behind: a dream machine (for it had given me plenty) that had fitted over my face so well it might have been made for me.

Later Dr Stone told me he had had to do more than just sew me. He had had to dig a hole in my head to pull the bones away from the brain, and I had had more ether for that.

I sat up one morning and there were the Houses of Parliament, with the boats racing back and forth in front of them, all in complete silence. After a while I got the idea that there was a visiting hour, but I went to sleep in the middle of all nonetheless.

The Houses of Parliament had disappeared when I woke up, and there was a supper of boiled ham next to me, along with a glass of beer. There were white screens around my bed, and the electric light was on. I had the feeling of late evening, and of Sister Purvis being close by. Standing at the end of my bed was the Governor, my landlady, and the policeman I had talked to at Nine Elms – the one who looked like a sea captain. Across all the years since then, I have always thought of him as the Captain, and it is possible that he actually was one – a captain of *police*, I mean, because they do have them.

At the moment I opened my eyes, he was looking at my boiled ham and beer so hungrily that he smiled when our eyes met. I started to tell all – for now I seemed to have everything straight – but I had only got over that it was Stanley who had crowned me and put me in a coffin, when they told me to stop, probably because things weren't coming out very clearly.

'Put it down as points,' said the Captain, and his voice was much lighter and less of a growl than I would have guessed. 'Give each point a number.'

They all went away, and a little while later the Captain came back with a pencil and a piece of paper which he put by my bed. It was funny to watch him creep towards me and creep away again, thinking that I was asleep. It was very good paper that he gave me. Across the top it said in fancy letters, 'From St Thomas's Hospital', and I thought about using it to write to Dad. It will just about make his day if I do that, I thought, but then I decided that he would probably not like to learn that I was in hospital, however beautiful the paper.

The next evening the same thing came about, except that I was eating my supper – steak and kidney pudding, this time – when the Captain and the Governor came along. I had my list of points but I think I went from one to three, so they stopped me again.

The third day brought hot pot, and it was all gone and the glass of beer was empty when the Governor and the Captain appeared again, and this time they had a third person with them – a man whose job was to write.

I would have liked to have had my diary by me, but it had gone. Stanley had taken it, along with my replacement pocket book and the brake handle, before putting me in the box. What he would have made of the writings in it I could not guess, for they were mainly scribbles, and mainly, until Stanley got himself in my sights, wrong. I was sure I had everything straight now, in any case.

'Number one,' I said, and I was in high force even before they were settled in their seats, for here was a chance to show my mettle, which I had not been able to get through railway work. 'Number one is Mr Stanley. He looks like a man in want of money, and that is exactly what he is. He speaks on interment for pay, and no other reason, but he was not paid enough. They agreed to keep his address weekly, even though the audiences were so poor, but he wanted more money. I heard him say at the address he gave on the day of Mr Smith's funeral that he had not been in the cemetery for almost four months, and he changed the subject double-quick afterwards. This would have put him there in August, and, I believe, on the afternoon of Wednesday 12 August Mr Stanley did travel to Brookwood – probably not on the funeral train which was running that day, but on a service of the common run from Waterloo.'

'Stopping train to Bournemouth?' said the Captain, and he

looked across at the Governor, who just nodded, and who I could tell was anxious on account of the greyness mixed in with the red of his face.

'The week before,' I continued, 'he had asked the board of the Necropolis Company by letter for an increase in pay, but he was refused.'

'How did you know this?' said the Captain, who'd been smiling and smoking a cigar all along and seemed, unlike the Governor, to be a man without a care.

'Because I went into the room at the Necropolis where the minutes are kept.'

'Regular spit-fire of self-dependence,' mumbled the Governor, then, more loudly to the Captain: 'No wonder Mr Smith brought him on!'

'It wasn't lawful to read the Necropolis minutes, though!' said the Captain, but his smile only widened as he did so, and the eye into which the smoke was streaming slowly closed – which I took to mean that I should go on.

'Sir John Rickerby, the chairman, had gone down on the funeral train, and Stanley, I suppose, knew that. Sir John made a habit of walking in the cemetery during his trips down there.'

'Ornithologist?' said the Captain, and he was delighted with that word, which I did not know the meaning of. He was not like a policeman at all.

'The trouble being that he was a creeping Jesus.'

The writer looked up at this, but immediately went back to his scribbling.

'He walked with a stick, I mean,' I continued. 'So Mr Stanley could smash his head . . . I mean the head of Rickerby . . . and it would look . . .' I did not like this talk of head-smashing that was coming from me, and the Captain could see it. He stood up and went away, returning with another glass of beer for me, which I drank while the writer, very mysteriously, continued to write. Maybe he had been so far behind that he needed all of my drinking time to catch up.

'Stanley smashed the head of Rickerby against a tombstone,' I continued, 'knowing it would look as though he'd fallen.'

The writer wrote; the Governor looked at the Captain.

'On the stone,' I said, 'were written the words "Thy Will Be Done."'

The writer looked up again at this and I put him down as a church-goer.

'This we do know', said the Captain.

'Number two,' I continued, 'Henry Taylor. Henry Taylor was at the cemetery on that same day.'

I looked at the Governor, who nodded and said, 'Rode out on the Red Bastard with Arthur Hunt and Vincent.'

'It is possible that he took a walk in the cemetery, because Hunt had given him a scolding. He liked the cemetery – Mike told me that – and Arthur Hunt was always chucking people off his engines.'

'You've told me all about this fellow Hunt,' said the Captain to the Governor.

'Socialist,' said the Governor, nodding.

'Here is the important connection: I believe Stanley saw Henry Taylor watching him doing the murder of Rickerby, or that's what Stanley thought; Taylor may very well have seen nothing.'

'Carry on,' said the Captain, and the smile was gone now. The Governor's I had not seen for some time.

'Taylor was killed a week later, and I reckon Stanley must have followed him about a fair bit before the right moment came along. He left his lodge, which is my lodge now . . .' Looking at the Governor here, I couldn't tell whether this was a new one on him. 'He left the lodge but never got to the shed. I think Stanley followed him, and got him somewhere along the river. There are some lonely spots behind the gasworks.'

The beer had made me sleepy, and my head was hurting. My sutures might have been of the finest silk but they did give me gyp. 'The next one was Mike,' I said.

'Is this number three?' asked the writer, although he did not look up this time.

I nodded at him, thinking Mike ought to have a number to himself. 'Stanley had seen Henry Taylor and Mike together around Waterloo or Nine Elms. Well, they were *always* together, best of friends. One foggy day he followed Mike to Nine Elms. By rotten luck, Barney Rose was under orders to let Mike take the Jubilee off-shed that morning, and he was alone on it for a while.'

'What's a Jubilee?' said the Captain.

'An 0-4-2 tender engine,' said the Governor in a thoughtful voice. 'Very fine motors.' For some reason the writer looked up at him on hearing this.

'Number four,' I said, which made the writer get back to writing, 'Mr Rowland Smith. A number of reasons here for Stanley to get him. He was not the new chairman of the Necropolis or even a director, from what I could see, but he was holding the purse strings at the time, and when Stanley again asked for more pay – and his second and third requests went into the meetings at the start of November and the start of December – it was Smith he blamed for saying no. Smith also wanted to sell Necropolis land; that was known, but he set about it at an amazingly fast rate, and maybe it began to look to Stanley as though in time he'd get rid of the whole show, leaving no call for an address at all. Finally, Stanley might have got wind that Mr Smith was set on finding out what had happened to Henry Taylor and Mike, and he *was* set on it. That was one of the reasons he'd brought me on – to be his eyes and ears on the half-link.'

'He wrote to you, didn't he?' said the Governor. 'He meant to ask what light you could cast on all this?'

I nodded, and then apologised to the Captain, for I had quite forgotten to show the letter to the police.

'We found a copy at the flat,' said the Captain. 'Some of his papers were in a safe that survived the blaze.' He glanced at the Governor, and continued: 'I've heard a good deal from

Mr Nightingale of the way Mr Smith pitched you in at the deep end . . . Now, is it your belief that Stanley started the blaze at Mr Smith's flat?'

'With paraffin,' I said. 'There's no shortage of it at any railway place.'

'A new sort of exploit for him, then, wasn't it?'

'Oh, I expect he bashed him on the head first.'

'I wonder', said the Captain, 'what gave Mr Smith the idea, up there in Yorkshire, that you would make such a great hand at detecting?'

I thought of Grosmont, Crystal's flowers, the hot waiting room, Rowland Smith's boots . . .

'I guessed that he was bound for London,' I said. I could not help but add, however, 'There again, he *was* on the up.'

'Maybe he'd forgotten about up and down,' said the Governor. 'Mr Smith has . . . He had, I mean, many good points, but he did not have the railways in his blood.'

'Above all,' I concluded, 'Stanley killed Smith because he knew Smith was trying to find out what had become of Henry Taylor.

You see, it is my belief Rowland Smith *liked* Henry Taylor.' I looked at the Governor and I looked at the Captain, and as I did so they both finished off their glasses of beer and I couldn't immediately bring to mind the word that Vincent had used of Smith. Then it came to me: Tommy Dodd. I did not speak it out loud, but said in a half yawn, although quite firmly, to the writer, 'Number six.'

Number six was me, and it turned out the longest, even though I was beginning to tire. I told them all about how each man in the half-link had had his knife into me. They thought I was Rowland Smith's man, just like Taylor, and that I would split on them. I was a bit careful about saying what I might split on them for: I mentioned Hunt's socialist ways, but not the mutual improvement class or the trade-union letters I'd seen. I said that Barney Rose 'perhaps seemed a little casual about his business', rather than go any further towards speaking of drink. Drunkenness, I was sure, had set in after the Salisbury smash that Vincent had mentioned, and his boozing had led to his mistakes, one of which had been seen and reported to the Governor by Taylor. As to Vincent, well, he covered up for both of them.

They also all lived in fear of being taken in for the murder of Henry Taylor, because they knew they all had reason to have done it. Taylor was not one of their London lot. He was Smith's man, and Arthur Hunt especially hated Smith. Taylor had reported Barney Rose, and he was likely to beat Vincent to the footplate. It didn't look good for them either when Taylor's great pal Mike – another out-of-town lad brought in by Smith – was jacked in.

The writer's hand was racing as I explained that I should have known the half-link were innocent because they could have had no real reason to crown Sir John Rickerby. Stanley, on the other hand, had cause to hate or fear everyone who'd been killed.

With the great confidence I now felt, I asked whose coffin I had been in, and the Captain said, 'Mrs Davidson-Hill's. There was a great deal of distress at the funeral when you were found.' I said I had no memory of any of that, but I was sorry, and the Captain said, 'You are hardly to be blamed.'

Two other questions occurred to me. 'How was I found?' I asked, for I was curious to hear what explanation Mack had come up with other than the truth, which is that he'd been trying to get his hands on the dear old lady's jewels.

'They heard you knocking,' said the Captain, and I smiled to myself at that.

Then I asked what had happened to Mrs Davidson-Hill herself, but I never did get to hear, for at that moment one of the sisters came to look at my gauze, and the Captain said, 'I would rather not say just at the moment.'

'Will you put salt on Stanley?' I asked, when the sister was gone. The Captain said nothing, but just smoked slowly, in a way that made me ask again: '*Will* you put salt on this man?'

'The difficulty', said the Captain, 'is evidence, and the other difficulty is finding him.'

'Doesn't the Necropolis hold an address for him?'

'We looked into that when you first mentioned him,' the Captain said. 'They have him down as being at a certain lodge, which he has lately quit.' He began digging something out of his coat pocket. 'I want you to go carefully until we can get to him. I've ordered the constables in your territory to keep a close watch on your lodge, and it's three blasts on this if you see him.' He had stopped rummaging at last and produced a silver whistle.

Well, I nearly burst out laughing. 'I would rather give him three blasts with a shotgun,' I said.

At this the Governor smiled for the first time, and said, 'It's more fun to watch 'em dangle.'

Later, my landlady was brought to my bed by Sister Purvis. They were as beautiful as each other: one second you would think one had the edge, another the other. I couldn't help thinking that it was like watching two Atlantics racing. After a long period of smiling on all sides, Sister Purvis left and my landlady remained. She sat on my bed saying nothing and it was a very happy time as far as I was concerned, except that shameful thoughts of Signal Street would keep coming back.

'I haven't yet managed to get any cocoa in,' she said after a while.

'Don't concern yourself on that score,' I said.

'I could make up the cocoa – when I get it – the night before and leave it in the range for you to pick up in the morning. It would still be hot – well, it would be *quite* hot.' She looked at the electric light over my head for a while before adding: 'I daresay it would not be absolutely cold, at any rate.'

'No need for that,' I said.

'I *would* do that,' she said, 'and I would be happy to do it, only I've been a little rushed.'

I nodded. 'Would you like to hear the whole tale?' I said. 'It comes in six parts.'

'Of course,' she said.

'Number one –'

'But not now, perhaps,' she said. 'You need to rest.' She made sure nobody was looking and gave me a kiss. Then she stood up. 'The room is now advertised in several papers,' she said.

After a long pause, as I recalled how I had attempted to escape from the casket, I said, 'I'm sorry for not having put up your notice at Nine Elms.'

The fact was, I hadn't wanted another in the lodge with the two of us.

She said that it was all right.

After a further pause, I said, 'I'll be out tomorrow, and I wondered whether you would like to come on another excursion.'

'With Mary Allington?' she said.

'Of course,' I said, and she turned away and suddenly laughed – a very short laugh but very beautiful.

She left shortly after.

The greatest astonishment came at six on my last day, just after I'd started on a plate of mutton and my bottle of beer. It was Arthur Hunt, still black from a day at Nine Elms, carrying a package roughly done up with string. Somehow things were the wrong way about between us, for he was very ill at ease in the hospital, as a man so full of strength and vigour could hardly fail to be. I asked him to sit down but he would not for fear of dirtying a chair, and nor would he take a bottle of beer, which I could have got for him easily. There was then a great collision of apologies, in which Arthur said he'd seen I was a decent sort, not sent in to sneak, on the ride out to Brookwood.

I said, 'I'd never have guessed that was what you were thinking.'

'In truth,' he said, 'I only thought it later, but the thoughts came from what I saw that day.'

'Why were you all going to twist me in the Old Shed, then?'

'Twist you? We were coming to improve you.'

'But you all looked fit to be tied.'

Arthur shrugged, saying, 'We might have taken a couple of pints. And Vincent clatters the engines as he goes – it's just a habit of his.' He looked at me solemnly for quite a while. Then he said, 'An engine man doesn't need as much imagination as you've got.'

'I'll try to put that straight,' I said, thinking: but how can a thing like that be changed?

'Buck up,' said Arthur. 'I've brought you a copy of the Bible.'

This was a turn up; I hadn't had Arthur down for anything in that line. But when I pulled away the wrapping from the package I saw a book called *Engine Driving Life* by M. Reynolds.

'You might look at the first page,' said Arthur.

There he had written, in a fine hand, but with some smudging:

> The steam is up; the engine bright as gold;
> The fire king echoes back the guard's shrill cry,
> The roaring vapour shrieks out fierce and bold,
> A moment – and like lightning on we fly.'

'I've had the whole story from the coppers,' he said – and I was glad he spoke at that point, for I could not have. 'I never took to that fellow Stanley and if I see him about I'll knock him into the middle of next week.'

'You know of him then?'

'I've seen him at the Necropolis station; I know him to be another parasite in a collar and tie.'

I nodded.

'It couldn't have happened if he'd been in a trade union,' said Arthur.

'But what union could Stanley ever be in?'

'In time there'll be one for every class of worker,' said Arthur.

By now I was ready to have a go at thanking him properly for the book, but again he cut me off in my stumbling attempts: 'You've got it in you to put up some good running,' he said.

'But I can't chuck coal to the front,' I said.

'No,' he said.

'And my fire-raising is not of the best.'

'It is not.'

'I can't read signals when they come in a jumble.'

'I noticed that.'

'And I'm no great hand at injecting.'

'No.'

'It is enough for now that I have a great affection for it all, and a determination to get on?'

'No,' said Arthur.

'So,' I said, 'How can you be sure I'll ever be up to the mark?'

He was buttoning his coat to go. 'Because I'm going to *make* bloody sure, that's how.'

Chapter Twenty-Seven

Monday 4 January
continued

I came out of St Thomas's on the Monday afternoon, and the wind from the river immediately started battering me. I turned a corner into the racing world of cabs and trams and horses, with their drivers in all combinations of moods, and thought: this is my home now. It was all the world of Waterloo. As I set off to Nine Elms, I resolved to take my first route, via the streets. But that would mean that Stanley had won, so I began to make my way by the side of the river, although I was not so brave as to chuck the whistle away.

In the Embankment gardens, a man was sitting completely still on a bench. He was leaning forwards and his high hat was tipped back. His hands were in his pockets, and I imagined that, in his head, he was flying through the air. I stopped and stared, and with the sight of him came a shuddering wonder at all I had been through.

I walked along the valley of the shadow of death, with the distillery and the gasworks on one side, the water on the other. A boat came swinging up, its black chimney bundling beautiful black clouds into the air, pumping out night-time. There was a man at the prow, a friendly looking sort, and this city sailor was making ready the ropes for landing. I nearly called out to him, in a cheery way, 'Cut that smoke out!' for I was happy in spite of my sutures.

Crook's eyebrows jumped at the sight of my stitches when I reached Nine Elms.

'I won't be booking on today, Mr Crook,' I said.

'Not at all, young Jim,' he said, 'not at all. Rest is what you need.'

'I want to walk around,' I said.

'You do that!' exclaimed Mr Crook. 'You take the air.'

As I walked out of his place I realised this was by way of being a joke.

On entering the shed I was met with such a hail of hellos and how are you's that I grew dizzy giving my greetings and thanks in return. Barney Rose was there, gabbling cheerily about the faulty fielding of the Australians which had permitted some new victory for England, and suggesting that he was going off, and would I take a pint with him directly. Arthur would be at the Turnstile, and somebody called 'Tiger' would be along too.

'Who's Tiger?' I asked, still in a daze.

'Why, it's Vincent,' said Barney, and there he was, with Arthur alongside of him, and Arthur looked like an uncle and Vincent looked like a nephew as they never had before.

I had to say no to the offer of the drink, as I was still pretty done up and I felt a pint would have knocked me out, but they left me in no doubt that the offer stood for whenever I was ready to accept. As I walked away from the mouth of the shed, I saw Flannagan limping towards me, grinning all round his head, and I thought: he's a good, brave fellow to be able to smile like that with legs like his.

I returned to Lower Marsh still in excellent spirits. All had been put straight at Nine Elms: I was not a spy, Smith was gone, and all the men stood above suspicion on that score as well as all the others. Stanley was the one, and the only thing left to do was find him.

As I approached my lodge I was feeling a want of sleep and a sort of dreaminess that lingered from my injury, so I was not as surprised as I might have been to feel, upon opening that door, a singular sensation of travelling backwards in time, for I could hear my landlady saying, 'Well, it's a pound down.' As I slowly climbed the stairs, I continued to listen: 'Wash day is Saturday, and you are to leave out your laundry on the Friday, if that is quite all right?' There came the voice of a man, which I could not hear clearly. 'There is a good supply of cocoa in the kitchen,' my landlady was saying as I reached the top of the staircase, 'or at any rate there will be presently, when I have a chance to arrange it, which is very beneficial on the cold mornings. You will notice that the ceiling is quite free from leaks.'

When I reached the top of the stairs I heard my landlady say, 'We have one other gentleman in the house. He works on the railways, not driving but cleaning the engines, yet he is keen to get on, and of a most amiable nature.' More fast words came from the man, but still I could not make them out. The two were in the unoccupied room, the one that was to be let. 'Might I ask your own occupation?' my landlady said as I moved along the upstairs corridor.

'Barrister-at-law,' said a light, fast voice. 'Advocate, that is. And yet the work is not of the common legal run but rather concerns the education of the public on matters touching –'

I seemed to stop him in his tracks as I stood in the doorway, for I was a dead man as far as he was concerned.

'This is Mr Stringer, the railway gentleman I was just mentioning,' said my landlady.

He was looking at the right side of my head, where the bandages held the gauze over the sutures. His eyes were orange, his face yellow and shining. He still wore the twisted greenish suit, but he had not shaved, and this time his papers were under his arm and he carried a cane.

'You were saying, Mr Stanley,' my landlady went on, 'that your work touched on . . .?'

'Interment,' he said, moving his gaze from my bandages to my eyes.

It was the cane, and the thought of it splitting my sutures, that was the main thing on my mind. At least it was at first, but then I looked at my landlady, who had suddenly somehow understood all. The fear on her face destroyed her beauty, but it was nothing to what this maniac might do to her.

'Every turn I take is a turn for the worse,' said Stanley, and then I heard a single, strange bird call. It was Stanley's cane, flashing through the air, and I somehow avoided it by taking a pace back. The next flash came, I ducked, and was upon Stanley, pummelling him about the face, wanting to hit harder but also wanting to hit faster, because I was like a man putting out a fire. For a moment he just seemed to take his beating, with the smell of old wooden halls rolling out of his mouth as he panted under the blows. He threw me off quite easily, though, as soon as he was minded to try, and I was more amazed by flying through the air than I was hurt by landing against the door, shutting it in the process. Stanley advanced upon me, slashed again, and I believed the tip of his cane stroked my eyelashes. He would have taken my eyes like somebody rubbing out a chalk line.

He came forwards again, and I could go no further back since I was already against the door. Stanley pulled back the cane again, readying himself for the next downward stroke, and as the cane climbed upwards, it made the same bird-call sound as before, except in reverse. He stood there with the cane held high in his hands, looking like a great, twisted tree, and began to bring it down fast, while starting up a slow roaring that contained the words 'You are all in darkness', or 'All is darkness': the cane was coming to snap my sutures this time without doubt. My landlady was moving towards Stanley from the side, slowly, prettily, with head held high.

And then came a fearful explosion of wood.

I saw that Stanley was on the stone flags of the kitchen below, looking like a broken star, with his papers fluttering to the floor around him, for they were slower than he had been. His eyes were open, and the fire was rolling upward through them, while the waves of blood moved away from the top of his head and out towards the chimney piece and the boiler.

One of his feet was facing the wrong way.

'The floor,' said my landlady, quite calmly.

It was no longer there. Half of it had gone, at any rate – Stanley's half – and my landlady and I remained standing on a sort of shelf over the kitchen. The door was on our shelf, and we were through it and down the staircase in a second.

My landlady was first into the kitchen, and on her knees with her hair in her eyes and a towel at Stanley's head. She had lost her straw hat on the way down, and as I blew the whistle I thought: how strange that she does not cry.

Stanley was quite dead by the time I had finished blowing the whistle, and my landlady was sitting on the floor beside him, staring into nowhere like a little doll. I began walking around the kitchen that had only half a ceiling, collecting the papers, and not being able to leave off reading them as I did so. I first collected a tiny advertisement from a newspaper: 'CASH ADVANCE' read the first, '£50 TO £5,000 ON NOTE OF HAND WITHOUT SURETIES OR SECURITIES'. Next I picked from off the smashed wood two longer items snipped from newspapers: 'COURT OF BANKRUPTCY', said one. Underneath these words was printed, in smaller type, 'before Mr Registrar Hope'. In larger type again were the words 'SCHEME OF ARRANGEMENT', and then the article began: 'His honour delivered judgement on the application made to the court to confirm the scheme of arrangement accepted by the creditors of Mr Adrian Stanley, late barrister-at-law of the Inner Temple. The scheme provides for the vesting of the estate in a trustee for the benefit of creditors.'

My landlady stood up and sighed. She told me to take my whistle outside and blow it again. I did so, getting some very queer looks, and when I returned there was a blanket over Stanley and my landlady's straw hat was back on her head.

From the grate, where it had drifted, I picked up an article headed: 'DIVORCE DIVISION', before Mr Justice Barnes and a special jury, 'EX-BARRISTER-AT-LAW A RESPONDENT'. It continued, 'Mrs Anne Stanley (*née* Hedley) sought a divorce by reason of the alleged cruelty of her husband, Mr Adrian William Stanley, an ex-barrister-at-law, formerly of The Maples, Guildford, Surrey.'

There was a banging at the door, which I had left open; the constables had arrived, so I read on rapidly:

Mr Clark, appearing for the respondent, said it was a shocking case . . . He asked Mrs Hedley: 'When did the cruelty begin?' and she replied 'With his anxieties at his chambers. He threw a pair of nutcrackers at me, later a carving knife that hit me on the third finger of my left hand. I was quite badly cut. Our servant gave him an egg that was not quite done; he cried out "Confound you!" and turned over the table. He would wander about the house at night, talking to himself; on one occasion I asked him to please stop because he had woken the children and he picked up a doorstop, saying, "I will give you such a knock on the head with this if you keep following me about."'

Three constables were now in the kitchen: one was talking to my landlady, one was over the body, and one was staring at the hole in the ceiling and saying, 'Strewth!'

I was reading the final article, headed 'AT BOW BEFORE MR KING':

Mr William Adrian Stanley of The Maples, Guildford, was charged with assaulting Mr Grant Low. Mr Unstead, for the complainant, said that on the 15th of June, 1900, the defendant, a barrister-at-law, had taken the complainant, his clerk, to task over the bundling of a brief. The defendant remarked, 'It will be necessary for you and I to talk this over,' whereupon he struck the complainant twice about the head with a large vase. After hearing witnesses, Mr King said there was no question that the complainant had been assaulted. The defendant must pay a fine of forty shillings, with one pound costs. Mr Stanley is to be proceeded against by the Bar Council.

It was some time later that I read the final three documents, which I found in the boiler after the constables and the Captain, who came on later to ask more questions, had all gone. The first two seemed to be rough drafts of letters. They were written in a very agitated hand, with many crossings out, capitals, underlinings. They had not been dated or addressed, but I had them down as some part of his plan to obtain higher wages for giving the address. I could make out nothing more than a few fragments from the two letters:

After the service that I have given . . . in view of my being required to go FAR beyond the common run of obligation that any employee however conscientious might owe to an employer . . . the mere continuation of the Address will not in itself be found sufficient . . . it will be noted that I adhere to gentlemanly language, and make free with such words as 'please' and 'I beg', but patience is short, and it is well if it is remembered that I am by profession a barrister-at-law, in short a master of many things pertaining to . . .

This ended with a word I could not make out except for the 'e' at the beginning.

The last of Stanley's papers was another advertisement from a newspaper: 'Unusually excellent furnished bed and sitting room offered to respectable person. Garden view. Thirty seconds from Waterloo Station. No servants kept. Every comfort and convenience. Very moderate terms.'

'But floorboards not of the best,' I said quietly. My landlady, however, lying beside me on my truckle bed, was fast asleep.

Chapter Twenty-Eight

Saturday 9 January

We took the District Railway to West Kensington, where we got off in a great crowd of happy people. We walked out of the station and onto a road packed with cabs. Over the road were the gates of the great outdoor theatre. The benches within were empty, and the curtain was across the stage, but there were posters against all the railings for 'A Tableau of Germania'.

We stopped in front of the posters for a while, which showed castles and some girls in pigtails.

'Do you fancy that?' I said.

'You should really say "them",' said my landlady. 'It's more than one. Anyway, it's not really my sort of thing.'

'Nor mine,' I said.

'And it doesn't come on until March,' said my landlady.

'*And* it's eight and six . . .'

'And that's for the cheapest seats,' said my landlady.

So that was it as far as 'Tableau of Germania' went. In any case, we were not in West Kensington to see an entertainment; we had come to ride the Great Wheel, and I was going to treat my landlady.

We walked past the theatre and through the Japanese garden, in which there was a tinkling little stream with a bamboo bridge going over. From here we could see the wheel, circling slowly with its forty cabins, and with the steam coming up from the engines at the bottom blowing against the great steel hub. As we watched, the cabins came to rest, and we stopped to look at the top one.

'You get a good long go up there, don't you?' said my landlady.

The Great Wheel started moving again, and so did we.

'Do you think it ever sticks?' asked my landlady.

'It would be nothing to me if it did,' I said. I meant because I would be with her, but she took it differently.

'You've found your backbone in all this business, haven't you?'

'Do you not think I had any backbone before?' I said.

'You had an uncommon talent for twitching and looking away,' she said, 'and as for those queer speeches of yours, all about life on the rails . . .'

I had told her the whole story, of course, in the house at Hercules Court, dividing the story into the six parts, as in the hospital. She had not said a word until the beginning of part six, when she began to make a pot of tea, but she was still listening, I think. Whenever I tried to go back to it later on, though, even to the most sensational parts, she would cut me off by saying, 'You should put it all in a book.'

With my landlady I felt that I was on the threshold of great things, but not perhaps a very relaxing time. In any event, I was not too young to see that she was good for me.

We were approaching the low, strange buildings under the Wheel, and I realised that some of them were just like the cabins that revolved above. It took two engines to drive the Wheel. The beats from their exhausts were not in time so that it seemed as though they were fighting, but the Wheel turned smoothly all the same.

A lot of the men among the crowd around the bottom of the Wheel were smoking cigars. A barrel organ was playing somewhere. My landlady said that there seemed to be quite a lot of Spanish-looking gentlemen, and there was a little dog running about that looked like a Pierrot. In the air was a smell of strange spices and fried fish. It was quite a low sort of entertainment that was going on all around, but, still, there were more toppers than anything on the heads of the men – and toppers of the best sort too. A crowd of johnnies on a beano were buying some fried fish from one of the huts, and one of them dropped his. People stopped to look, while another johnny cried out to them all: 'Head full of wine! Head full of wine!'

'He has a head full of wine,' said my landlady who was also looking on, 'but he's rather handsome, nonetheless.'

'Perhaps you would like to go and ask him to pay for your ride on the Wheel,' I said.

She laughed, and said, 'You get in the queue. I'm off to buy you a present.'

So I joined the back of the queue, following the lines of my sutures with my fingers.

When my landlady returned, all in a fluster, I was at the front of the queue. One of the forty cabins had just swung down before me, and I was being shown towards it by a man in a blue coat. (All the men who had anything to do with the Wheel were dressed in blue coats.) She handed me a paper bag, and as I took it she kissed me on the cheek that was not sewn. 'It's not the one you like,' she said, 'but it *is* cocoa.'

'Well, I'm sure I shall like it,' I said, and I started to read the words on the tin: it was called 'Vi-Cocoa', which I had never heard of before. 'In tiring work,' I read, 'there is nothing like Vi-Cocoa.'

'Never mind about that, mate,' said the fellow in blue. 'Are you for a turn on the wheel or not?' Then he said, 'What happened to your bonce?'

'Somebody knocked me into the middle of next week,' I said, at which my landlady suddenly turned to me and said, 'If, two weeks ago, you were knocked into the middle of next week, then what week are you in now?'

It was a good question.

I paid the money and stepped into the cabin. With my beautifully sewn face, my cocoa and the girl I was stuck on, I felt like . . . well, King Edward himself, I would have wagered, was never happier.

Twenty other people or thereabouts were shown into the cabin with us, and as soon as my landlady stepped aboard she said, 'Electric light!' The cabin was like a wide railway carriage with seats along both sides and looking glasses

217

above them. The doors were slammed, the cabin gave a jerk and we began to rise up, but had gone hardly any distance before we stopped again.

'We are neither up nor down,' I said, turning to look out.

'No,' said my landlady, and she was holding my hand very tightly, 'we are up!'

We started to rise once more, and somehow there were violins in my head. I thought: this must be the sound that balloonists hear all the time. We were above the roofs of the houses now, level with the chimney pots, and then we carried on, rising with the smoke that came out of them. The higher we climbed, the more we saw of their back gardens, and very nice ones they were. I saw my landlady looking at them, and there was an expression on her face that I would almost have called sadness, so I put my arm about her waist and said, 'We will have a garden like that. You can get them out Wimbledon way. I know, because I've seen them.'

We continued to climb, and the large gardens slowly became quite small, and then the whole of West Kensington station could be seen, and the streets beyond going on for miles. Looking down the line of the District, I said, 'You can see the next train to come into the station from London, and the one after that.'

My only disappointment was that I could not see the edge of the city. There was no end to the houses and that was all about it. Our cabin stopped again, and my landlady and I walked towards the windows, for now we were at the top – just in the nick of time, too, because the light was going and the lamps were coming on.

'Look at the lines of electric lights,' said my landlady. 'They spread across town like necklaces . . . I wonder whose electricity it is.' That was always one of her strange concerns.

'Can you see Waterloo?' I asked her.

'I do not *want* to see Waterloo,' she replied, full of indignation.

Looking down, I could see the crowd around the base of

the Great Wheel, and the walkers in the Japanese garden. Beyond the gardens were some tennis players, who looked comical as they dashed about in the gathering darkness, and not at all good at the game, but they were trying their best and my heart was filled with good wishes for them and with love for my landlady.

Then something made me go back to the Japanese garden. A man was walking slowly along one of the paths. He wore a very fine grey felt hat. As I watched, the Japanese lights in the garden around him came on in one soft, swift burst. They were all colours and very pretty but they seemed to have vexed the man in the fine hat, who stopped and looked up at the Great Wheel, then down again, before continuing. He seemed to walk very lightly, almost floating; his clothes were of the latest cut, and I believed he was smoking a cigarette, for he kept bringing his hand to his face. The gentleman was moving towards the bamboo bridge now. Watching him walk was like listening to funny music.

A woman was coming over the bridge towards him, and when the man lifted his hat I expected his hair to spring up, which it did not, and I expected not to see a beard, which I *did*. But he was Rowland Smith all the same.

My landlady was saying, 'I think I can see St Paul's! But if that is St Paul's then *that* can't be the Houses of Parliament.'

He has put Brilliantine on his hair and grown a beard so as to start again as a new person, I thought quite calmly as our cabin began rolling past the buildings at the base of the Wheel and the Japanese garden disappeared from view. We began to climb again, far too slowly, and with the garden gone I became sure I had made a mistake. But here was the Japanese scene again, and, yes, there was evil and not just sadness behind the mysteries of the Necropolis, and I had a dizzy sense of beginning a fall that has lasted me, in a way, the rest of my days.

For there was Smith again on the bamboo bridge, with his hat back on his head, the lady far away.

I called to my landlady, so loudly that everyone in the cabin took fright.

She came over, saying, 'Is it your head?'

I said, 'Look down there. You see that man with the beard on the little bridge?'

She nodded; she was anxious now. I had taken away all her fun and the others in the cabin were all looking at us.

'That is Rowland Smith,' I said.

'The one who's dead, you mean?'

'The one who *was* dead.'

I saw all the bad shots I'd made in hospital over this business, and for these I immediately blamed the ether. But I was now haring down a second trail, and I turned to my landlady and started on what must have seemed to her the queerest of all my speeches: 'Mack's little friend who could not grow a moustache told me in the bar of the North Station at the Necropolis that corpses had been dug up, and some left lying about the place. Mack – well, it had to be him; he was on the fly as everybody knew – would have been under orders to find the body of a man the size of Smith; others he could abandon, knowing they'd be put down to the work of grave robbers. He would have been well paid for it. Why, he told me in the Citadel that he was poor as a rat, but he was always in funds, and those brain dusters in the Kingdom of Italy did not come cheap.'

'What are you talking about?' said my landlady.

'But no,' I said. 'Smith lived in a flat, with a gatekeeper at the door. The coroner's report had said so. How could a body be got in?'

My landlady, still looking down at Smith, had somehow caught up with me. 'I thought,' she said slowly, 'that when you told me of that coroner's report, you said the firemen had played their hoses through doors giving on to a garden.'

'You're right!' I said. 'I hadn't thought you were listening. Not long before, Smith bought a new flat – I heard him telling Erskine Long so – and he'd done it for one reason only: to get a garden!'

In my mind's eye I saw the swanky flat with the beautiful garden facing away from the road. I saw Mack, with some of his friends who were out of the straight, turning up after dark with the right sort of dead man after leaving some of the wrong sort lying about in Brookwood or other places. Maybe he had brought paraffin too. I saw Smith, talking of being tired to the gatekeeper. I saw him light the fire and leave.

'But why did Smith *do* it?' I exclaimed, at which some of the others in the cabin who'd left off staring at us began to do so again.

The Great Wheel rolled upward once again, and my thoughts roamed as wide as the view from our cabin, a hundred ideas coming into my mind. I revolved in my mind the words that Vincent had used of Smith on the coal heap at Nine Elms, and the sort of scandal that might go along with it. That I did not like to mention in front of my landlady. I was now at a height to see where the buildings merged into grey greenness at the edge of the city, and this brought the land sales flooding into my thoughts.

'There was something wrong with the land sales,' I said out loud. I pictured the name of White-Chester in the Necropolis minute book, and that brought me to it. 'Smith was selling off the land at cut-price rates to his friends, or perhaps even to himself in a roundabout way. There's this fellow at the Necropolis: Argent. He has sound looks, and seemed up to snuff. I saw him at Smith's funeral. He was not in the least downcast; he was swishing the grass with his black cane!'

'Calm down,' said my landlady. 'And where does he come in, anyway?'

'He was against the land sales. All the Necropolis board had doubts over it, but Argent led the way. After the funeral, he said to the chairman, Long, that it was the terms on which the lands were sold that he was particularly against. Long asked him what he might bring it to and he said a vote. They were all on to Smith. They were going to set things to rights, and Smith could see where it would all end.'

I pictured myself as a boy at the West Cliff marshalling yard in Whitby with Mr Hammond explaining railway mysteries to me. Had there been a vote in the background of his disgrace? However it had come about, he had been stopped from ever being involved with companies, and it had been the finish of him. Smith must have feared the same thing: the vote, then open court, or worse yet.

'Gaol?' said my landlady.

'Probably,' I said, 'and he could not have kept up his exquisite ways in stir.'

Now our cabin was at its fullest height, and I could see trains cutting crazily through the streets in all directions, as if each was saying, 'My way is best!' or they were ever-growing pointers of clocks, driving the world forward into the future.

A new thought brought me down to earth. 'Yet Stanley did the murders,' I said. 'I must have been right over that. *He* finished off Sir John Rickerby, Henry Taylor and Mike all right. Why else would he have crowned me and locked me in a coffin?'

'Yes,' said my landlady, 'but who put him up to it?'

I looked down into the Japanese garden, at Smith, still there, smoking a cigarette and looking all at once like a man who cared not a rip for anything but himself.

I nodded. 'Smith was the true killer,' I said, 'and poor Stanley was just the tool with which the job was done.'

'I'm sure you have that right,' said my landlady, although of course she was the one who had got to it first. And this was what Stanley had meant by darkness: he had seen from my diary that while I had known enough to send him to the gallows, I had not got the thing straight.

'Smith asked him to bash poor old Sir John Rickerby so as to give himself control of the Necropolis Company so that he could start selling the land,' I said. 'As for the next part, it was as I said in the hospital: Stanley was seen by Henry Taylor, or at any rate he thought as much, and so Taylor was done too. Then Mike, for what he knew, or might have known.'

'Or what he might have told the detectives who would never leave him be,' added my landlady.

Our cabin was once more descending. I looked at Smith again, and there seemed to be a white flash in the darkening air around him. He began looking in the stream below the bridge – and then was gone, for we were now too low to see him.

And with the loss of the vista, more doubts came. I was sure Sir John Rickerby had been killed on the say-so of Smith, but whether Smith had also ordered the destruction of Henry Taylor and Mike I could not guess. That might have been the private business of Stanley, for the noose was more closely about his neck – he had done the deed, after all. Smith, realising that he was in Queer Street too should the police be put on to Stanley, might have gone along with these other killings, or he might have been furious at them.

The two had made a deal: why else would Stanley's address have been allowed to continue every Tuesday, there being so little call to hear it?

'Stanley really was as poor as a rat,' I said.

'That's why he wanted my room,' said my landlady sadly. She was at my shoulder. I was ashamed to think that I had forgotten about her for the minute. 'It was the only one he could afford,' she added, and I realised then – which I had never thought before – that she knew very well that her rooms were not excellent, or whatever hopeful words she had used.

'He needed the money that Smith could pay him for the killing,' I said. 'But he botched the job by doing it in full view, or so he thought, of Taylor, and Smith likely told him he could sing for any true reward.

'He was a madman,' said my landlady. 'I could see that; I would still have given him the room, though.'

'Yes,' I said, 'Stanley was off his onion. And Smith was at the mercy of a madman likely to tell all, or do worse than that, so he had another good reason to disappear.'

I thought of those half-finished letters among Stanley's papers: they were meant for Smith, and I was sure some of the same sort had actually been sent. I reminded my landlady of them, and that Stanley had spoken of himself in one as an expert in some matter beginning with 'e'.

We could not answer that, but it was obvious to me now that those letters were in some way threats. Of course, by making these, Stanley ran the risk of being jacked in himself, but Smith was a wily worm. I had him down as quite cautious in the killing line.

Our cabin was right at the bottom now, passing the queue forming for the next ride. As we climbed again, I fixed on the question of why Smith had brought me down from Yorkshire. I turned to my landlady, who was looking straight ahead at nothing but sky, and again I felt sorry for spoiling her day. 'Why did Smith want me as his little detective?' I asked her. 'Why would he want me snooping among the murders he himself had caused to be done?'

My landlady turned to me and said, 'I don't know.' Then she said, 'You must learn to be smart.'

That helped because it was true, and the answer came to me double-quick: 'Because that would make him look innocent.'

My landlady nodded.

'The police were questioning everybody. It would be good for him if he could seem as keen to find the answer as any-body else. That *has* to be it. At the Necropolis station, Erskine Long was standing behind us when Smith said he would like to quiz me about events at Nine Elms. Smith didn't exactly speak in an under-breath: Long had been *meant* to overhear.'

The rest came to me in rapid thoughts. Before disappearing behind a wall of flame, Smith had written the letter asking to see me on the same point. He had kept the letter – in which he had put a down on the half-link – in his safe for the police to find after the fire. He wanted to make himself seem keen as mustard in the search for the truth, and in this he had gulled the Governor into helping.

It was the strangest thing of all that thoughts of the Governor should have come to me at that moment, for we were now at a height to see the Japanese garden once again, and there was the very gentleman, alongside Rowland Smith on the bamboo bridge.

Well, I knew that London could serve up no more shocks now.

Smith was pointing to the stream and saying something. The Governor had stopped laughing and was coughing, which, as ever, brought his colour up. He had always looked to me a very fine man, but now, though his body had not changed a jot since I had last seen him at the hospital, he looked a true fiend, with the redness not of Father Christmas but of the very devil.

Just then, the Governor and Smith, with one last look down into the stream, stepped off the bamboo bridge. My landlady and I watched them walk in the direction of the railway station, and as we did so the wheel gave a jolt, and my landlady fell against me.

'There is no cause for alarm,' I said.

'Oh, don't be ridiculous,' said my landlady. 'I'm not in the least alarmed.'

A second later, the wheel continued as smoothly as before, but by then the Governor and Smith had been lost to view.

Chapter Twenty-Nine

Saturday 9 January
five minutes later

As we stepped off the Great Wheel, the crowd waiting to get on looked at us with envious eyes.

I was coming to the end of telling my landlady, in a kind of daze, as if it was nothing out of the way, that I had just seen the Governor in the garden with Rowland Smith, and she said, 'I know a little of what it is like to live in the thick of coal dust and smoke, and your Governor was getting on in years. He would want something back in return.'

This notion came to me as though in a dream, and I said, more or less to myself, 'He made true engine men eat dog, but even though he hated the half-link, he also needed them. He needed them to take the knock for Stanley's exploits.'

We were walking by the buildings at the foot of the Wheel. There was a good deal of fried fish paper blowing about, and the Pierrot dog was eating the scraps. Everything seemed scruffier than before, and it was as if the cabins around us had lately crashed from the Wheel above.

'I remember how the Governor put his knife into the half after the murder of Mike,' I said, 'with the Captain listening in. The Governor, I shouldn't wonder, set that one up for Stanley himself. He ordered Barney to take Mike off-shed into the middle of the fog, perhaps hoping that Barney would drift off for a stiffener.'

My landlady turned to me and smiled. 'Do you think the two of us should do the same?' she said.

'But you won't drink,' I said.

'Oh, tea will do the job for me,' she said.

'First let's take a turn in the Japanese garden,' I said. 'I think I saw Smith drop something in the stream.'

'Hawk eyes,' said my landlady.

We walked towards the little red gates – Japanese gates, they were, I suppose. All was now slowly, sadly becoming clear.

'The Governor was keen to make the Captain think of Mike's death as being down to the half,' I said, 'and it suited his programme to put it about that the fire at Smith's place might be their work too. He showed the police the letter Smith sent me, warning me of the half, and after Smith's funeral he ordered me to stay about the shed for fear of what the half might do. And this time there was Nolan around to hear.'

'He always made sure there was a witness to hear him say the right things,' said my landlady.

'That is it exactly,' I said. 'It was the same game that his friend Smith was playing. The Governor wanted at all times to make it seem as though he suspected the half, but he would never go too far into the details in case somebody should stumble over the truth. I can see now that he didn't like it when I asked about Taylor's last ride out.'

I held open the little gate for my landlady. She laughed and said, 'The Japanese are smaller than us.'

'After all, that last ride had taken Taylor to the cemetery on the very day that Stanley had started on his line of murders. The Governor could hardly fail to answer my question, because Nolan was there watching, but in the event he needn't have worried. The book he took down showed him, or maybe it *reminded* him, that Arthur Hunt and Vincent had been on hand at the cemetery –'

'Landing themselves in it like ducks on a dough pile,' said my landlady, most surprisingly.

We walked on, following the paths that went under the lights, which I thought of as being all colours, but were in fact only blue, red and green.

'It must have scared the Governor', my landlady went on after a while, 'to hear that you had got on to Stanley in spite of all.'

I nodded. 'Now that I think of it, he was like a cat on hot

bricks in the hospital.' I pictured him at the end of my bed looking like a man with the noose already about his neck. And had he not at one moment made a bloomer in saying 'Smith *has* many good points,' not 'Smith had . . . '? I had not returned to work since my accident, and had not seen the Governor since being in the hospital. I could not be sure, but I guessed that he would have heard of Stanley's death, and now Smith would know of it too. They would have been glad to hear of it. Now that all was fixed on a dead man, they would think the matter ended.

But in that they were wrong.

We were walking beneath the branches of a tree in which were some of the paper lanterns. 'You couldn't do that with gas,' said my landlady, looking up.

But my mind was going back to Grosmont, and the start of it all. The muttering in the ticket office, the growling of T. T. Crystal, and the smoothness of Smith's voice. Crystal would have been apologising for the delay in selling Smith his ticket and would have been blaming me, damning me with half curses, calling me a layabout and a blockhead. If so, Smith could have been sure that I would not be any great hand at detecting. Maybe I was a blockhead, and maybe I had still not got the Necropolis mysteries quite straight, even now, but I would put salt on those fellows who wanted to turn beautiful land into houses for little men.

We had now arrived at the bamboo bridge where Smith and the Governor had been standing.

'Smith dropped something into the water,' I said again.

'And there it is,' said my landlady.

The stream was no stream at all, just something to keep the bridge from looking lonely. It was a trench with a rubber mat at the bottom and a foot of water that did not flow. The red lantern on the bridge cast a broken picture of itself into the water, and there in the middle of the redness floated a scrap of paper.

I moved to the bank, bent down and scooped it up. As I did

so it wrapped itself about my finger, and I peeled it away by degrees, reading aloud as I did so. 'It's touching on railways,' I said, for the first thing I saw were the words 'London & North Western Railway'. 'He's with this show now,' I said. But the next words I read out were 'Received with Gratitude'. 'It's a receipt!' I exclaimed, and carried on reading: 'Received with Gratitude, the sum of twelve shillings and . . .'

'Oh, do come on,' said my landlady.

'It's for twelve and sixpence ha'penny,' I said, when I had finally made out the words, which were handwritten in ink that had run.

'It's for a ticket,' said my landlady. 'But does it show his name? My receipts, on the few occasions I have cause to write them, carry the names of both parties.'

'It is not commonly done like that on the railways,' I said, still examining the paper.

'I might have known it would not be,' said my landlady.

'Twelve and six, it says, in respect of . . . first-class single . . . Euston to Manchester.' The thing was now stretched out in the palm of my hand. 'This will help put the fixments on him,' I said, 'although it will not be easy. There's so little evidence.'

'Evidence,' said my landlady. 'That was the word in the letter from Stanley to Smith.'

'Stanley had the evidence; Stanley *was* the evidence, but he's dead.'

'Then you must get what you can from his papers,' said my landlady. 'They will be a start. And finding a no-name in Manchester will be a lot easier than finding one down here.'

'The Necropolis Board will help,' I said. 'I'm sure they would love to see him brought to book.'

'And you will have the police force to provide such little assistance to you as they are able,' said my landlady.

I laughed. 'It *is* crazy to think I will do the job on my own,' I said.

But my landlady looked quite grave as she said, 'Oh, I don't know, you seem to have got everything else you wanted.'

We both looked up at the Great Wheel, with all its cabins lit up against the dark-blue sky, thinking our own thoughts for a moment before turning back to face each other, ready to kiss.

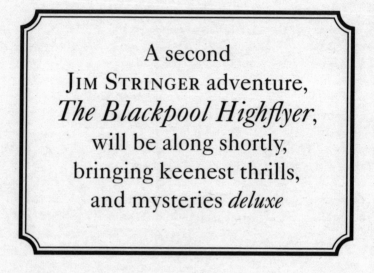

A second
JIM STRINGER adventure,
The Blackpool Highflyer,
will be along shortly,
bringing keenest thrills,
and mysteries *deluxe*